JUST ONCE

Other Life-Changing Fiction™ by Karen Kingsbury

Baxter Family Stand-Alone Titles

The Baxters—A Prequel
Truly, Madly, Deeply
Someone Like You
Two Weeks
When We Were Young
To the Moon and Back
In This Moment
Love Story
A Baxter Family Christmas
Coming Home
Forgiving Paris

The Baxters–1–Redemption Series

Redemption
Remember
Return
Rejoice
Reunion

The Baxters–2–Firstborn Series

Fame
Forgiven
Found
Family
Forever

The Baxters–3–Sunrise Series

Sunrise
Summer
Someday
Sunset

The Baxters–4–Above the Line Series

Take One
Take Two
Take Three
Take Four

The Baxters–5–Bailey Flanigan Series

Leaving
Learning
Longing
Loving

Other Stand-Alone Titles

A Distant Shore
Fifteen Minutes
The Chance
The Bridge
Oceans Apart
Between Sundays
When Joy Came to Stay
On Every Side
Divine
Like Dandelion Dust
Where Yesterday Lives
Shades of Blue
Unlocked

Angels Walking Series

Angels Walking
Chasing Sunsets
Brush of Wings

9/11 Series

One Tuesday Morning
Beyond Tuesday Morning
Remember Tuesday Morning

Lost Love Military Series
Even Now
Ever After

Forever Faithful Series
Waiting for Morning
A Moment of Weakness
Halfway to Forever

Women of Faith Fiction Series
A Time to Dance
A Time to Embrace

Cody Gunner Series
A Thousand Tomorrows
Just Beyond the Clouds
This Side of Heaven

Red Glove Series
Gideon's Gift
Maggie's Miracle
Sarah's Song
Hannah's Hope

Life-Changing Bible Story Collections
The Family of Jesus
The Friends of Jesus

Children's Chapter Books Ages 8–12
Best Family Ever—Baxter Family Children (Book 1)
Finding Home—Baxter Family Children (Book 2)
Never Grow Up—Baxter Family Children (Book 3)
Adventure Awaits—Baxter Family Children (Book 4)
Being Baxters—Baxter Family Children (Book 5)

Children's Picture Books
Let Me Hold You Longer
Let's Go on a Mommy Date
We Believe in Christmas
Let's Have a Daddy Day
The Princess and the Three Knights
The Brave Young Knight
Far Flutterby
Go Ahead and Dream with Quarterback Alex Smith
Whatever You Grow Up to Be
Always Daddy's Princess

Miracle Story Collections
A Treasury of Christmas Miracles
A Treasury of Miracles for Women
A Treasury of Miracles for Teens
A Treasury of Miracles for Friends
A Treasury of Adoption Miracles
Miracles—A Devotional

Gift Books
Forever Young: Ten Gifts of Faith for the Graduate
Forever My Little Boy
Forever My Little Girl

e-Short Stories
The Beginning
I Can Only Imagine
Elizabeth Baxter's 10 Secrets to a Happy Marriage
Once Upon a Campus

KAREN KINGSBURY

JUST ONCE

A Novel

ATRIA BOOKS

New York London Toronto Sydney New Delhi

An Imprint of Simon & Schuster, Inc.
1230 Avenue of the Americas
New York, NY 10020

Published in association with the literary agency Alive Communications, Inc., 7680 Goddard Street, Suite 200, Colorado Springs, Colorado, 80920, www.alivecommunications.com.

First Atria Books hardcover edition November 2023

ATRIA BOOKS and colophon are trademarks of Simon & Schuster, Inc.

For information about special discounts for bulk purchases, please contact Simon & Schuster Special Sales at 1-866-506-1949 or business@simonandschuster.com.

The Simon & Schuster Speakers Bureau can bring authors to your live event. For more information or to book an event, contact the Simon & Schuster Speakers Bureau at 1-866-248-3049 or visit our website at www.simonspeakers.com.

Manufactured in the United States of America

1 3 5 7 9 10 8 6 4 2

Library of Congress Cataloging-in-Publication Data

Names: Kingsbury, Karen, author.
Title: Just once : a novel / by Karen Kingsbury.
Description: First Atria Books hardcover edition. | New York : Atria Books, 2023.
Identifiers: LCCN 2023021030 (print) | LCCN 2023021031 (ebook) | ISBN 9781982104443 (hardcover) | ISBN 9781982104450 (paperback) | ISBN 9781982104467 (ebook)
Subjects: BISAC: FICTION / Christian / Romance / General | FICTION / Christian / General | LCGFT: Christian fiction. | Romance fiction. | Novels.
Classification: LCC PS3561.I4873 J89 2023 (print) | LCC PS3561.I4873 (ebook) | DDC 813/.54—dc23/eng/20230505
LC record available at https://lccn.loc.gov/2023021030
LC ebook record available at https://lccn.loc.gov/2023021031

ISBN 978-1-9821-0444-3
ISBN 978-1-9821-0446-7 (ebook)

Dedicated to Donald, the love of my life, my husband of thirty-five years. And to our beautiful children and grandchildren. The journey of life is breathtaking surrounded by you, and every minute together is time borrowed from eternity. I love you with every breath, every heartbeat. And to God, Almighty, who has—for now—blessed me with these.

MARCH 2018

Prologue

A wicked nor'easter crippled Washington, D.C., that March afternoon, closing down the entire federal government under a snow emergency. But one order of business remained:

Today the spies of World War II would finally get their recognition.

In a ceremony at the snowed-in U.S. Capitol's Emancipation Hall, thirteen thousand members of the Office of Strategic Services would receive the Congressional Gold Medal, the highest civilian honor awarded by the government.

Audra Mitchell could hardly wait.

Back then, four thousand agents of the OSS had been women, and one of those was Audra's grandmother Irvel Holland Myers. Never mind the blizzard, Audra wasn't going to miss a minute of the celebration.

Her husband, Tom, pushed through the last steps of the snow-covered walkway to the building's entrance and held the door so Audra and her parents could enter first. The four had walked two blocks from their hotel to be here.

Once inside, they brushed the snow from their coats and boots and made their way to the ceremony room. Already the front was filled with senators and representatives, each of them having tackled the weather so they could declare for all time the honor due the members of the OSS.

That these men and women were, in the words of OSS founder General William "Wild Bill" Donovan, the "glorious amateurs" of World War II. Heroes who deserved their day in the sun.

Audra and her family took their seats in the third row, in the section reserved for the twenty living OSS members who would attend today, and the children and grandchildren of many others who had passed on. Audra settled in between her husband and her father. She turned to Tom. "I still can't believe it."

Tom looked deep into her eyes. "Soon everyone will know."

He was right. A thrill ran through Audra and she faced the front again. Her grandmother, the sweet, genteel Irvel Myers, the one who finished her days at Bloomington, Indiana's Sunset Hills Adult Care Home drinking peppermint tea, had lived out World War II not as a nurse or a volunteer for the Red Cross.

Her grandma Irvel had been a spy.

And until three years ago, the only one who ever knew was Irvel's beloved Hank. Audra's mother had no idea, and neither did Irvel's only son—Audra's father—Charlie

Myers. Irvel's secret was one that she and Hank took to the grave—Grandpa Hank, first, in 1995, when he died of a heart attack while out fishing.

And Grandma Irvel, a decade later.

For fifteen years, Audra had lived in Hank and Irvel's Bloomington house not far from Indiana University. Through the seasons while Audra attended school at IU, and then while she got her master's degree in writing, and later when she stayed on as a professor. Audra lived in the house after she married Tom, and the two stayed there as they welcomed their twin boys—both home with Tom's parents this week.

Then three years ago, Audra and Tom decided to remodel the old place, and that's when they found the wooden chest. Audra closed her eyes and she was there again, crawling through the cobwebs of the dusty attic, intent on reaching the old box. It was splintered and weathered, but it was still intact.

Tom helped her bring the chest down the ladder and into the living room.

Painted across the top in fine black lettering was a simple message:

The story of Hank and Irvel . . . a love that could only happen just once.

Working together, Audra and Tom removed the fragile lid of the chest and took from the box a sealed plastic bag containing five Super 8 videotapes, each labeled simply *Our story 1, Our story 2,* and so on. Audra took the cassettes to a video transfer shop near the university, and a week later she and Tom sat down and watched the footage that had been so precious to Irvel and Hank.

Ten hours of a story that had taken Audra's breath away. And to think the wooden box had been in the attic all that time, since long before Audra moved in as a twenty-year-old college sophomore.

The first lines of the video had taken residence in Audra's heart, where they would live forever. In the video, her grandma Irvel sat straight and dignified and beautiful, her intelligent, kind blue eyes as clear as they would ever be. Her voice never wavered.

MY NAME IS IRVEL MYERS.

THIS IS FOR MY SON, CHARLIE, AND HIS WIFE, PEGGY, AND MY PRECIOUS GRANDDAUGHTER, AUDRA. IT IS ALSO FOR ME, AND FOR WHOEVER MIGHT WANT TO KNOW THE DETAILS OF MY LIFE, AND MY LOVE STORY WITH HANK MYERS.

YESTERDAY, I WAS DIAGNOSED WITH ALZHEIMER'S DISEASE. ALREADY, I FEEL ITS EFFECTS, SO HANK BOUGHT THIS CAMERA. HE THOUGHT WE SHOULD TELL OUR LOVE STORY . . . WHILE WE STILL CAN.

ALSO, THERE IS SOMETHING NO ONE KNOWS ABOUT ME. FORTY-SEVEN YEARS AGO, I WAS RECRUITED BY THE OFFICE OF STRATEGIC SERVICES TO WORK FOR THE U.S. MILITARY DURING WORLD WAR II.

THAT'S RIGHT, I WAS A SPY. BUT OUR STORY DOES NOT BEGIN THERE. IT BEGINS THE SUMMER OF 1940.

Commotion in the room was settling down and the memory of Grandma Irvel's voice faded. Audra opened her eyes. The ceremony was about to begin.

Five American flags stood at the front of the room, and off to the right, a color guard waited. The Speaker of the House, the honorable Paul D. Ryan, stepped up to the podium.

"Ladies and Gentlemen, welcome to the United States Capitol. I want to thank you for braving the elements to get here." The Speaker looked over the crowd. He went on, talking about the privilege of Congress to bestow Congressional Gold Medals in recognition of extraordinary deeds. "Today, we present the medal to the members of the Office of Strategic Services for their indispensable contributions to victory in World War Two." He paused. "The men and women of the OSS have never been collectively recognized for their heroism until this moment."

Audra squeezed Tom's hand. If only her grandparents could be here.

The next person at the podium recalled some of General Donovan's speech in 1945 at what was the final gathering of the OSS before the group was disbanded. "We have come to the end of an unusual experiment," the general had told the group that long-ago day. "An experiment to determine whether a group of Americans made up of different races, temperaments, and talents could perform America's first intelligence work, and by doing so, defeat their enemies."

None of this was news to Audra. She had done her research. The OSS had not only succeeded in aiding the victory in World War II, but then led to the creation of the current-day CIA.

It was time to hear from a number of actual OSS operatives, and the children and grandchildren of late OSS members. Each speech was emotional, ripe with the emotion these heroes and their family members had carried for decades.

Finally, a white-haired, retired OSS code breaker finished his talk and introduced Audra. "There was some speculation," the man still had a twinkle in his eyes, "that the U.S. was using spies to gain an edge in World War Two." He looked at Audra. "But back then no one would have guessed so much of our intelligence group was comprised of women."

The man held up a hardback book—an advance copy that Audra had mailed to him weeks ago.

"Soon, you will all know the name of our next speaker," the man said. "She spent the last few years writing a novel based on her grandmother's days in the OSS, a novel that will be in stores everywhere next week." He motioned to her. "Please welcome author and Indiana University Professor of Writing Audra Mitchell."

Audra smoothed the lines of her long skirt and adjusted her sweater jacket. For the next five minutes she could only ask God to give her grandma Irvel Myers a window from heaven. She deserved it.

The audience seemed extra intent on what Audra had to say. "I'm here today to honor my grandmother Irvel Holland Myers and to tell you a little about her story."

Audra touched only the most heartfelt points, enough so that the people in attendance were smiling and wiping away tears by the time she took her seat again.

When the ceremony was over, Audra and her family walked through two feet of snow back to their hotel. With the blizzard still bearing down, and their flight home canceled, her parents returned to their room for a nap. When they were gone, Tom sat in front of the TV to watch college basketball—Indiana vs. Gonzaga.

Audra found another advance copy of her novel in the front pocket of her suitcase. The copy she had brought in case she wanted to give it to someone at the ceremony. With the craziness of the storm, she hadn't remembered to take it. She changed into sweats, grabbed the cozy chair near the window, and settled in. She turned to the first page.

For Irvel and Hank, that your daring, heroic love story might be remembered forever.

She ran her hand over the image on the cover, a young couple much the way her Grandma Irvel and Grandpa Hank might've looked during World War II. And below that, the only title that could ever have worked. The one Irvel would've given it, had she been here.

JUST ONCE.

OCTOBER 2, 1989

1

Red was the last color, the very last. That's what Dr. Edmonds was saying.

Irvel Myers's mind would splinter and fracture and fade under the burden of Alzheimer's, and she would forget the love that long ago caused her world to stop and stare in awe. Irvel and Hank. In little time, she would no longer know his face or his voice, or Hank himself, the one who had held her hand when she said, "I do," and who had stood beside her that rainy Wednesday morning in Bloomington, Indiana, when she delivered their son.

Her brain would release to nothingness the name of that boy, the one she had cherished for thirty-two years, and also the smell and feel of the wood and walls and windows of the house where her life had taken shape for the past four decades, and it would do something else. It would erase entirely her years as a spy for the Office of Strategic Services.

But until the very end, it would remember the color red.

That's what the doctor was saying.

Irvel Myers adjusted her sweater and tapped both feet on the floor beneath the doctor's desk. The tick of the clock on the wall was louder than before. Deafening. The doctor stopped talking. For a long time, he didn't say a word, just stared at them. And Irvel wanted to scream. How could this be happening? Her strong and glorious mind was dying? Through the years of fighting for her life and her heart, Irvel could always count on three things.

God. Hank. And her mental acuity. Until now . . .

Tall, strong Hank released a guttural sound. Like someone had kicked him below his ribs and he was still trying to figure out how to inhale. He tightened his hold on Irvel's hand and whispered his next words. "How . . . how long?"

It was the only question that mattered.

Dr. Edmonds looked down at Irvel's file and after a beat he lifted his eyes. "Since your first exam, your degeneration has been happening at a rapid pace."

Her first exam. Irvel blinked and stared out the window. Two months ago today, Hank had brought her to this same office. Irvel had been acting scattered. That's how Hank had described it. "You're just a little scattered, my love."

Setting dirty dishes in the refrigerator. Pulling into the driveway of the wrong house. Calling Hank from a pay phone and asking if he remembered the name of their favorite grocery store. "I know what I need to make chicken piccata." She had forced a nervous laugh. "But for the life of me, I can't remember where the store is."

Now the doctor exhaled. He hesitated, as if the news was only real and true and terrible if he spoke it out loud.

Finally, his answer pushed its way through. "By my estimation, you'll need full-time care sometime in the next year, Mrs. Myers."

A year? The word hovered over her and screamed at her and consumed her in a single instant. And as it had done all her life, Irvel's mathematical brain imagined that time in increments. Precious, passing, dissolving, disappearing sections of time. *Three-hundred and sixty-five days . . . fifty-two weeks . . . twelve months.*

"I have to be honest here." The doctor lifted his eyes to Hank and then to Irvel. "You may only have six months."

Hank was holding on to her hand so hard now she was losing feeling in it. She slid her chair closer to his, so their arms were touching. Hank's arm against hers, his skin against her skin. Because the two of them were only halves of a greater one. So that if he were close by, if she could feel him next to her, then maybe she would be okay after all.

The doctor was going on about a host of medications, two of which he'd like to try. The side effects included sleepiness, dizziness, mood swings and confusion. Which, of course, sounded a lot like Alzheimer's, itself. Irvel stared at her hands and then at her husband. The doctor was still talking.

"Though slight, there is an increased risk of brain bleeds and therefore, a greater chance of premature death with these drugs, I have to tell you that. But we hope that over time they prevent the progression of disease for at least—"

"Excuse me." Hank held up his hand. "I have a question."

The doctor fell silent.

Hank blinked. "Will . . . the drugs reverse Irvel's symptoms?" Hank looked at her, and then at the doctor again.

For a few seconds, Dr. Edmonds stayed quiet, his face slack. Then he took a slow breath. "Mr. Myers, there are no drugs that cure Alzheimer's disease, no drugs that reverse symptoms. Good evidence exists that certain medications can slow progression for a while, maybe ease symptoms. But there are no guarantees. With the medications I'm recommending, some people experience favorable results. Some suffer worsening levels of dementia." He paused. "It's a personal choice."

Hank nodded. His eyes told Irvel he was sorting through his options. Fast. Like a man running out of time. He made a fist with his free hand. "Do we have to decide now?"

Dr. Edmonds hesitated. "If the drugs are going to make an impact, they need to be taken on the front end of an Alzheimer's diagnosis. We'll need to act quickly to accomplish that. Your wife is already struggling to remember."

Irvel sat straighter in her chair. "That's not true." She blinked, her eyes locked on the doctor's. "Forgetting my keys or . . . or putting the milk in the cupboard does not mean I'm struggling to remember." She looked at Hank. The hint of tears made her voice waver. "I remember everything."

A perplexed look came over the doctor's face. He

closed Irvel's file and leaned back in his chair. "We can hold off on the medications. I want you both to be comfortable with your decision."

Hank nodded. "Thank you." He stood and helped Irvel to her feet. "We'll be in touch."

On their way out of the office, Irvel stopped at the door. "Our car's to the left, yes?"

"Actually it's to the right." He smiled. Then he put his arm around her and opened the door. "It's a confusing building."

That was it. Very confusing. Irvel stayed close to Hank as they walked down the hallway and out into the parking lot. Anyone could struggle to recall where they left their car. But she didn't say that. She didn't say anything and neither did Hank. When they reached their blue Ford Escort, Hank stopped and turned to her. He took her purse and set it on the ground, then he drew her into his arms. In a voice almost too quiet to be heard, again and again, he said the same thing. "It'll be okay. God has us, Irvel. It'll be okay."

Then he opened the door for her and when they were both inside, Irvel saw proof that Hank was only trying to convince himself. Her decorated World War II vet had tears streaming down his cheeks. He swiped at them with the back of his hand and smiled at her. "It'll be okay."

Irvel couldn't bear to watch. She looked out the passenger window at the medical facility growing farther and farther away. What were they doing here, anyway? She squinted her eyebrows and focused. Really focused. They were at the doctor's, that's what. They had just finished getting her diagnosis.

An aggressive case of Alzheimer's disease.

She leaned into the seat and watched the trees pass by, each of them decked in brilliant oranges and reds. *Red. The last color*. See, there? Irvel felt herself relax. The doctor was wrong. She could remember just fine. Not just small details like that one, but the bigger ones. The details that made up the story of her life. What about sixth grade? She opened her eyes again. Did she remember that year? The year she and Hank Myers became friends?

A myriad of vividly familiar sounds and smells and images filled her mind and she smiled. She could feel the soft grass beneath her white tennis shoes and hear the rushing creek that ran through that part of town. Young Hank was there beside her, most handsome boy she'd ever seen.

Yes, she definitely remembered. It was spring, 1931. She and Hank were twelve years old, and since he lived three doors down on the same street, the two of them walked home together. Every day. But that April afternoon, they took a different route. The one Irvel's parents had warned her never to take, because it meant walking alongside the rushing creek.

"The earth could give way and you'd wind up in the water," her mother had said. "Stay away from that path, Irvel."

But the sky was blue and the sun warmed the afternoon. The maple trees were in full bloom. A little adventure seemed like a good idea, so instead of turning toward the sidewalk, she turned the other way, toward the sound of the water. "Come on." She could feel the way her eyes sparkled. "Just once."

Like always, Hank could no sooner say no to Irvel than he could stop breathing. He had grinned that day and found his place beside her.

"I saw Tommy Fuller talking to you at recess." Hank picked up a stick and dragged it through the long grass as they walked. "The guys say he has a crush on you."

"No." Irvel felt her cheeks flush. She shaded her eyes against the brightness of the sun. "Tommy Fuller likes Betty Owens."

"I don't think so." Hank cast her a look.

"It's true." Irvel looked long at Hank. His eyes were the most beautiful she had ever seen.

He didn't give up. "Would you hate it? If Tommy Fuller liked you?"

"Yes." She batted her eyelashes at him. "I'd hate it, Hank Myers. That's all I'm going to say."

She kept her word, the two of them too young to understand the crush that had developed between them that school year. So they switched to talking about the upcoming spelling test and the book they'd been assigned to read—*Floating Island* by Anne Parrish. "I like reading about a family of dolls." Irvel lifted her face to the sun. "It's adventurous."

"I'd rather read about pirates." Hank stuck out his chest. "I'd be one of the good ones."

Irvel laughed, but she believed him. Hank was good at everything.

Ten minutes was all it took to get home along the sidewalks, but along the creek that day the walk took longer. In some areas, brush and trees had overtaken the earthen path, and they had to take careful steps around the branches to keep from falling in.

"This is why we aren't supposed to do this." Hank's deep blue eyes didn't look worried. "Be careful, okay?"

"I'm fine. The creek isn't more than a stone's throw across." She laughed again. "It's safe."

Irvel had no sooner finished her response when the dirt beneath her right foot gave way. Before Hank could stop her, she dropped her bag, fell into the cold water and slipped beneath the white, choppy surface. She tried to scream, but the water was deep and the current faster than she could swim.

For a moment, Irvel wondered if she might die in the rushing creek, her last act one of utter disobedience to her parents. She poked her face above the water and grabbed as much air as she could. Her yellow and white sundress was pulling her down, and jagged rocks at the creek's bottom cut hard against her legs.

Another breath, and another. Just when she wasn't sure she could force herself above the water one more time, Hank was beside her. Panic screamed from his eyes, but his actions were calm and sure. He put his arm around her waist and swam her back to the creek's edge. Then he helped her scramble up onto the grass.

For a long moment they lay there facing the sky, drenched and trembling, their hearts beating out of their chests. The shivering started then and Hank reached for his sweater a few feet away. He must've thrown it off before he jumped in after her because it was still dry. "Here." He slipped it over her shoulders. "Come on. We need to get you home."

When they were both on their feet, he searched her eyes. "You okay to walk?"

"I'm c-c-cold." Her teeth were chattering. She could barely feel her hands and feet. "I'm s-s-sorry, Hank."

"It isn't your fault." He picked up both their bags. "I shouldn't have let you get so close to the edge." He put his free arm around her shoulders and pulled her close.

"Th-th-thank you. For saving me." She glanced up at him as they walked. His body was warmer than hers, and for the next few minutes, Irvel could hardly breathe. Not because she was cold and wet and terrified. But because Hank Myers was so close.

Long before they reached Irvel's house, Hank stopped and turned to her again. He ran his fingers through his still wet hair. "You stopped shivering."

"I'm . . . fine." Warm rays of sunshine washed over them. "Because of you." Irvel surveyed him, still drenched, water running from the cuffs of his pants. Their shoes were drenched, also. Another reality hit. "We're going to be in big trouble."

"No. It'll be okay." He started walking again and motioned for her to follow. "Come on."

It'll be okay. His words played in her mind again, and Irvel nodded. *Yes, that was it.* Five minutes later they headed up the sidewalk to Irvel's house. Her mother met them halfway, eyes wide and panicked. "Where have you been?" She stopped short and looked Irvel and Hank up and down. "What happened? You're drenched!"

Before Irvel could open her mouth, Hank was talking. "I'm sorry, ma'am. It was my fault. I asked Irvel to walk home along the creek because, well, you know it's such a nice day and all." He seemed to gulp back a breath. "I distracted her and she fell in the creek. But just for a moment and then I helped her out."

Irvel and her mother both stood stone-still on the sidewalk, staring at Hank. Her mom spoke first. "This was your idea?"

Hank didn't hesitate. "Yes, ma'am." He nodded and took a step back. "Again, I'm sorry. Truly." He backed up, but before he turned around, he cast Irvel a quick smile.

Irvel's mom missed it. She put her arm around Irvel's shoulders. "Let's get you inside." Her mother led her into the house. "You need to warm up. You'll catch your death of cold."

Irvel kept the truth to herself. After being rescued by Hank, after walking halfway home with his arm around her shoulders, she wasn't cold at all. And in the end, it wasn't Irvel who got sick, it was Hank.

So sick he caught pneumonia and nearly died.

He missed two weeks of school, and lost ten pounds. The whole time Irvel felt terrible. Every night after she shut her bedroom door, she would drop to her knees and pray for Hank. And every time she heard Hank's words again. *It'll be okay*.

God must have heard Irvel's constant prayers because Hank survived. When he returned to class, he was thinner and his pale skin didn't have its usual glow. But he was whole and healthy and alive, and that day, Irvel couldn't stop thanking God.

On the way home Hank's first day back, they took the sidewalk. And there, while they walked, Irvel had the chance to say what she wanted to say. "I'm sorry, Hank. It was all my fault."

"Nah, silly girl." He grinned at her. "You didn't force me to jump into that ol' creek."

"Yes, I did." She stopped and turned to him. "I walked too close to the edge."

"I'd jump in again every time." He flipped his blond bangs and searched her eyes. "You know why? Because when we grow up, I'm going to marry you, Irvel Anne Holland. You wait and see."

For a few seconds, neither of them looked away or blinked or breathed. But then at the same time they both tipped their heads back and laughed, the innocent laugh from the precipice between being a child and being old enough to fall in love. They kept walking, talking about something funny and letting the more serious conversation fade.

After all, being grown up was millions of minutes away.

Irvel blinked and the memory faded. Hank turned the car into the driveway of the home where they'd lived for forty years. As Hank parked, Irvel reached for his hand. "I remember, Hank. I still remember."

He nodded. "I know." He leaned close and kissed her cheek. Then he said the same thing he'd said after he pulled her from the creek that long-ago spring day. Before war or loss or heartbreak had anything to say about life. The same thing he'd said this morning at the doctor's office. "It'll be okay."

And she loved Hank Myers for it.

OCTOBER 2, 1989

2

He couldn't have this conversation at home with Irvel listening, so Hank waited until his wife was asleep before driving to the local Best Buy and parking in the back row. It had been six hours since the doctor appointment, and not until now did Hank feel okay leaving Irvel at home alone.

Their only child, Charlie, answered on the first ring. "Dad . . . what did they say?" His voice was heavy with worry. "I've been praying."

Hank tried to make himself speak the words, but his lips wouldn't work. Tears flooded his eyes and he held his breath.

"Dad?"

"I'm . . . sorry, Charlie." Hank closed his eyes. He would give anything to avoid this conversation. They could talk about the weather in California or the economy or Thanksgiving coming up and whether Charlie and Peggy and young Audra would fly to Bloomington or whether Hank and Irvel would take the trip to Los Angeles. As long as they were together.

Anything but this.

Charlie was waiting. Hank took the slowest breath.

God . . . give me the strength. Please, God. And gradually an inexplicable peace came over Hank. "The news isn't good, Son. I'm so sorry."

"No . . . don't say that." Charlie was an in-house attorney for one of the top studios in Hollywood, but here he was just Irvel and Hank's boy. The one who called twice a week and missed his parents every day. Charlie exhaled. "I talked to her yesterday. She sounded fine."

Hank shook his head. "She . . . she has good moments." He put the phone on speaker and stared out the windshield. The parking lot was busy, people stopping in for a new television or refrigerator or laptop computer. The ones still in the race. Making the most of their lives, the way Hank and Irvel had done with theirs, one decade upon the next since they married in 1945.

"Dad." Charlie sounded sick. "Tell me about the tests. Please. I want to know everything."

For the next fifteen minutes, Hank rehashed all the doctor had told them. How her test results were worse than they'd been before and how her decline appeared to be on a rapid trajectory. "If she focuses, she's okay." Hank felt like he was betraying Irvel by telling Charlie this part. "But I'm worried about her."

Then Hank gave his son the details to back that up. Irvel's strange behavior at home, misplacing things and leaving items in odd locations. Keys in the freezer, a hairbrush in the china cabinet, her purse in the bathroom closet. As if the easy things were no longer so.

"She couldn't find her way home the other day." Hank squeezed his eyes shut.

"Okay, so what do we do?" Charlie was rebounding, using his professional voice. As if by sorting through the details he might find the answer they'd all been missing. "They must have a plan . . . next steps, a way out."

Hank breathed in sharp through his nose. The sun was warm that second day of October, and Bloomington's fall was showing itself to be one of the most beautiful ever. If only he could be with Charlie right now, look their son in the eyes and hug him. "There's no way out, Charlie. The doctor said she has a year, maybe more, maybe less. After that, she won't remember anything . . . or anyone."

For a long beat, Charlie didn't say anything. He sniffed a few times, and Hank realized his son was crying. For a family like theirs, the news couldn't have been worse. In a car accident or a fatal heart attack, death would be swift. Here one minute, gone the next—home to heaven, where they would all spend eternity.

But this . . . this slow taking of Irvel's mind and memories, their marriage and her motherhood . . . Hank couldn't imagine anything worse. And clearly, Charlie couldn't, either.

"I'll talk to Peggy about getting out there next week." Charlie seemed to compose himself. His wife ran a skin care business from home. "She could work from your house." Charlie hesitated. "We can take Audra out of school for a few weeks, maybe homeschool her through the fall semester. And I can work remotely, fly back to L.A. for any in-house depositions."

After a few minutes Charlie fell silent again. "I can't lose her like this, Dad. I can't."

A single tear slid down Hank's cheek. "Me, either, Son." He waited till his voice was steady. "Me, either."

Before they hung up, Charlie agreed to call later that night with his plans. "I wish I could blink my family there right now." He sighed. "None of this makes sense."

The call ended and for a long suffocating minute, Hank sat there, staring out the window. *Let me wake up, God. Let it all be a terrible nightmare*. He squinted at the Best Buy sign and the truth fell over him like cold rain. It wasn't a dream. Irvel had no more than a year before her memory would die, even as her body kept living.

Hank stayed seated in his car. He still had time, since Irvel would sleep for a few hours. He gripped the steering wheel and pictured the fear in Irvel's eyes earlier when they walked into the house from the doctor's appointment. He could still hear the terror in her voice. Terror and determination. *I remember, Hank. I still remember.*

As they made lunch, she had told him what she had been thinking the entire ride home, how she had allowed herself to go back to junior high, to that spring day when they went against their parents' wishes and took the walk home along the creek.

"I can still feel that sundress wet against my skin," Irvel told him. She sat at the kitchen counter while Hank made turkey sandwiches. Her eyes looked distant, like she was still back in that time.

"You were always one for adventure." Hank winked at her.

"Definitely." A glimmer of daring sparkled in her eyes. The Irvel he had fallen in love with. "You jumped in after me, Hank . . . remember?"

"Are you kidding? Of course I remember." He leaned on the counter and looked long into her eyes. "I nearly caught my death from that pneumonia."

She tilted her head, lost in his gaze. "You said you'd do it all again. When you came back to school after you were sick. I can still hear your voice."

"And I told you something else that day." He leaned closer and kissed her forehead. "What did I tell you?"

"That when we were grown up, you were going to marry me." She smiled. "You always keep your promises, Hank. Back then and still today."

Irvel went on another ten minutes about that walk home along the creek and the rescue he'd pulled off, and how her parents had talked to her that night about finding other friends. How maybe Hank Myers wasn't the best influence on her.

"They were right about a lot of things." Irvel laughed. "But they were wrong about that."

"They loved me in the end." Hank finished the sandwiches and handed Irvel a plate. He paused long enough to get her attention. "I'm glad you remember, my love."

"I remember it all."

Which was why Hank was here at Best Buy this afternoon.

He grabbed his keys and wallet and took the long walk to the front of the store. Every step, every breath reminded him of the truth, of the reason he was here this October day. If Irvel had only twelve months left to remember the people and places and wildly daring moments of her mysterious life, then there were two things Hank wanted to do.

For sure, he would take her to the lake more often, the place where she loved spending time with him. But before that, he would journey with her on another kind of trip, one down memory lane.

Hank entered the store and walked to the far side, the place where a forever long display of video cameras lined a glass counter. He looked over the lineup. Where to begin? A young man in his twenties approached. "Sir . . . can I help you?"

"Yes." Hank wore a fedora, something he'd done most of his life. He took it off, smoothed his hair back and replaced it again. "I need a video camera. A reliable one."

"That's our Super 8." The young man motioned to Hank. "Let's look at the ones over here."

Hank followed and with the man's help, he chose a camera that cost twice as much as what he'd planned on spending. But what did money matter now? He and Irvel weren't going to spend the next decade taking trips to

California and bringing their son and his family on cruises or to Disneyland.

This was it, this next year. A Christmas and a spring, a summer and the beginning of another fall. By then there was no telling what the cruel disease would have done to his beloved Irvel. He added a tripod and a spare battery to his cart along with a five-pack of Super 8 cassettes. Enough for ten hours of video recording.

If that wasn't enough, he'd buy more.

On the way home, he let his mind drift back to that spring day along the creek. He pictured the way Irvel had looked when he pulled her out of the raging water. Her lips were blue, her blond hair matted to her head, her eyes wide with fear. He always downplayed the moment to Irvel whenever they talked about it. But the truth was, Irvel had been in a heap of trouble.

If he hadn't jumped in when he did, she would've been pulled under a fallen tree branch and there wouldn't have been anything Hank could've done to help her. The same thing could've happened to him. Jumping into the creek to save her meant he could've died. The current had been stronger than he was, so the possibility had been very real.

But Hank hadn't hesitated, not for a single second. Before his feet hit the water that day, he had begged God to help him. He could still see himself, uttering the silent prayer as he dropped his bag and jumped. *Let us live, God! Please, help me get her out of the creek before she drowns.*

And God had met him there, giving him a strength and precision beyond his own capabilities. Before he knew it, Irvel was in his arms and the two of them were on the shore again. He remembered thinking that her parents were going to be furious, but he had decided long before they were at Irvel's house that he would take the blame.

What he'd told Irvel's mother hadn't been a lie. Not really. Her accident *had* been his fault, because if he'd taken better care of her, she never would've fallen in.

Hank stopped at a light and narrowed his eyes. He remembered Irvel's mother, the look on her face and the sound of her voice when he brought Irvel home. He chuckled to himself. He didn't think the woman would ever forgive him.

But she did. Both of Irvel's parents forgave what he'd done, and in no time, her mom and dad actually came to love him. Hank was Irvel's best friend, the two of them inseparable. But Hank's father was relocated to Indianapolis for their junior and senior years of high school. By the time his family returned to Bloomington, Irvel had a boyfriend.

Even then, Hank had every intention of keeping his promise. As long as he was breathing, he was going to marry Irvel one day. If only it had been that simple.

His mind found its way back to now. If only he could do something to save Irvel today. He parked in their driveway and brought the Best Buy bags into the kitchen. Irvel was up, searching from one cupboard to the next. She looked at him over her shoulder. "Have you seen the tea?"

"Tea?" Hank set the camera gear on the counter and moved to her side. He gazed up at the cupboard. She was still sifting through plates and bowls. He turned to her. "Did you move it?"

"No." She exhaled hard. "I hate this. It was just here."

She was wrong about that. He crossed the kitchen and opened a drawer they'd used for years. The tea drawer, Irvel had always called it. Sure enough, her assorted tea bags were still there. Right where they had always been. "Here they are, love."

Irvel spun around and stared at the open drawer. "They weren't there before. That's where the silverware is supposed to be."

She was wrong about that, too. He opened the adjacent drawer. "The forks and spoons are here."

Fear tightened the creases near the corners of her eyes. "You didn't move things around?"

"I didn't." Hank went to her and eased her into his arms. "Don't worry about it, Irvel. People make mistakes about things like this all the time."

But they both knew that wasn't true. Irvel loved tea. Peppermint tea, most of all. She would never have forgotten where she kept her tea. And a few months ago, she could've found her way to the silverware drawer in her sleep.

Hank took her hand and together they walked back to the tea drawer. "Here we are. Peppermint. Your favorite." He pulled a packet of tea from one of the small cardboard boxes. "I'll make it for you."

"Thank you, love." Irvel seemed humiliated. She stepped back. "I knew the tea was there. Of course."

Hank could feel her watching him as he filled the kettle and set it over a flame on the stove. He turned to her, willing himself to hide his concern about this latest manifestation of the disease.

She took hold of one of the Best Buy bags and peered inside. "What's this?" The camera box spilled from the bag, followed by the other new purchases.

"I thought we might shoot a few videos." He came to her and took her hand. "You know, tell our love story on camera. For us to watch. And for Charlie and Peggy and Audra. For whoever might want to know. Just once. So we'll have it forever."

Hank watched her process this. Clearly, she understood the point of this. "While I still remember, you mean." She lifted her eyes to Hank. Hers were watery now, the sadness almost too much for him to take. She nodded. "Right? That's why?"

"It is." He leaned down, kissed her, and brushed his cheek against hers. His voice was little more than a whisper near her ear. "Does that sound like a good idea?"

She waited a few seconds, but then she nodded. "Our story is too beautiful not to tell."

He stood again and searched her eyes, her face. "Exactly."

The teakettle was whistling, so Hank poured the boiling water into a floral mug and added the peppermint tea bag. He brought it to her and set it on the counter. How much longer until he wouldn't be able to do this? Until hot water would be a danger to her? Hank didn't want to think about it.

"Thank you." Irvel pulled the cup close and looked at Hank. "Will we tell *all* of the story?"

A sense of relief came over Hank. Because if Irvel could ask a question like that, then her memory of the past was still crystal clear. "Yes. All of it."

"But Charlie and Peggy . . . Audra. They don't know about . . ."

"We don't have to tell them yet. We can wait until we're ready." Hank took her hand in his, their eyes locked once more. "But people need to find out, Irvel. One day the whole world should know. Irvel Myers, special operative, spy."

She thought for a moment and then slowly, she nodded. "Member of the Office of Strategic Services." A sense of exhilaration seemed to fill the moment. Her eyes sparkled. "You really think it's okay to talk about it?"

"After forty-four years?" He felt the warmth in his smile. "I'd say it's more than time."

Irvel cupped her hands around her tea. "This will be a good story, Hank."

"The best." He couldn't take his eyes off her. Even now, she was the love of his life. She always would be.

She stood and straightened. "When will we start?"

"Tomorrow." He came to her and took her in his arms. "I thought we could take the camera to the park. Way in the back where we'd be by ourselves. That way we wouldn't have anything to distract us." What he meant was, nothing to remind Irvel that her memory was going. But he didn't say that.

"Yes." The corners of her mouth lifted ever so slightly and her eyes softened. "I'd like that. We'll tell the story at the park. All of it."

Irvel took her tea into the living room and sat on the sofa facing the large picture window. Outside stood a large oak tree and a pretty picket fence framed the same yard where Charlie had played as a little boy. Hank watched her, studied her. She was thinking, remembering. He could see it in her eyes. Probably getting ready for tomorrow and the story they would tell. Their beautiful love story.

Hank figured they could take turns. He didn't want them to miss a single detail, because some far-off day, Charlie would find the tapes and play them and he would finally know the truth. And he and his family, Audra and hers and future generations would remember forever the story of Hank and Irvel.

He didn't want to leave her, didn't want to be anywhere but nearby. So he found his Bible and settled into the recliner opposite the sofa. He couldn't see the front window, but he had all the view he needed. His precious Irvel.

At first, he found his way to Psalm 23, and the comfort of God. Even as a person might walk through the valley of the shadow of death. But eventually he closed the leather cover and studied his dear wife. Every now and then she would catch him looking and they would share a smile. But otherwise she was quiet. Something new for her. Irvel had always been bubbly, chatty, the life of the party and the energy in any room.

But not now.

He didn't look away, completely captivated by her. And suddenly he wasn't looking at the beautiful sixty-nine-year-old Irvel Myers. He was looking at the young girl, the one soaked to the skin as they headed up the walkway of her parents' home. The feeling he'd had that day was still as close as his own heartbeat. He had jumped into that rushing water and saved Irvel, no matter what it cost him.

His throat felt tight and a wave of emotion came over him, one as cold and fast as the creek that day. Because once more she was caught in the tumult of a raging river, one that would soon pull her under. This time around, Hank would have jumped in and saved her, even if it cost him his own life. He wouldn't hesitate. But with her diagnosis, he could only stand by and watch her fight for her life, for her very identity and existence.

And there wasn't a thing he could do about it except take her to the park tomorrow and capture every detail of the life they'd shared.

Before the disease pulled her under the water once and for all.

3

Hank made scrambled eggs, wheat toast, and sliced avocado that morning, but he skipped the orange juice. This would be their new way of eating, because yesterday, in a follow-up call, Irvel's doctor had told him to cut back on their carbohydrates. Juices, candy, baked goods. There was new cutting-edge research that suggested sugar could speed the process of Alzheimer's. "Focus on protein," the doctor had told him. "Protein and fats. As much as possible."

This was new information to Hank, so as soon as the call ended, he had gone to the fridge and found the orange juice. Then he took off the cap and dumped it down the drain. He would've walked over glass to keep Irvel with him even a single day longer. If protein and fat would help her, then that's what they would eat.

Irvel breezed into the kitchen and Hank felt his heart catch in his throat. She was still a vision, still the striking woman he had loved all his life. The way she looked, he could've convinced himself this was any other fall day, that they were merely celebrating a breakfast together before going to the antique mall in downtown Bloomington or taking a picnic lunch to the shores of Lake Monroe. That they weren't, in fact, setting out to record their love story before Irvel didn't remember it anymore. He would've believed that except for one thing.

The dress Irvel was wearing was red.

She stopped and lifted her eyes to his. "How do I look?" She turned one way, then the other. "I found this in the back of my closet."

"You look . . . stunning." Hank came to her and hugged her. Then he stepped back. His eyes must've held the words he didn't say because she put her hand alongside his face.

"Red, right?" Her voice was soft, tender. Resigned. "That's what the doctor said? Red is the last thing to go?"

"Yes." Hank hugged her close again. He ran his hand over the back of her still-soft gray-blond hair. "Red is the last color."

"So that one far-off day, you and I can sit together and watch our movie, and I'll remember, Hank. I'll remember it all. Because of God's grace and my red dress."

"Exactly." He could've dropped to the floor and wept for a day. But he wanted this to be a happy outing, so he smiled. "It's the perfect dress."

Irvel didn't ask why there was no juice that morning. Maybe because she didn't care for it much, anyway. Or maybe she didn't remember. Hank chose not to think about it. Over breakfast they talked about their granddaughter, Audra. Irvel set her fork down. "Peggy called this morning. She said they're coming for a visit."

"Right." Hank took a bite of his eggs. "Charlie said it'll be soon."

"That's nice." Irvel sat back in her chair. She didn't seem very hungry. "Were they here for the Fourth of July? They were, right?"

They were not. "Yes. We saw them for the Fourth." Hank grinned. It had been the previous Fourth, but there was no sense in saying so. The realization that she had forgotten something else would only upset her. And that wouldn't be any way to start the day.

When breakfast was over, they drove to Winslow Woods Park on Highland Avenue. The grassy acreage was dotted by hundred-year-old elm trees and meandering paths. Irvel had worn pretty black heels, so Hank parked at the front of the lot near the main walkway. It had rained a few days ago. The grass would be too soft for her shoes.

Irvel didn't seem to register any of his efforts on behalf of her heels. As if she figured public park or not, if she was going to go on camera to tell her part of their story, then she was going to dress the part.

They found a picnic table at the back of the park near a tree with leaves bright orange and yellow. The perfect backdrop. Hank breathed deep. As much as whatever they captured on camera in the coming days, Hank would hold the feel of this moment in his heart forever. He and Irvel together, braving the coming storm side by side. The way they always had.

Hank had charged the camera overnight, so now he attached it to a short tripod, set it up on top of the picnic table, and slipped a single videotape into the side compartment. He turned to Irvel and held his hands out to his sides. "You want to go first?"

Irvel grinned. "Yes, please." She looked almost giddy, as if now that they were here, she was truly looking forward to this. Like it was her last and greatest assignment. "I think the love part of our story starts with me."

He laughed. "Yes, my love. I believe it does. You were the one who didn't wait for me."

"Now, now." She came to him and put her hands on his shoulders. And like she'd done when she was a college coed, she batted her eyes at him. "Hank Myers . . . you were the one who left town."

"Okay, you're right." He had brought two white folding chairs, and he set them up now, one facing the camera and the picnic table and the other beside it. "Go ahead. You start."

Irvel took a deep breath and settled into the chair. She sat straight and poised, her hands folded. Hank had brought a blanket, in case the breeze picked up. But for now warm sunshine streamed through the branches of the nearby tree.

After a beat, Irvel lifted her eyes to the camera and began to speak.

"My name is Irvel Myers." She hesitated, sadness coloring this part. "This is for my son, Charlie, and his wife, Peggy, and my precious granddaughter, Audra. It is also for me and Hank, and for whoever might want to know our story, our beautiful, breathtaking love story."

Hank watched, hanging on every word.

Irvel continued. "Yesterday, I was diagnosed with Alzheimer's disease. Already, I feel its effects, so Hank bought this camera. He thought we should tell our love story . . . while we still can.

"Also, there is something no one knows about me. Forty-seven years ago, I was recruited by the Office of Strategic Services to work for the U.S. military during World War Two.

"That's right, I was a spy. But our story does not begin there. It begins the summer of 1940."

Hank was drawn in by her words, taken by her. Irvel was ready for this. She had clearly practiced and rehearsed, without ever saying a word. For a few seconds, she closed her eyes. Like she was allowing herself to journey back in time, intent on remembering every detail.

Finally, she opened them and from the beginning, the story came to life in vibrant moments and fully detailed memories. Not just for Irvel, but for Hank, too. Never mind Alzheimer's disease or the reason they were shooting this video or the impending heartbreak. Here and now, it was the summer of 1940, for both of them.

As if it were all happening again right before their eyes.

• • •

THE INVITATION FROM Hank had come when Irvel Holland least expected it. That July morning in 1940, she was getting ready for a date with Gary Walsh, the boy she was seeing, when the phone rang.

Irvel's mother answered it. "Why, Hank, hello!" She covered the mouthpiece and motioned to Irvel in a whispered voice. "Irvel! It's Hank!"

Boyfriend or not, Irvel's heart took wing when she heard Hank's name. She was ironing her skirt for her date that night, but at the mention of Hank, she set the iron down and hurried to the phone. "Here." She held out her hand.

But her mother wasn't finished talking to him. "Yes, Hank, it's been a lovely summer. How's life at University of Michigan?" She listened, and then laughed. Over the years, Irvel's mother had grown quite fond of Hank. Much more so than the way she felt about Gary, a soda hop at the local diner. "Yes, we've missed you, too."

"Mother!" Irvel whispered as loud as she could. "Please!"

"Okay, Hank. Just a minute. I'll find her for you." Her mother grinned and handed the phone to Irvel. "Here."

Irvel wondered if Hank could hear her heart pounding in her chest. "Hi." She tried to sound casual, like the world hadn't stopped because of his call. "Are you in town?"

"I am. Home for the weekend!" He sounded older, somehow. Older and more handsome. If that were possible.

Irvel absently wrapped the phone cord around her fingers and leaned against the white-tile kitchen counter. "You haven't been home since Christmas."

"Way too long." There was an intentionality in Hank's voice, as if he was calling for more than mere social reasons.

Irvel closed her eyes, willing her heartbeat to slow down. "How was your spring semester?"

He hesitated. "Honestly? I missed you." He paused. "I was wondering if we could take a walk at the lake. If you weren't busy."

"I'm not." She'd been best friends with Hank since they were twelve. She wasn't worried about sounding too eager. "I'd love that." Her answer was out before she could remember her plans for the night or that she had a boyfriend. "What time?"

"Can I pick you up in an hour?"

"Perfect." As Irvel hung up the phone she couldn't feel her feet on the floor. Not until she turned around did she remember the iron. By then the skirt was smoldering beneath the hot surface. Irvel screamed and ran to grab it, but she was too late.

An iron-shaped mark was forever burned into the pale yellow material. Proof that though they lived five hours apart, and though they'd never officially dated, Irvel's heart belonged to Hank Myers.

He picked her up in his father's old blue Ford truck, and between their two seats was a picnic lunch, which he'd made for the occasion. When they pulled away from her parents' house, Hank leaned back in the driver's seat and glanced in her direction. "So . . . how was your sophomore year?"

"Good. I still like being close to home." Irvel attended Indiana University right there in Bloomington. She felt her cheeks flush under his gaze. "What about yours?"

"I really like it there. Two years of college left." He grinned at her. "Then I'll have my degree in government studies."

Irvel nodded. The sky was the brightest blue it had ever been and a heavy humidity hung in the July air. "So . . . you going to be president one day, Hank?"

"That's the plan." He looked confident, like he believed fully in this plan. "But for now, I'm president of a dairy farm in Ypsilanti, half an hour from campus." He laughed. "Humble beginnings are good for a man. That's what my daddy tells me."

Dairy farming looked good on Hank. He had grown another inch or two and his muscled arms were tanned from what must've been a great deal of outdoor work. His blond hair had grown dark with age, and his blue eyes took her breath. He caught her attention again. They were almost at the lake. "What about you, Irvel? What are you studying?"

"Math." She angled herself so she could see him better. "I love numbers. Same as back in sixth grade."

"You were always brilliant." He chuckled, the air between them easy like always.

"Numbers are fun, that's all." Irvel looked straight ahead. The hills leading up to Lake Monroe were in full bloom. Everything about the moment felt perfect.

"Fun, huh?" Hank uttered a quiet laugh.

"Sure." She looked at him. "They're a puzzle. There's always an answer." She lifted her chin, proud of herself. "Next semester I'm going to tutor junior high math a few hours a week."

"And you'll be the best, Irvel." He winked at her. "The very best."

They parked not far from the shore and Hank carried the picnic basket. He spread a cloth over a table near the water and left their lunch on the ground nearby. "Let's walk first. Before we eat."

"Okay." Irvel walked beside him. She wore a pale pink skirt, a white sleeveless fitted blouse and pink Oxfords. Again, she felt like she was floating.

"So . . . what have you been up to?" Hank's expression told her he knew more than he was saying.

"Not much." She decided to play it coy. "Me and the girls have been at the city pool almost every day."

"I can tell." He brushed his arm against hers. "You look like you've been to the beach."

She smiled at him. Her heart somersaulted within her. "You're only home for the weekend?"

"Actually, until mid-August. Just before school starts."

They headed south along the path to the prettiest part of the lake. Their pace was slow, leaving room for whatever was on their minds. Hank talked about the war in Europe. "Hitler won't stop until he owns the world." He stared up at the blue sky. "It all feels so far away."

"It does." Irvel took a slow breath. The war terrified her. "A guy in my history class dropped out to volunteer. He left last week for Europe."

Hank nodded. "I've thought about it. Dropping everything and helping somewhere." He turned to her. "Either way, I'm pretty sure my turn is coming."

Irvel's heart skipped a beat and fear shot storm clouds over the moment. She couldn't imagine the United States joining the awful fight overseas. The two walked in silence for a few minutes, the slightest breeze drifting across the water. Irvel found her most positive tone. "President Roosevelt says we're staying out of it. It's not our war."

"It will be." Hank shot her a wary look.

"I don't know. The *Star* says FDR is in peace talks." Irvel shrugged. "Don't you believe that?"

"The president means well." A sad chuckle came from deep inside Hank. "But there won't be peace with Hitler. He's evil."

"True." The thought made Irvel sick to her stomach. "Like the devil, himself." She had overheard her parents talking about something else, a detail most people weren't openly discussing. "What he's doing to the Jewish people in Germany . . . it's hard to imagine."

"Hitler is forcing most of them out of the country." Hank looked down for a moment. "The things I hear are unthinkable."

"I bet it's worse than we know." Irvel's chest felt tight. "He blames the Jews for World War One."

Hank looked out over the lake. "The war isn't just Hitler and Germany. It's Italy, too. Mussolini. And Japan. We're bound to be involved."

Hank was right. Already, Italy had joined forces with Germany, declaring war on France and Britain. And Japan was attempting what seemed to be a takeover in the Pacific. "It all scares me to death, Hank."

"Hey." He slowed to a stop and turned to her. "Remember eighth grade?" A grin lifted Hank's mouth. "The teacher had us memorize Bible verses?"

"Of course." Irvel tilted her head. Time had stopped here on the lakeshore with Hank. "*Scripture is our best weapon when we're afraid*. I can still hear her voice."

Hank brushed his thumb against her cheek. "Remember this one? 'Be strong and courageous. Do not be afraid . . . do not be discouraged, for the Lord your God will be with you wherever you go.'"

The words from the Bible ushered a new and deeper peace for Irvel. She could breathe right again. She met his eyes. "Joshua 1:9."

"The most reassuring truth." He searched her eyes. "Don't be afraid, Irvel. Whatever's ahead . . . just hold on to that truth. We're all going to need it."

She smiled and they kept walking. Neither of them brought up the war again. But there was a different type of battle they still hadn't talked about. The one raging in their hearts.

Hank broached the subject first. "So . . . tell me about Gary Walsh."

There it was. He did know. Irvel took her time responding. "Someone told you."

"Three people, actually." Hank grinned like it didn't matter. But his eyes told a different story. "I remember that football game my senior year. You and your friends walked by and Gary whistled at you."

She felt her cheeks grow hot. "He was just teasing."

"No." Hank chuckled. "Gary Walsh always had it bad for you." He stopped walking and faced her. His voice grew softer. "It was my fault. I should've asked you out before anyone else had a chance."

She tried to keep things light. "That would've helped."

"I always thought . . ." He seemed to change his mind about whatever he was going to say. "You wanna tell me about it?"

"Not really." Irvel sighed. "Gary reached out to me a week after I heard about you and that pretty Michigan coed . . . Maggie Wright."

"We had one date." Hank laughed. "So, Gary seized the moment. The moment that wasn't even a moment. Is that it?"

"I figured if you'd moved on with Maggie . . . I had no reason to tell Gary no." She searched Hank's face. "Gary *wanted* to date me."

Hank took hold of her hand for a few seconds and then released it. "You really thought I was seeing another girl?"

"Of course. You're the one who left for Ann Arbor, Hank." She could feel the hurt in her eyes. "I figured we would always only be friends."

"I got a scholarship to U of M." Hank put his hand alongside Irvel's cheek. "Otherwise I never would have left you, Irvel. You should've known that."

Despite the situation, Irvel felt the slightest happiness in her heart. "You never said anything."

"I would have. Eventually." Hank held her gaze for a

long moment and they started walking again. "Gary Walsh, huh?" His tone was lighter now. "Gary hasn't been serious a day in his life. You deserve someone better." He leaned closer. "And that someone will be coming home to Bloomington the minute he graduates from Michigan."

"Interesting." Irvel tried to hide the way his words filled her heart.

"I mean it, Irvel." He slowed his pace. "The minute I graduate." He hesitated. "So you and Gary . . . how long have you been together?"

Despite the sun casting diamonds on the water, and the summer breeze warm on her face, Irvel's heart felt heavy again. "A few months. He asked me to be his girlfriend and . . ."

Hank nodded, slow and thoughtful. "And so you are."

"So, I am." Irvel looked at the ground for a few seconds. Hank didn't ask if she had plans with Gary that night, and she didn't offer the information. Later she would learn that Hank had known all along. He and Gary had spoken earlier that day. Before Hank called her.

But in that moment, walking along the shore of Lake Monroe, it was just the two of them. Neither of them brought up Gary's name the rest of the afternoon. When they reached the south side of the lake, Hank spotted an old tire swing. "Maybe we should reenact it." His eyes sparkled. "Come on, Irvel. There's no current today."

He was right. The water was calm and clear and before Irvel could think of a reason to say no, she and Hank were laughing and running for the swing. They took turns flying out over the water and dropping into the cool lake below. At one point Hank took her hand. "Let's do it together!"

Being that close to Hank sent chills over her skin and gave her feelings she hadn't known before. She shouldn't be doing this, here on the far side of the lake, just the two of them. Gary wouldn't like it. Her mama wouldn't, either. But even so Irvel didn't let go of Hank's hand.

The two of them climbed up on the swing, and Irvel sat on Hank's knee as they pushed out over the lake. They landed together ten yards offshore, their arms and legs tangled together. Irvel laughed so hard she gulped down a few mouthfuls of water and started coughing.

"Here we go again." Hank was laughing, too, but he was a stronger swimmer, so he wasn't choking.

"I'm okay." Irvel coughed again. She could've made it safely back to the shore. But when Hank looped his arm around her waist and helped her to the shallow edge of the lake, she didn't stop him.

Later, they sat shoulder to shoulder at the picnic table Hank had chosen. He had brought cheese and crackers and grapes, so they snacked on those and looked out over the water.

A few times, Hank turned to her to say one thing or another and their faces were only a breath apart. Was he going to kiss her? Out here at Lake Monroe, even when she had a date with Gary Walsh that night?

As wrong as it was, Irvel wished he would. Before he took her home, he turned to her one last time, his breath sweet against her cheek. "You remember the two things I told you after I came back to school from my pneumonia? After I rescued you from the creek that day?"

"Yes." Irvel would never forget. Still, she wasn't sure where Hank was going with this. "I remember."

"I said I'd do it all again . . . I'd jump in that creek to save you every time, Irvel."

"Right, yes." She swallowed. If only he would kiss her, and they would both know for all time that this was the only right thing besides God and family they would ever know in all their lives.

"Well, I still mean that." Hank lowered his voice. He was so handsome, so close. "And that other thing I told you that day . . . you remember that?"

"Yes, Hank." Their faces were closer now.

"Irvel," he whispered. "I still mean that, too."

He paused, but he left the words about wanting to marry her unspoken. They both knew what he'd said. Hank slid a few inches back, putting distance between them. Then he collected the leftover cheese and crackers, grapes and napkins, and placed them in the wicker basket. "Well, that'll do it for today." He grinned at her. "Let's get you back, Irvel Holland. I hear you have a hot date."

"Hank." Irvel felt her heart sink. "I . . . it's complicated."

"I know." Hank stayed at her side as they walked back to his truck. "You let me know when you're single again, okay?"

She managed what felt like the weakest of smiles. "He's a good guy, Hank. He is."

"I don't doubt it." For a flash of a moment, Hank

looked hurt, but he changed the subject. "So, while you've been dating Gary Walsh, I've been hanging out with cows. They're still warming up to me, though. Almost got kicked in the head yesterday by old Betsy."

On the drive home, Hank told her a handful of funny stories from his time working at the dairy farm. How he had brought a bucket of sudsy water into the holding area, thinking it was fresh milk and how the farmer had drunk half a cup before spitting it out. "It's amazing I still have a job."

They laughed, the wind in their hair, and for a few quiet minutes it seemed they were both secretly certain that somehow all of life would eventually work out for the two of them.

Even so, as they neared her house Irvel could sense the closeness between them slipping away. At least for now. By the time he walked her up to the front door, they were just a couple of best friends, not sure where life or love would take them. But Irvel knew one thing for sure as she watched Hank Myers drive away. She could never give herself fully to anyone else.

Because he hadn't just taken the picnic basket with him from the lake that day.

He had taken her heart.

OCTOBER 3, 1989

4

Irvel blinked and fell silent as if a pivotal scene in a movie had just come to an end.

Hank hit the stop button on the camera and they faced each other. So compelling had her version of that day been that Hank long ago forgot he was listening to a story. He was there, the lake water on his skin, the feel of Irvel close beside him.

She stood and smoothed the wrinkles in her pretty red dress, a dress much like she would've worn back in 1940. Then she came to him and touched his cheek, their faces as close as they had been that day at the lake. "I should've canceled my date with Gary Walsh." Irvel looked straight into his soul. "My heart could never belong to anyone but you."

"I know." He kissed her lips and then her forehead. This spot at the back of the park was private, as if all the world existed just for the two of them and this retelling of the pieces of their love story. "It's okay. God worked it out."

"He did." Irvel smiled. "It just took us a while to get the timing right."

Hank hit the record button again. "My turn."

"Which part are you going to tell?" Irvel looked young again, like the remembering was doing her good.

"You'll see."

He moved to the chair in front of the camera. The next piece of their story came as easily for Hank as if it had happened last week.

Because where Irvel was concerned, his memories were always just a whisper away.

• • •

NOVEMBER 1940

BY THE FALL of 1940, Germany was bombing Britain practically around the clock, and President Roosevelt had declared that all men eighteen to forty-five must register for the draft. That meant Hank; his brother, Sam; and their father had to fill out paperwork and be ready to serve. When the selection process began, each person called up was required to serve one year in duty to the U.S. military.

The peacetime draft was the first of its kind for the United States.

Clearly, the American leaders were preparing for war.

Hank and his family weren't chosen in the first round, but Hank was only frustrated by the fact. He still wanted to volunteer, fly overseas to fight the Nazis, anything to help. Instead he returned full-time to University of Michigan and listened to updates every night on the radio. Because if the US joined the war, he wanted to be ready. Irvel stayed in school at Indiana, where—despite their day at the lake—she kept seeing Gary Walsh.

Because of that, eventually Hank moved on, too.

That semester, Maggie Wright was in his English class, and after studying together most Monday afternoons and hanging out most Friday and Saturday nights, by November, the two were an item. Even then Hank didn't ask Maggie to be his girlfriend. That spot belonged only to Irvel.

If she'd ever have him.

Still, Hank was fond of Maggie, and there was no telling how serious things were with Irvel and Gary. When Thanksgiving came around, Hank heard from his older brother, Sam, that Irvel and her family were going to visit her aunt in Kentucky. Typically, they would join Hank's family for dessert on Thanksgiving Day. But not this year.

So without giving his parents any warning, Hank brought Maggie home for the holiday.

Snow was falling the day the two of them pulled into his family's driveway. The house where Hank had grown up was spacious and warm, nestled on a pretty tree-lined block of homes in the shadow of Indiana University and around the corner from Irvel's. Hank's mother looked surprised as she met them at the door and gave Maggie a hug. "Hank's told us so much about you. We're glad you could join us."

"Thank you." Maggie beamed under the compliment.

Not until after Maggie was settling into the family's guest room did Hank's mother find him in the kitchen. She looked concerned.

"There's a problem." She glanced over her shoulder and then back at Hank. This time she lowered her voice.

"Why didn't you tell me you were bringing Maggie?" Her shoulders sank. "I invited Irvel and her family for dessert tomorrow. Like always."

Hank could only stare at his mother. "I thought they were spending Thanksgiving in Kentucky?"

"No. I don't know where you heard that." His mother put her hand on Hank's arm. "Also . . . Irvel and Gary ended things three weeks ago."

This was terrible. Hank sighed. "You're sure?"

"Yes," his mom whispered. "Irvel is bringing her famous apple pie. Her mother said she was looking forward to seeing you."

"Perfect." Hank paced a few steps away from his mom and then back again. "Maybe Maggie and I should just head back to Michigan."

For a few seconds, his mother said nothing. Then she took a step closer. "Son . . . you used to tell us you were in love with Irvel Holland. You were going to marry her. But you haven't acted on that. Not ever." She paused, studying him. "Is there a reason?"

Hank stared at the floor for a moment. "When she didn't break up with Gary . . . " He hated this. "I figured she'd lost her feelings for me."

"You know what I think?" His mother's tone was kind, but certain. "I think you and Irvel are both okay being just friends."

She was wrong. Hank started to shake his head, but the gesture died off. Why would his mom think any differently?

Why would anyone? She was right. He could've asked Irvel out years ago, and because he never did, this predicament was his fault. "I don't know, Mom."

"Exactly." His mother seemed to relax a bit. "Let's have a nice Thanksgiving."

They heard Maggie exit the guest room and walk in their direction. Hank's mother still talked in a whisper. "Your girlfriend is wonderful, Son. I really like her."

Hank nodded. He was dizzy and sick to his stomach and anxious. He didn't want to hurt Maggie. But all he could think about was spending the holiday with Irvel. If only she had let him know about ending things with Gary. Now he'd have to find a way to get through the next few days. It wasn't his time with Irvel, that was all. Soon . . . someday soon they'd find their way together.

"Did I miss anything?" Maggie entered the kitchen and smiled at Hank and his mother.

"Not at all, dear." His mom pulled a loaf of bread from the top of the refrigerator. "Maybe you and Hank could help with the stuffing."

Maggie's eyes lit up. "I'd love that."

"I'm the best bread ripper in the family." Hank grinned. He couldn't stay upset. There was no point. This was his Thanksgiving with Maggie, no matter what else happened. One day, when he married Irvel Holland, the two of them would laugh about this Thanksgiving of 1940, and how the timing had been off.

Hank and Maggie tore the loaf of bread into small pieces and seasoned the bowl with rosemary, sage, and thyme.

After that, they played cards with his parents and Sam. The group laughed and then grew more serious as they talked about final exams and the war in Europe and the plight of the Jewish people. They shared the dreams they had for the coming year. Anyone watching would've thought Hank and Maggie were a longtime thing.

But all the while Hank could only think about Irvel.

When it was time to turn in that night Hank and Sam headed to their room, on the opposite side of the house from where Maggie was staying. The brothers had shared a room since they were little, and when they were both home from college, they still did.

As soon as the door closed behind them, Hank sat on the edge of his bed and looked hard at Sam. "What made you think Irvel and her family were going to Kentucky?"

The brothers had always been close. Just two years apart. Hank, tall and slender, and Sam shorter and stockier. Hank had played football and basketball in high school, and Sam had been a wrestler. Both played baseball and both excelled in the classroom. Either of them would have laid down his life for the other.

Hank had been waiting all night for this conversation.

Sam slipped into a T-shirt and shorts and sat on the opposite bed, so they were facing each other. He was a senior at Indiana, preparing to be a math teacher. Just like Irvel wanted to be. Sam shrugged. "That's what I heard."

A possibility dawned on Hank. "Did you hear it from Gary Walsh?"

Sam thought for a moment. "You know, I think I did. I saw him at church a few weeks ago."

There it was. The pieces all added up. Hank leaned back on his elbows. "Did he happen to mention that he and Irvel broke up?"

"No." Sam's surprise was genuine. "Really?"

"That's what Mom said." Hank could see it all very clearly. Gary would have known that Hank was seeing Maggie. He may have figured Hank would bring Maggie home if he thought Irvel was out of town. If so, Gary had thought right.

"Speaking of Irvel . . ." A nervous look came over Sam. He wrung his hands together for a moment. "She, uh . . . she and I have a few classes together."

Deep in his chest, Hank's heart skipped a single beat. He chuckled. "I figured as much. You both want to spend your lives teaching kids about numbers."

"Right." Sam laughed, too. For a moment they were in high school again. Their laughter faded. "Anyway . . . I was thinking . . . you're with Maggie, and . . ."

Hank's heart was pounding now. He blinked. *Where is this going?*

Sam squinted. "You and Irvel . . . you've always been just friends."

Had he been listening to Hank's conversation with their mother earlier today? Hank nodded. Their bedroom felt like it was spinning.

"So . . . is that all you feel for her?" Sam wiped his palms on the edge of his bed. "Because I don't know . . . I mean if she'd go, I'd like to ask her to dinner. If she and Gary aren't together."

Hank sat up straight. How could this be happening? His mind raced, searching for an answer. It took no time to reach the only one possible. If his brother wanted to ask Irvel out to dinner, Hank couldn't stop him. "Heck, Sam." Hank remembered to smile. "Irvel couldn't have a better dinner date anywhere, in all the world."

"Really?"

"Sure." Hank felt sick to his stomach.

"Okay. Good." Sam visibly relaxed and he laughed again. "I wasn't sure how you felt about her. She's always been your friend, but if you wanted her to be *your* girl . . . I'd never think of asking. You know that." He paused. "And Maggie Wright, she's a real peach, Hank. You gotta keep her around!"

"Right." Every word felt forced. "She is. A real peach."

"I'm glad I asked." Sam stretched out on his mattress, hands linked behind his head. "I might ask her tomorrow. Like I said, I see her all the time."

Sam was the best person Hank knew. "Tomorrow. Sounds good." He stretched out on his bed, too. His heart was still racing. *Just dinner,* he told himself. Sam would just take her out for dinner and that would be that. And eventually . . . eventually everyone would see things the way they were supposed to be. Irvel and Hank, together forever. Just not yet. He swallowed, searching for the right words. "You . . . you ask her to dinner, Sam. That'll be great."

There had been no way then for Hank to grasp or

comprehend where such a statement might go. He was seeing Maggie. How could he do anything but approve a single dinner date between Sam and Irvel? So, tomorrow, on Thanksgiving Day, his brother, his best friend, would ask the love of Hank's life to dinner. And that would be that. One time, right?

Long after Sam was asleep, Hank stared at the ceiling and wondered why he hadn't been honest with his brother. Just because he had brought Maggie home, didn't mean he wasn't in love with Irvel. How could he have made such a terrible mistake?

Then a different reality hit him. He didn't have to worry about Sam's dinner date idea. Because Irvel would never agree to dinner with Sam. Of course not. She would smile and her blue eyes would fill with kindness. But she would politely tell Sam no. What with her feelings for Hank, dinner with Sam would be too strange.

Hank felt himself relax. Yes, that was it. He had nothing to worry about. Even so, when Hank finally fell asleep he was no longer looking forward to Thanksgiving Day.

He was dreading it.

Sure enough, the next afternoon, things were off from the beginning. He and Maggie helped make the mashed potatoes and dinner rolls, but when it came time to sit down at the family table, their conversation felt awkward and uncomfortable. Hank looked at the front door so often, Maggie finally asked about it.

"Are you expecting someone, Hank?" She tilted her head and cast a glance to the door, then back at him.

Hank's parents were talking with Sam about his teaching opportunities in Bloomington. Hank set his fork down and forced a smile. "Actually . . . yes. My good friend Irvel and her family are joining us for dessert."

"Okay." Confusion flashed in Maggie's eyes. "So . . . until then can you focus on us?"

"Sure . . . sorry." Hank put his arm around Maggie's shoulders. "I just . . . Irvel and I . . . we haven't seen each other in a while."

Maggie stared at him for a long moment. Then she turned to Hank's mother and found her way into that conversation, instead. Occasionally she would shoot Hank a look. Like she still didn't understand the distance that seemed to be growing between them with each passing minute.

Hank clenched his jaw. What was he doing? He finished his turkey and kept his attention on Maggie. She was intelligent and beautiful and kind. And this holiday weekend, she was his date. He had cared enough to bring her home for Thanksgiving, so no more thinking about Irvel.

The rest of dinner Hank worked hard to be himself around Maggie. Later, they washed dishes together and took turns whipping the cream for the pumpkin pie. By the time Irvel's family arrived, Hank was determined to make Maggie feel special, no matter how things played out that night.

Instead, the moment Irvel walked through the door she took Hank's breath. She wore a navy-blue dress and a matching fascinator angled to the side of her blond hair. Her high-heeled dark blue shoes had little bows on them.

Not that Hank was looking.

He took Maggie's hand and led her over to where Irvel was standing on the far side of the kitchen. "Irvel, I'd like you to meet Maggie." He didn't dare linger on Irvel's eyes. Instead, he turned back to Maggie. "And Maggie, this is Irvel. My longtime friend."

Longtime friend? The words felt like sandpaper on his tongue. Hank could practically see Irvel bristle at the title. *What in the world was happening?* he asked himself often that night. But he was also mindful of Maggie. None of this was her fault, and again he determined not to hurt her, no matter how difficult things were.

As they settled in for dessert, Irvel was gracious. She asked Maggie about her time at Michigan, and then Irvel asked her about Hank. There were a number of conversations playing out at the long table, but Hank had ears for that one alone. The two girls didn't seem to notice him listening.

"I just think the world of him." Maggie leaned closer to Irvel. "I think he'll ask me to be his girlfriend by Christmas."

Girlfriend? Hank stared at his half-eaten pumpkin pie. He had no intention of making things official with Maggie in a month. But then, why had he brought her home? His feelings were like a ball of tangled fishing wire.

Half an hour later it happened. Hank watched Irvel and Sam have a conversation near the dessert table. This was it . . . the moment Sam was going to ask her to dinner. Hank couldn't hear a word but he was certain about what would happen next. His older brother's face would fall. Sam would nod in defeat, and Irvel would angle her pretty head, apologizing for telling him no. But of course, she simply could not go out with him.

But that's not how it played out.

Instead Irvel was the one nodding. Nodding and moving her hands, laughing and hanging on Sam's every word. A little later that night, Hank was making a cup of coffee in the kitchen, when he saw Irvel step out back by herself. She seemed to not want anyone to see her.

Hank set his coffee down and followed.

Out back Irvel stood at the edge of the patio, her eyes fixed on the starry Bloomington sky. She turned at the sound of him and their eyes held. "Hi."

"Hi." He slid his hands into the pockets of his trousers. He waited a long moment. "I saw you talking to Sam."

Irvel turned her confused eyes to him. "You knew?"

"I did." Hank wasn't sure what to say.

He couldn't betray Sam, couldn't confess his feelings here . . . now. But anything less would be practically a lie. Surely, nothing would come of Irvel and Sam. Not when Hank and Irvel were destined to be together. Hank mustered up his courage. What should he say? Nothing had changed. He would still love Irvel till the day he died. He dug deep, from the bottom of his heart. "Sam's the best guy I know."

He could feel Irvel's eyes on him for what felt like a hundred seconds. "I told him yes. About dinner."

"Good." His response was out before he could consider the outcome. He felt dizzy and sick and upside down. Like all of this was only a nightmare. "You two will, uh . . . you'll have fun."

"Yes. Sam's great." The hurt in her eyes was instant. "And you . . . with Maggie. You two look very happy."

"Sure. Yeah." Hank gazed up at the stars. What else could he say? The decision was made. Irvel was going out to dinner with the best guy in the world—Hank's brother, Sam. He felt like he was driving a hundred miles an hour toward the edge of a cliff. How had they gotten here?

"I guess that seals it." Irvel faced him. "You're my best friend, Hank." Tears filled her eyes, but she smiled, anyway. "No matter what happens from here . . . I hope we keep that."

All he wanted was to take her in his arms and kiss her, tell her everything he never seemed to get around to telling her. That it might not feel like it now, but he hadn't been only talking when he had told her he wanted to marry her someday. He still felt that way.

But Maggie was waiting inside . . . and Sam. Both of them probably wondering what was happening out here. He pulled her into a hug that lasted a moment longer than he intended. Then he stepped back and looked all the way to her heart. "We will keep that, Irvel. You'll always be my best friend."

As they walked back in the house and joined the others, as she returned to Sam and he took his spot next to Maggie, and as their families shared dessert and stories from the old days and conversation about the war, Hank was plagued by a very specific, visceral feeling.

The feeling that he had made a terrible mistake and this time he *was* drowning.

And there was no one in all the world coming to save him.

MAY 1941

5

Irvel's date with Sam Myers turned into a string of candlelit winter dinners in downtown Bloomington and springtime picnics along the creek at Lower Cascades Park, until the thing she never saw coming, happened.

She had actually fallen for Hank's brother.

No, she didn't long for Sam the way she had for Hank. But she cared deeply. Which had to mean something. Besides, Hank didn't want her, anyway. He had made that clear on Thanksgiving night with Maggie Wright waiting inside the house. The two were still dating. Irvel wondered if there'd be an announcement coming soon. An engagement or a wedding before 1941 ran out.

But through every date and picnic with Sam, every Sunday church outing and dinner at her parents' house, the threat of war loomed. Like a ticking clock or a pounding heartbeat, a distant drum or gathering storm clouds. The threat seeped into daily life like an invisible toxin penetrating every conversation and casual outing and quiet moment. By then, Hungary, Romania and Bulgaria had joined the Axis powers and Germany had taken Yugoslavia and Greece.

And everyone guessed that Hitler's real goal might be an invasion of Russia.

For now, Irvel was more concerned with her growing fear of the war and whether Hank and Sam would be drafted than where her relationship with Sam was headed. What if the Germans started dropping bombs on Indiana the way they were still doing in London?

With wars and rumors of wars consuming life all around them, Sam finished his fifth year of college, graduated with his teaching degree, and took a job teaching math at Bloomington High. "A couple years from now, you can join me," he told her at his graduation party that night. "Can you picture it, you and me teaching down the hall from each other?"

She smiled and slipped her arms around Sam's shoulders. "Yes. I can see it all, Sam." And she could.

By then she didn't feel sad or awkward or confused when she was at Sam's house. But the graduation party was the first time she'd seen Hank since the spring semester ended. He found her in the kitchen, and this time there was no hug, no reaching for her hand.

"Hi." Hank simply nodded. "Good to see you, Irvel."

"Hank." She felt suddenly shy. "Nice party for Sam."

"It is." He took a step closer, his eyes locked on hers. "He deserves everything he has."

Was it her imagination or did Hank hold her gaze longer than necessary? They hadn't spent time together in months, so the best friend thing hadn't really worked out. Maybe that accounted for the longing in Hank's eyes that night. Or maybe it was her imagination, a figment of what might have been that hadn't quite cleared the cobwebs of her yesterday's heart.

The junior high girl, dripping wet on her front porch, had believed she would always be friends with Hank. That she'd tell him her deepest secrets as long as she lived. But the twenty-one-year-old college junior knew better. Irvel was falling for his brother, and Hank was in love with Maggie. Clearly.

Those realities left no time for friendship between Irvel and Hank.

Even with the concerns about war, the summer of 1941 kicked into high gear in Bloomington. Irvel's heart still skipped a beat when she saw Hank, but she understood things would never be what they had once been between them.

That summer, Hank worked baling hay at a farm in Bloomington rather than go back to milking cows in Michigan. As for Sam, with his first day of teaching months away, he took a job at the farm, too. Both of them grew strong and tan, working outdoors in the Indiana sun.

Like Hank, Maggie was home from Michigan, living less than an hour away outside Indianapolis, so on the weekends, Maggie and Hank would sometimes double-date with Irvel and Sam. Seeing Hank with Maggie never became totally normal for Irvel, but they had both moved on. The days of summer flew by and over the Fourth of July, the four of them were playing cards at the Myerses' house when talk of the war came up—as it often did.

"The news says the Germans are trapping tens of thousands of Jews in Polish ghettos." Maggie looked at the others. "I saw a photo . . . a little boy with bone-thin legs and a gaunt face. People are starving to death."

Irvel's heart started to race. *Don't be afraid,* she told herself. *Stay calm.* She focused her attention on Maggie's words. No wonder Hank was in love with the girl. Maggie was going on about how the Bible was clear that the Jews were God's chosen people. Something that had been called into question culturally in the past decade. Hank's girlfriend took a deep breath. "Maybe Hitler is the antichrist."

"I've heard that." Sam turned his attention to Irvel. "At the teachers' summer meeting last week, that's what a couple people were saying. Apparently, Hitler is forcing the Jews to bow down to him."

Irvel hated this. How could any of this be happening? She drew the slightest breath. Her heart beat so hard she figured everyone at the table could hear it.

Hank laid his cards facedown. "I read that in the paper last week. Hitler doesn't just want the Jews out of Germany, unable to work or buy food." He looked around, his eyes somber. "He wants them punished."

"Some people think he wants them dead." Sam crossed his arms. "All of them."

A tight feeling wrapped itself around Irvel's throat and shoulders. There it was again. That crippling fear. The feeling that was becoming more familiar every time they talked about the war. "We . . . we can't let that happen."

Hank and Sam agreed they'd sign up for the Army today if it meant rescuing the Jewish people. But for now, the United States wasn't involved like that. There would be no way to get into occupied Poland to free the Jews. And things had definitely grown more troubling a few weeks ago when—like everyone thought—Germany invaded the Soviet Union.

"It's all getting worse." Maggie shuffled the cards. "Hitler has to be stopped or . . . I can't imagine it."

Irvel tried to exhale but a suffocating panic crashed over her like a ten-foot wave. She could no longer feel the sandy bottom, couldn't get her footing or breathe or think. "I'll . . . I'll be back." She pushed herself away from the table and headed for the bathroom. *Breathe,* she ordered herself. *Breathe, Irvel.*

Once inside, she shut the door, grabbed onto the counter and stared at herself in the small oval mirror. Drops of perspiration had formed on her forehead and above her upper lip.

It was happening again.

Her mother had taken her to the doctor last week for these very same symptoms. After checking her heart and her lungs, after measuring her pulse and drawing blood, the results were not altogether surprising. Irvel was fine physically.

The episodes were panic attacks. "It's all in your mind," the doctor told her. "You need to find a way to deal with your fear."

Irvel's mother had nodded, sympathetic. "It's the war

in Europe," she told the doctor. "Lately, every time she thinks about it, this happens."

"I think that goes for all of us." He chuckled. "Let me just say . . . you aren't going to die. Panic attacks can't kill you." The doctor patted Irvel on the shoulder and smiled. "Let me put you at ease, young lady. *We're* not in the war. You can relax. It's all someone else's problem."

Even now in the middle of a card game on a holiday weekend, the doctor's words stayed with her. *Someone else's problem.* Was that the right way to look at what was happening in Europe? Or the way Japan was showing aggression in the Pacific? Or the plight of millions of Jews in Poland?

Stop! The walls felt like they were closing in, and her lungs still wouldn't work. She was scared to death and getting more afraid with every passing second. Fear was like an avalanche and she had no way to outrun it.

Irvel stretched her arms high over her head and forced herself to breathe out. *Just keep breathing.* What had the doctor told her to do? If it happened again? Irvel's mind raced. There were exercises, actions meant to bring herself out of an attack.

Bend at the waist, right? Wasn't that it? Irvel's heart pounded so loud she could barely think, but she followed his advice. She bent at her waist and held her breath. Nothing. The tight feeling remained and she gasped for her next breath. What else had he said?

Irvel straightened and leaned on the bathroom counter again. Something else . . . what was it? Irvel's mind was moving too fast to focus. Shove something . . . no, that wasn't it. Push . . . yes, push! She held her breath again and pushed down on the counter as hard as she could. Like she was trying to move it through the floor.

She could hear the doctor's cavalier voice. *You won't die.* How did he know? If she couldn't breathe, then she actually could die. *Breathe out, Irvel. You have to breathe out.* Never mind breathing in, as long as she could exhale, she wouldn't pass out. At least that had been true for her in the past. *You won't die, Irvel,* she told herself. A panic attack couldn't kill her. The situation was getting worse, her breathing fast and shallow when she heard it.

My daughter, peace . . . peace, be still. I am with you.

The voice was louder than a whisper, but who had spoken? Irvel dropped her arms to her sides and looked behind her. No one was there. This was a bathroom. Once more she stared at the mirror and a thought hit her. Could it be . . . ?

"God?" She kept her voice low. Her hands trembled. "Is that You?"

My peace I give you, my precious one. I am with you always.

Like a switch had been flipped, a surreal calm came over her. The pain in her chest and shoulders eased and she could breathe again. As if the attack had never happened. She closed her eyes. God was the answer . . . why hadn't she thought of that before? She felt her body relax more with every passing breath. She was His . . . and He alone could give her peace.

"Okay . . . okay, I can breathe." Her whisper was warm with relief. She filled her lungs full and exhaled. More peace . . . enough to make her forget that moments ago she was in a raging attack. One more easy breath, then another. Irvel blinked back tears. Maybe this was her answer for whenever panic struck. "Thank You." She whispered. "Thank You, Father."

Irvel returned to the others, and they got back to playing cards. Sam took her hand and gave her a look the others missed. *You okay?* his eyes seemed to ask. She nodded. The feeling of supernatural peace remained and throughout the night fear left her alone. But never for long.

Every time she was with Sam, they talked more about the war. How Jews were being rounded up and massacred and the fact that the British government had ruled out any chance of peace negotiations with Germany. Fear would come and with it the panic. Irvel would pray, and eventually that would help. Until the next time.

Once when the four of them were sharing lunch at Lower Cascades Park, Sam brought up the idea of military codes. "One of my buddies told me the United States military is communicating with troops overseas via codes." He nodded. "It's happening in Europe and the Pacific."

They were sitting near the creek that ran through the park. Hank stood and paced closer to the water's edge.

Instantly, Irvel remembered him at her side along this very creek, that time in junior high. She let the thought go.

"I like that." Hank turned and stared at his brother.

"We should do that. Join the Army and help make codes for the troops."

"We all should." Sam reached for Irvel's hand. "We could work on ships or overseas. I'd sign up in a minute."

The thought of moving a single step closer to the places where the war was actually taking place brought another rush of fear to Irvel. "I couldn't." She felt her heart pick up pace. "You men can do that. If it comes to it, Maggie and I will help from here. Whatever we can do." She nodded at Maggie. "Right?"

"Yes." Maggie took a drink from her iced tea. She uttered a slight laugh. "I can sew, but I'm terrible at math and making codes."

The next week when Sam picked her up for dinner, he told Irvel how American code makers were gaining intelligence on Japanese plans to attack Southeast Asia. "They're calling it Operation Magic." He put his arm around her as they walked to his car. "Things are getting worse."

Irvel turned to Sam. "Please . . . can we talk about something else? I . . . I can't think about the war. It makes me sick."

This seemed to hit Sam like a revelation. His tone softened, and regret filled his eyes. "I'm sorry, love. I didn't mean to upset you."

She nodded. "Thank you. It's just . . . I can't find peace when I'm thinking about it."

"I won't bring it up again." He leaned close and kissed her cheek. "I promise."

Through the fall, with Hank and Maggie back at the University of Michigan, Sam kept his word. At times it felt like they were dancing around the most dangerous elephant. But they didn't talk about the war. Maybe it was Irvel's imagination, but it seemed things had quieted down overseas. There was talk of peace with Japan, and the United States had announced an oil embargo against "aggressors" in the war.

And so, America seemed no closer to joining the war, even though the persecution of Jewish people continued. Jews were being ordered to wear armbands embroidered with a yellow Star of David, and their treatment was growing worse every week. In September, word made it back to Bloomington that Hitler's SS troops had killed more than thirty thousand Jewish people because of their efforts of sabotage.

When Irvel heard the news, she succumbed to her most fierce panic attack yet. Not until she took herself alone to the back corner of her family's yard and cried out to God did the fear let up.

Later that week she and her parents attended the alumni basketball game at Bloomington High. *Something normal,* Irvel told herself. She wore a light blue dress and a matching pillbox wool hat. If there was one place they wouldn't talk about the war it was at their local school gymnasium. A storm raged outside that night, but there in the stands, routing for the home team, Irvel felt like a teenager again.

Hank and Sam both played for the alumni team, but

Hank was the star. His days of dominating the court as a high school kid seemed only a blink ago. Maggie had stayed back in Michigan, unable to get away for the game, so both Hank and Sam seemed to look Irvel's way when they hit a basket.

With two seconds left, and the score tied, Sam passed the ball to Hank, who fired up a shot just before the buzzer. The basketball fell straight down the middle of the net, giving the alumni team their most exciting win in a decade.

Irvel was on her feet, clapping and cheering for the brothers. Sam started high-fiving his teammates, but it was Hank who spun in her direction and pointed at her. Just like he used to do when he played basketball in this very gym five years earlier.

She pointed back at him, their eyes and faces lit up by the happiest smiles. As if the world wasn't at war and people weren't being tortured. As if evil rulers weren't trying to take over neighboring countries.

Sam never noticed the moment, and neither did Irvel's father. But her mother did. When Irvel sat back down, she caught her mom's glance and a warning that was unmistakable. *Be careful, Irvel,* she seemed to say. *You're supposed to be in love with Sam.*

Her mother didn't need to worry. The moment was merely a flashback to another time. Not a sign that Irvel's heart could still take flight whenever Hank smiled in her direction. Even if she had to work to convince herself of the truth. Hank was merely treating her like the sister he didn't have. Nothing more.

Still, when she fell asleep that night, it was Hank's grinning face that filled her mind, and there wasn't a thing she could do about it.

The next week, she and Sam celebrated six months of dating. By then Irvel's head was clear again. Hank was probably about to propose to Maggie, and Irvel was in love with Sam. Irvel was sure about this.

At the restaurant that night, Sam took her hands and looked long into her eyes. "There's something I want to ask you, Irvel."

Her heart slipped into a strange rhythm. She wasn't ready, couldn't promise him her whole life. Not yet. She reminded herself to smile. Sam was waiting. "You . . . you do?"

"Yes." His eyes were nothing but kind and trusting. "But I'm going to wait until you finish your undergrad schooling. Next May." He kissed her hands, his eyes never leaving hers. "That way you can be finished with school and completely sure. About us."

Irvel felt herself relax. "Okay." She could flirt a little, now that the seriousness of the moment had passed. "You have my attention, Sam."

"Good." Sam sat back in the booth, a grin tugging at his lips. "You're the best thing that's ever happened to me, Irvel."

The rest of the night and their time at the movies later was filled with easy laughter and an attraction Irvel definitely felt. But she would remember forever his line about waiting . . . so she could be completely sure. Because if Sam had been certain of her answer, he would have asked her to marry him right then. On their six-month anniversary. Instead, it was almost like he could see a hesitancy in her that even she hadn't acknowledged.

But it was a hesitancy that faded a little more every day. Sam was wonderful, and by October, with Hank back in school in Michigan, Irvel's feelings for Sam continued to grow stronger.

Unfortunately, just like her panic attacks.

Especially after Irvel learned that German forces had fired on the USS *Kearny*, killing eleven sailors—some of the first U.S. casualties in World War II. But Irvel also discovered a way to combat her panic. She remembered something her teacher had said back when they were given Bible verses to memorize.

"The Word of God is your sword," she had told them. "An invisible sword able to handle any battle, any difficulty you face. That's why we memorize Scripture."

And so Irvel renewed her work at committing to memory the Bible verses that spoke most of peace and God's hand of protection. When her breathing would get tight and her heartbeat faster, she would silently repeat the Scriptures, and the attack would fizzle before it became full-blown.

That night sitting on Sam's parents' sofa near the radio, they heard more details about the USS *Kearny*. Irvel turned to Sam. "What do you think's going to happen?"

"I think . . ." He touched the tip of her nose. "God is in control. That's what I think." His smile warmed her heart. "Don't worry your pretty little head, Irvel. Really."

She held on to that. Ten minutes later, the Abbott and

Costello show got underway. The two of them had planned their night around listening to the performance.

Anything for a reason to laugh.

As November came and the holidays neared, something beautiful happened. Irvel's fearful spells grew less frequent. *The result of using my invisible sword,* Irvel told herself. Sam wasn't talking about the war like before, and Hank wasn't around to unwittingly challenge Irvel's feelings for his brother. Irvel could see graduation only six months in the future, and for the first time she began to look forward to Sam's question.

Once again, Hank brought Maggie home for Thanksgiving. Peace talks were happening between FDR and the Japanese leadership, and talk of the United States joining the war again seemed further and further away.

As they enjoyed turkey and mashed potatoes and Irvel's apple pie, they had no idea that quietly and under the cover of misleading military codes, Japan had authorized an attack fleet of more than thirty ships and throngs of bomber jets to set sail for Hawaii.

At the table that Thanksgiving night, Irvel noticed the way Hank looked at Maggie Wright and the feel of Sam Myers's hand in hers. This was the way life was going to be, and it felt right. By the time dessert was served, Irvel could almost feel herself letting go of Hank once and for all. Her heart was with Sam, where it should be. Thinking about the future she and Sam would build and the way she truly was falling for him.

Because she loved Sam Myers, truly she did.

DECEMBER 5, 1941

6

Hank broke up with Maggie Wright that first week of December 1941.

He had tried all he could to convince himself that he was in love with Maggie. Like he'd told his brother a year earlier, the girl was a peach. She was. The two spent most of their free time together and in all the months they'd dated, they hadn't had a single fight. Not one. But no matter what Hank tried to do, there was one problem that wouldn't go away.

He didn't love Maggie. He loved his brother's girlfriend, and there wasn't a thing he could do about it except break up with Maggie. Because the dear girl didn't deserve to be loved less.

So, on Friday, the fifth of December, he took her to a quiet bench at Allmendinger Park near Keech Street, and with his heart pounding, he turned and faced her.

Maggie's brown eyes sparkled as their gaze met. "It's the most beautiful day." She lifted her face to the chilly blue sky. "We'll have snow before Christmas, don't you think?"

Hank studied her. She had no idea what was coming.

"I . . . I'm not sure about snow." Hank didn't look away. As much as this would hurt both of them, he had to get on with it. "Maggie . . . this is serious."

That's when Maggie seemed to notice something was wrong. Her smile fell, and she took his hands in hers. "Hank?" Her voice fell. "What is it?"

He hated himself for waiting so long to do this. Always he had figured his feelings for Maggie would grow, that one day he would wake up and laugh at the idea of marrying Irvel Holland. Especially now, when that was not even remotely possible. Now, when he'd never seen his brother so happy.

But he had never woken up to that day, and Hank couldn't wait any longer. He ran his thumbs along the tops of her hands. "It isn't working, me and you."

"What?" Maggie couldn't have looked more shocked.

"It isn't you." If Hank could've stopped her pain, he would have. But there was no other way.

Maggie shook her head. "I . . . I was going to marry you." Tears filled her eyes and spilled onto her cheeks. "I can't believe this."

Hank would always remember Maggie's face, the shock and betrayal that played in her eyes. She was one of the kindest, prettiest girls on the U of M campus, smart and intellectual and fun to be with. And she knew it. Her confidence had stopped her from seeing Hank's hesitancy, though it had been there all along.

The conversation lasted only another ten minutes, and then Hank took Maggie back to her dorm. They had six months till graduation, and after that they wouldn't see each other again. No point in being friends, they had agreed. It was over. No looking back.

That weekend, there was just one place Hank wanted to be: back in Bloomington. His mother would make him his favorite roast and potatoes and he and Sam could go out to the woods and shoot targets. The breakup might've been his idea, but Hank was hurting, too. Time with family was just what he needed.

That and time alone. So he could ask God the question that burned in his heart. How was he going to spend his life watching Sam and Irvel live out theirs?

Sure enough, his parents and Sam welcomed him and he shared his sad news. Sam was saving up to buy a house, but for now he still lived at home. "You'll both be okay." He patted Hank on the back. "God has other plans for you. That's all."

Hank agreed. That night while they ate their mother's pot roast, conversation quickly found its way to the war. "Irvel hates when it comes up." Sam shook his head. "She used to get so afraid she could barely breathe." He shrugged. "She's doing better now, but she still hates talking about it."

A memory flashed in Hank's mind. Irvel, when he pulled her from the creek that day, shaking and shivering and struggling to breathe. He had seen Irvel like that. Deeply afraid. He kept the detail to himself and smiled at Sam. "I'm glad she has you to help her deal with it."

Sam stared at him a beat longer than usual. His smile

seemed to mark his appreciation that Hank truly was in favor of the relationship between Irvel and Sam. "Thanks, little brother." Sam pulled Hank into a hug. "I'm glad she has me, too."

On Saturday, unbeknownst to anyone in the United States, the ominous Japanese fleet pushed through the Pacific toward Oahu. At the same time, Hank and Sam were standing at the edge of the woods shooting targets in a nearby field when Hank asked the question. He had to know.

"So, you and Irvel?" He lowered his rifle and turned to his brother. "It seems serious."

"It is." Sam grinned. He aimed his gun at the farthest bull's-eye and pulled the trigger. The ping of the hit was distinct. As if he couldn't contain his joy, a laugh sounded in his chest. "I'm hoping to ask her to marry me."

"Really?" This time the panic was Hank's, but he didn't let it show. "That's . . . amazing." He picked up his rifle and aimed for the same target. Like Sam, he hit it square in the center. Then Hank set his gun down and gave his brother a light slap on the back. "Congratulations. When's it happening?"

"Not till she finishes her undergraduate in May. I want her to have more time . . . just to be sure . . . but I wish it was tomorrow." Sam grinned. "I'm in love with her, Hank. The other day at school we had a group of kids on campus getting a tour. Irvel got into a conversation with one of the high school girls, encouraging her to do her best and aim for high marks. She even told her to be sure to look to

God when she was fearful about the future." Sam let that sink in. "Once she finishes her training year, I think Irvel will be the best math teacher . . . and one day, the best mother for our kids. Don't you think?"

"Yes . . . I do." Hank half expected to see his heart fall out of his chest and break into a thousand pieces on the ground. Something Sam had just said stuck out. "So . . . you think she's not sure?"

"Sometimes." For a moment Sam stared out at the field. "It's not the two of us. I mean, I don't think it is. It's just a sense I have. Probably just her age. Anyway, it makes sense to wait. She's focused on finishing school." Sam shifted gears. "Hey, I'm really sorry . . . about Maggie."

"Yeah." Hank aimed his rifle and fired shots at two targets. He wasn't missing today. "We were together a long time."

"I think I know what it was." Sam waited until Hank faced him again.

"What?" Hank set his gun on the ground and turned to his brother. The two knew each other so well. A single look and the one knew what the other was thinking. When Sam threw a ball through the front window, Hank took the blame. And when Hank got ketchup on their mother's favorite white sofa, Sam claimed to be the one who dropped his plate.

So here . . . Hank held his breath.

"With Maggie . . ." Sam gave him a sad smile. "You didn't really love her."

After a long beat, Hank nodded. "You're right. I didn't."

"But you tried. I watched you try." Sam angled his head. "She just wasn't the one."

"No." Hank wanted to change the subject or run to the far edge of the field and collect the targets. Anything but travel to where this conversation seemed to be headed. If Sam asked about Hank's feelings for Irvel, he wasn't sure he could lie.

Instead, Sam picked up his rifle and fired at a different target. "Well." He gave Hank a quick glance. "You'll find your girl one of these days. She's out there."

The tension left Hank all at once. His brother was so in love with Irvel, that for the first time Sam couldn't read what Hank was thinking. He couldn't see that Hank was in love with Irvel, too. Which had to be a good thing. At least for Hank and Sam.

Hank tried to push thoughts of Irvel from his mind. "Maybe I'll move to the West Coast after college. Get a job in Hollywood, somewhere. Find a girl out there."

"I like it." Sam laughed. "They'd take one look at you and put you in the movies! And then the girls would be lined up around the block."

"Sure." Hank tried to laugh, but it fell short. Because there would be one girl *not* in line if that happened. Hank's dear, sweet Irvel. By next year at this time, she and Sam would be engaged. Hank clenched his jaw and fired off another round. The metal pinged again. "Yeah, I think that's exactly what I'll do. Move to Los Angeles."

They were still talking about the idea when they got

home that afternoon and again over dinner, when Irvel joined them.

"You never said anything about moving out west." That night Irvel sat next to Sam, across from Hank. "Indiana was the best place to live, remember? You were going to stay here forever."

There was a moment of awkward silence, as Sam and their parents seemed to remember that Irvel's heart had belonged to Hank first. Even if they had never been an official couple. "Yes, well . . . I changed my mind." Hank smiled at his parents and then at Sam. Anywhere but at Irvel's eyes. "It's a new plan, right, Sam?"

Sam raised his glass of water. "Right!"

That night they listened to the radio. Everyone agreed that the Grand Ole Opry was worth tuning in to, but Hank and Sam shared a look as they got settled. The guys cared more about war updates than music. So maybe tonight they'd hear the latest news from overseas, if there was any.

Hank couldn't tell if it was his imagination or not, but he kept feeling Irvel's eyes on him. Once he even caught her looking, and her eyes seemed to be filled with all the questions she couldn't ask. About Maggie and why Hank had broken up with her, and about whether he still had feelings for her.

Or maybe that was just Hank's imagination, his wishful thinking.

As the next hour passed, Hank couldn't focus on the

radio music program. Was it possible Irvel might break up with Sam before she graduated, before Sam proposed? That could happen, right? Sam, the analytically minded brother, might shrug off the heartache and laugh about how Irvel had always belonged to Hank, after all. They could all stay close and move on with their lives. Hank and Irvel together, and Sam on the lookout for someone better suited for him.

But, as soon as the idea formed in his head, Hank caught Sam looking at Irvel, and he knew he was wrong. If Irvel broke up with Sam, things would never end well. Sam would be forever hurt, and Hank would have to move to the West Coast—away from Irvel—to keep from harming his friendship with Sam.

There were no emergency broadcast interruptions that night as they listened to one song after another. They laughed about the comedy of Fibber McGee and Molly, NBC's top-rated radio show, and before the night was up, they played an hour of gin rummy. With every passing hour, the idea of leaving felt better to Hank. Moving to Los Angeles was a very good way to put distance between him and Irvel.

So that the love story of his brother, Sam, and Irvel would play out the way it was supposed to play out. Of course, maybe—if Sam could see a bit of doubt in Irvel—their relationship would end naturally. Years from now, the pain would lessen and Hank could ask Sam if maybe he could have a turn dating Irvel.

However he tried to see a way out, there was none.

Moving would give him a new life. By the time he fell asleep in his old bed that night, with Sam across the room already sleeping, Hank was locked in on the idea. Next week he'd talk to his professors about getting his résumé out to some studios in Hollywood.

• • •

DECEMBER 7, 1941

HANK GOT UP earlier than the rest of his family that Sunday morning. He found *The Indianapolis Star* in the driveway, boiled himself a cup of coffee, and sat at the kitchen table. He snapped the newspaper in front of him and stared at the top corner. The weather was going to be sunny and forty-five degrees. Cold, but not terrible.

He breezed through the front section. Several movies were coming to the Talbott Theater in Indianapolis. Always a fun night out while he was home on break.

In the second section there were ads for Christmas gifts, everything from floor-model radios to home appliances and women's clothing. Halfway through the paper, Hank stopped. In giant bold letters, the next page read, WAR IS DECLARED!

What? His heart thudded into double time. It took a few seconds to realize that a furniture store was declaring war on the prices of its competitors. Whew. Hank closed the paper and stared at the front page. The headline showed a photo of Japan's Emperor Hirohito, and a three-word headline: WAR OR PEACE?

Would they have their answer soon? If Japan's messaging

meant anything, the goal seemed to be peace. Hank drank his coffee and stared out the window. What were God's plans for this world? So many battles and acts of aggression breaking out. Was it the end of the world?

He folded the newspaper. There were no answers, none that God was handing out this morning. An hour later, Hank and Sam and their parents walked to church—just a few blocks from where they lived. They sat with Irvel and her family. The message was on making a difference.

The pastor was an older man, but that morning he had the fire of a minister half his age. "With the power of God, we need not sit on our hands while so many battle afar." He grabbed a quick breath. "We are in an international crisis of light versus darkness, and there is a very real and spiritual battle playing out alongside the tangible one." He took his time here. "The war is coming, and you will be called to act. Even if God only calls you to pray for your fellow man, for the persecuted Jews, and for families across Europe whose lives have been torn apart by the Axis powers. Whatever it is, God is calling each of us to do something."

His words were sobering. Hank shot a look down the row at Irvel, and he could see the fear in her eyes. Sam was sitting next to her, but he didn't seem to notice. Hank turned his eyes back on the preacher. The man was wrapping up. "I'll end with this." He paused a long moment. "The war is coming. Don't let it catch you off guard."

After church, Irvel's family and Hank's mingled in the

aisle for several minutes. Hank heard Irvel tell Sam she wasn't feeling well. "I might come by your house later. We'll see."

"If you're feeling up to it, come over by three or so." Sam put his hand alongside Irvel's cheek. "We can listen to *Sunday Down South*." He grinned. "And maybe string popcorn for the tree."

As they finished talking, Irvel once more caught Hank's attention. What was that look in her eyes? Was it fear or pain? Confusion? If only Hank could ask her about it. But that sort of conversation would be completely inappropriate for him to have with a girl nearly engaged—to his brother, no less.

Once they were home, his parents set about trying to fix a belt on the washing machine, Sam settled near the radio with a stack of student papers to grade, and Hank stepped out back by himself.

His heart felt heavy, maybe more than just because of Irvel. Was it despair? Or a distant kind of impending doom? He waited, but no explanation came to him. The sadness had to be about Irvel, of course. What else could it be? He drew a long breath. In time the feeling would pass. After graduation, he would find a job out west, or anywhere far from here. So long as he didn't have to live out his days watching his brother and Irvel, wondering the whole time if Irvel still longed for him as much as he longed for her.

If Sam was going to give her a ring, then Hank would show up for the wedding. But he'd have to make his life somewhere else. Hank looked at the empty spot beside him. It was little more than a year ago that he and Irvel had stood in this very place, here in his family's yard. Back when the only thing at stake was a simple first dinner with Sam.

"Stupid man," he uttered to himself. "Why didn't you tell her the truth then?" Hank crossed his arms and stared at the sky. Clouds were moving in, a reflection of his broken heart. What was the worst that could've happened back then if he'd been honest? She would have canceled the date with Sam, and Hank would've told his brother the truth. Of course he loved Irvel. He had always loved her.

Oh, if only he could go back in time. Right now he would be sitting on the edge of his bed, looking across the room at Sam. And Sam would be asking if it was okay to ask Irvel out for a meal. Only this time, Hank would get very serious with his brother. "Look, I might be seeing Maggie. But I'm going to marry Irvel Holland." He would give his older brother a single nod. "Thanks for asking."

It would've been that simple.

Instead, here he was, making plans to move from the place he had always loved. *God . . . what am I supposed to do? Maybe You could change Sam's feelings for Irvel . . . so he could see the two of them aren't right together. Because no matter where I go, I'll never love—*

The back door swung open.

"Hank!" Sam was standing there, his face ash white. "The Japanese just bombed Pearl Harbor. In Hawaii."

And suddenly, all the world stopped spinning.

It was one of those moments Hank would remember as long as he lived. That when the news about the attacks on Honolulu hit, he was out back praying to God about Irvel. In seconds, he and Sam and their parents were gathered around the radio. A symphony was playing, something popular and upbeat.

Hank crouched near the sound and looked back at Sam. "Are you sure?"

"I heard it, too." Their father wiped his hands on his trousers and set a dirty wrench on the fireplace mantel. "It was fast, but I heard it."

They sat huddled around the radio for what felt like forever, none of them talking. Breathless for information. The Japanese had been in peace talks with the U.S., right? Wasn't that the most recent news? Hank let that thought settle in his gut. How dare the Japs attack the American fleet at Pearl Harbor? Unwarranted. Without any hint of a warning.

Finally, at just before five o'clock, when the first round of *Sunday Down South* should've been getting started, a man's voice broke through. His words were hard to understand. "This battle has been going on for three hours." He paused and something like explosions seemed to go off in the background. Sam and Hank shared a desperate look. The man continued. "It's no joke. It's a real war."

At that moment, the broadcast was cut off by an operator. Something about needing the line for an emergency call. And like that, the music of the symphony played again.

"Did you hear that?" Their father looked at them. "Those were bombs. I'd know that sound anywhere."

Their dad had fought the final year of World War I. Only a few times when the brothers were growing up did he ever talk about what he experienced and saw while serving in the military back then. Now, the look in his eyes told Hank and Sam more than any conversation ever could have.

What did this all mean? Hank looked at Sam again. Already, anger burned in his brother's eyes. "What do we have at Pearl Harbor? How many ships?"

"Our entire Pacific fleet." Again, their father had known. He stood and took the nearest spot on the sofa. For a long time, he stared at the floor, until finally he looked from Sam to Hank and back again. "If the attacks happened at eight this morning in Hawaii—on a Sunday—no one would've been expecting it."

Their mother put her hand on Dad's knee. "So . . . you think they killed some of our men?"

"Some?" He choked on the word and shook his head. "Thousands of men live and sleep on those ships."

Thousands of men? Hank felt sick and dizzy and furious. On a Sunday morning without any warning of a coming attack, the Japanese had dropped bombs on America's entire Pacific fleet? How could this be happening? Hank tried to imagine it. A sunny day in Hawaii, the early morning calm over the water, rows of men asleep on their battleships.

Then the quiet, broken by a division of Japanese bombers?

Hank couldn't decide if he wanted to go throw up, or run as fast as he could to wherever it was he could sign up to serve. His head was spinning, but he tried to focus. Sam was telling their parents he was going to enlist and Hank was nodding, agreeing. "We have to go. As soon as we can."

The look on their mother's face that late Sunday afternoon was also something Hank would never forget. His mom was ashen and quiet, tears falling down her cheeks. Not once did she try to add reason to the conversation or disagree that—probably in days—Sam and Hank would both join the military. It was a foregone conclusion. The time for speculation was over.

The United States was at war.

DECEMBER 7, 1941

7

Panic was Irvel's constant companion from the moment the radio interrupted with the news about Pearl Harbor. She and her parents hovered around the radio for two hours, until Irvel knew there was only one place she'd rather be.

When she reached the Myerses' house, she joined them in doing the same thing.

These times were hard enough with Sam and Hank both registered for the draft. But this? This unwarranted attack on Hawaii meant that life as they knew it was over. Forever.

That night both the Holland and Myers families met with others at church and prayed for everyone across America who had lost someone at Pearl Harbor. They begged God for wisdom and protection and an end to the war.

But it wasn't until the next day while Irvel was on campus at Indiana University that the nation first heard from President Roosevelt on the matter. Students gathered around a number of radios to hear what he had to say. Irvel was walking down the hallway of the math building when Ruth Cohen, one of her friends, stuck her head out of one of the classrooms and waved her in. "FDR's going to speak, come on!"

Ruth was a Jewish immigrant from Germany and a math whiz, like Irvel. The two had become good friends that fall semester. Irvel had a feeling there was much more to Ruth's story. But for now, all that mattered was what was happening in Hawaii.

Irvel skittered into the room and found a seat near Ruth. A man was talking in a low voice, saying the president was about to take the podium. This was FDR's unprecedented third term. He was a president all the people loved.

This would be his most tested hour.

For a few seconds, Irvel closed her eyes. *Help him, dear Lord. Please help our president lead us through this disaster.*

And like that, FDR was speaking. "Yesterday, December 7, 1941—a date which will live in infamy—the United States of America was suddenly and deliberately attacked by naval and air forces of the Empire of Japan." He paused and all around Irvel, the kids who had gathered murmured and whispered. If they'd had any doubt about the news reports yesterday, there were none now. The president continued, talking about false efforts of peace on the part of the Japanese leaders.

"It will be recorded that the distance of Hawaii from Japan makes it obvious that the attack was deliberately planned, many days or even weeks ago. During the intervening time the Japanese Government has deliberately sought to deceive the United States by false statements and expressions of hope for continued peace."

Irvel's heart began to race, pounding out an unnatural rhythm within her. Not now. Panic welled inside her, the attack sudden and intense, which was only fitting given the situation. But then Irvel remembered Hank's words at Lake Monroe that summer day, when he was home from school.

Be strong and courageous. Do not be afraid . . . do not be discouraged, for the Lord your God will be with you wherever you go. The Scripture they had memorized in junior high. The Bible words that held a living power different from any other words.

Irvel let the words work their way through her heart and soul. Over and over again. *Be strong and courageous. Do not be afraid . . . do not be discouraged, for the Lord your God will be with you wherever you go.*

And suddenly she could breathe again. God was with her. She didn't need to be afraid.

FDR was talking about the impact now. "The attack yesterday on the Hawaiian Islands has caused severe damage to American naval and military forces. I regret to tell you that very many American lives have been lost."

"Very many?" One of the boys in the math department turned to three others. The whispers repeating those two words carried around the classroom. *Very many American lives have been lost.* What did that mean? Hundreds? Thousands?

A sick feeling seized Irvel, but she was no longer afraid. *Be strong and courageous. Do not be afraid . . . do not be discouraged, for the Lord your God will be with you wherever you go.*

President Roosevelt added that other American ships had been torpedoed on the high seas between San Francisco and Honolulu, and that the Japanese had also launched an attack against neighboring islands including Malaya, Hong Kong, Guam, and the Philippine Islands. "This morning," the President's voice was beyond somber, "the Japanese attacked Midway Island."

Roosevelt's anger simmered in every word. "Japan has, therefore, undertaken a surprise offensive extending throughout the Pacific area. The facts of yesterday and today speak for themselves. The people of the United States have already formed their opinions and well understand the implications to the very life and safety of our Nation."

Silence fell over the classroom. The students hung on this next part. What did the attack on Pearl Harbor and these other attacks in the Pacific mean for them, for their classmates? For every American citizen?

"As Commander in Chief of the Army and Navy I have directed that all measures be taken for our defense." He paused, his delivery stronger with every passing moment. "But always will our whole Nation remember the character of the onslaught against us."

The silence among the students grew louder.

"No matter how long it may take us to overcome this premeditated invasion, the American people in their righteous might will win through to absolute victory." FDR then took his pronouncement a step further. "I believe that I interpret the will of the Congress and of the people when I assert that we will not only defend ourselves to the uttermost but will make it very certain that this form of treachery shall never again endanger us."

A rousing cheer came from the thirty students gathered around the radio that day. FDR was a strong leader, and it would take that sort of strength—that sort of declaration—to inform all enemies of the United States that together we would not stand for this.

The applause died down. The president was still speaking. "Hostilities exist. There is no blinking at the fact that our people, our territory, and our interests are in grave danger. With confidence in our armed forces," he paused, "with the unbounding determination of our people we will gain the inevitable triumph so help us God."

"Amen!" A boy at the back of the room raised his fist.

A chorus of students responded in kind.

The entire speech came down to the next moment. Irvel was sure FDR's next words would live on for all time.

"I ask that the Congress declare that since the unprovoked and dastardly attack by Japan on Sunday, December 7, 1941, a state of war has existed between the United States and the Japanese Empire."

As the president's speech ended, Irvel dropped her elbows to the desk and covered her face with her hands. *Do not be afraid . . . do not be discouraged.* A hundred questions rushed through her mind, but the one that screamed loudest was this: *What was going to happen to Sam and Hank?*

She felt Ruth put a hand on her shoulder. "It'll be okay. We're going to win this war." Ruth's voice was strong, certain.

Irvel let her hands fall to her sides and she turned to Ruth, searching her eyes, the confidence there. "You think so?"

"I do." Ruth pulled her sweater tight. She was shivering a little, though the room was toasty warm. Determination rang in her voice. "It'll cost us. But we'll win." She hesitated. "I know what it's like over there. The American spirit is too great to be defeated."

For the first time since long ago when talk of war first began, Irvel did not feel panicked. The Bible verse filled her soul once more. *Do not be afraid.* She drew a deep breath. Her heart ached deeply for the losses ahead, and she couldn't imagine saying goodbye to Sam and Hank, when they most certainly would leave any day to join the fight. But she wasn't afraid. She steadied her voice. "Well, then . . . we need to do whatever we can to help."

"Exactly." Ruth nodded. She didn't quite smile, but she was no longer shivering. "Whatever it takes."

One of the other girls in their math class, Jackie Conrady, joined Irvel and Ruth. "I can't believe it." Jackie was one of Irvel's favorite people, a great friend who loved to laugh. But she wasn't smiling now. "I'd sign up right now if they'd let me."

That didn't surprise Irvel. A week ago, Jackie had come to her house two hours before class—before the sun was up—so they could study for a big math exam.

"Women won't be on the battlefield." Ruth crossed her arms. "I wish."

"Me, too." Jackie was clearly seething over what had

happened at Pearl Harbor. "Give me a gun any day. I took a class once. I know how to use one."

"Not me." Irvel couldn't fathom such a thing. She'd be terrible out there in combat. "We need to help from here. In Bloomington." She looked at her two friends. "Maybe working with the Red Cross or helping raise money for our troops."

The three talked awhile longer, dreaming up ways to help and trying to imagine what was next for the United States and for their guy friends. "I can sing and dance." Jackie stood and did an impromptu ten-second tap number. A few of the kids sitting in clusters nearby turned and watched. One of them chuckled, but Jackie didn't care. Like Ruth, she was brimming with confidence.

"See?" The girl sat back down. "We could find a dozen other girls and put on a show. Sing or dance, do a skit. Charge for tickets and give all the money to the U.S. Army." She looked at Irvel and then Ruth. "What do you think?"

Ruth rolled her eyes. "I think I'd rather fight."

Classes were called for the day. By the time Irvel got home, her father had gone to the local police station to try to sign up. "He's too old, I'm pretty sure." Her mother was making dinner. She stopped and faced Irvel. "Everyone wants to join the effort."

"Of course." Irvel set her books down on the kitchen counter. If her father wanted to sign up, then that meant . . . "Hank and Sam must be down there, too."

"They are." Her mother wiped at a stray piece of hair.

She looked ten years older than she had two days ago. "I spoke with their mom earlier."

Irvel steadied herself. "What about us? The women?"

"We're still learning the details." Her mom sighed. "Life will change for everyone. I expect we'll get to work in factories, making uniforms and parts for ships and planes."

Irvel hadn't thought of that, but her mother was right. There were manufacturing plants all across Indiana, and the United States. Places where machines could now make whatever was needed for the war.

"Okay." Irvel stared at the floor and then at her mother. "I can't believe this is really happening."

"It is, Irvel, dear." Her mother took her hand. "We need to pray every day, all day for our troops." There was a catch in her voice. "For the safety of the boys we love."

"Yes." A steadiness filled Irvel, a calm she had never known before. As if God really and truly was with her, and now, facing the worst crisis of her life—of all their lives—she could actually *be* strong and courageous. She didn't know what to make of this new and divine bravery, but she was thankful for it.

Irvel helped her mom with dinner, then she walked to Sam and Hank's house and waited with their mother in their living room until the guys got home. From the moment the brothers and their father walked through the front door, Irvel could sense something was wrong with Hank.

He looked at her for a long beat and then he shook his

head and—without saying a word—he stormed to the back of the house toward his bedroom.

Sam and their dad looked defeated as they took the other sofa. Their father broke the silence first. "They won't take me or Hank. I'm too old for this first wave of recruits." Their father hesitated. "And for now they only want one son per family. At least at our recruiting office."

"Hank can sign up later. Just not now." Sam ran his hand through his hair. "He's pretty upset."

Irvel felt a rush of relief. Hank wasn't going to war! Not yet! But just as quickly sorrow hit, because she would still have to bid Sam goodbye. Irvel looked at Mrs. Myers and saw in her eyes the same mix of emotions, both heartache and hope. Yes, Sam would face death in the coming days, but not her husband or her younger son.

"Did they say anything else?" Their mom was on her feet. Mr. Myers pulled her into an embrace and they stayed that way for a long moment.

Sam helped Irvel to her feet and he wrapped his arms around her. "They might call Dad and Hank up, even in a few weeks." He kissed the top of Irvel's head. "Also . . . I guess some branches are letting multiple men from one family go."

His father looked at the group of them. "They told us we could go to Indianapolis and see if someone would take us." He looked into his wife's eyes. "But I told Hank . . . God has a reason for everything. If we're not supposed to go now, we won't."

Irvel knew how upsetting all this had to be for Hank. She lifted her face to Sam's. "When do you leave?"

His hesitation lasted only a few seconds. "Tomorrow. A bus will pick us up at the fire station in the morning and take us to Indianapolis. We'll have three weeks of training, and then we'll ship out."

The pounding in Irvel's heart was back. But this time it wasn't fear, it was anger. How dare the Japanese do this? And how many American boys leaving tomorrow would never come home again? She tried to focus. "Where . . . where will they send you?"

"No telling." Sam took her hand. "Let's take a walk."

They left through the front door, headed down the sidewalk and along several neighboring streets. "I want to spend every last hour I have with you, Irvel."

"Me, too." Irvel cared so much for Sam, but she realized something now. She had never quite felt like she was in love with him. Maybe because she had always been Hank's closest friend. Either way, she wouldn't tell Sam that now. And she couldn't bear the thought of losing him. They kept walking. "If you had your choice, where would you go? Europe or the Pacific?"

"That's tough." He kept the pace slow, their hands warm together.

"Ruth and Jackie and I were talking about it today in math class. The two of them would sign up right now if they could." Irvel remembered the sincerity in her friends' faces. "If I had to fight, I'd go to Europe." She knew for sure. She could imagine it now, as if she were an entirely different person from the one who wanted to stay home and sew uniforms if the United States ever joined the war.

"Why Europe?" Sam stopped and turned to her. His eyes told her how much he loved her.

She hesitated. Hank wouldn't have had to ask the question. Hank knew her better. Maybe he always would. Irvel started walking again and Sam kept up. She felt her own courage begin to rise. "So I could help the Jewish people." She was quiet for a moment. "I have a new friend. Ruth Cohen. She's a Jewish immigrant from Germany. I want to get to know her better." She shrugged one shoulder. "Maybe we can do something to help. From here."

"You can." Sam gave her hand a gentle squeeze. "You can sew, just like you told us a while back. Remember?"

The idea sounded fruitless. "I want to do more than sew." Irvel had an idea. "Let's go to the hospital! I bet we can give blood!"

Sam stared at her. "Right now?"

"Yes." She had never been more serious. "What better way to spend your last night here? We might save a soldier's life."

"Okay. Sure." Sam seemed to catch her enthusiasm for the random idea. The hospital was around the corner, so they changed direction and walked to the emergency room double doors. It was after closing time for the main entrance.

Inside, Irvel took the lead and approached a nurse behind a desk. "We'd like to give blood." She barely paused. "Right now, if possible."

The woman's smile told Irvel she understood. "We're having a drive in the late morning tomorrow."

"I won't be here in the late morning, ma'am." Sam put his arm around Irvel. "We only have now. Tonight."

"Joining the war?" The nurse turned to Sam.

"Yes, ma'am." Sam turned on the charm—something he rarely did.

At first the woman looked like she might send them away. Then she asked them to hold on, and a few minutes later they were both giving blood. An hour later they were on their way home again.

"That's what I love about you, Irvel." Sam had his arm around her again. "The way you care about people."

"I had to do something." She looked at the bandage on the inside of her elbow. "I just kept thinking of all the people overseas who must need blood. Right now. I'd do anything to help."

"I know you would, my love." The look in Sam's eyes said all she needed to know about how he felt. As if in all the world, Irvel was the only one he would ever love.

If only she could say the same thing about him.

DECEMBER 8, 1941

8

When they got home from their walk, Hank was no longer angry, Irvel still knew him well enough to tell. Instead, he looked determined. Just like Sam and Ruth and Jackie. And now Irvel. Their parents were at the market getting food for dinner. At one point, Sam left to pack his bag and Hank and Irvel had a few minutes alone in the kitchen. Hank was finishing the lunch dishes, so Irvel stepped in beside him to dry them. It had been months since they'd had a chance to talk, just the two of them.

Irvel broke the silence first. "I'm sorry." She ran the dish towel over a plate and cast him a glance. "That they wouldn't take you right away."

"It's okay." He finished the last dish and handed it to her. Their hands touched in the process.

The feeling was electric.

Under her breath, Irvel gasped a little and then covered it with a cough. "Good." Irvel felt her cheeks grow hot. "I'm glad. I hated seeing you so upset."

"I have an idea." If he had registered the touch of their fingers, he didn't let on. Hank turned to her. "You can test out of your classes and graduate early. You're the smartest one on campus, Irvel. I already know that."

"Okay." She liked where this was going. Maybe there was something more she could do, after all. "Then what?"

"Go with me to Indianapolis. One of my buddies at the police station today was turned away, too." An intensity built in Hank's voice. "He said a bus of college kids was going to Indianapolis in a few days. To work at the manufacturing plant there." He paused. "They need all the volunteers they can get."

"Where . . . where would I stay?"

"The girls are sharing a few apartments. The guys will be on the same floor down the hall. Someone has it all figured out. All we have to do is show up on Thursday near the police station."

In a rush of certainty and anxiety, Irvel set her towel down on the counter and reached out her hand to shake Hank's. The handshake was meant to be an act of friendship and solidarity, the two of them satisfied to have something they could do to make a difference.

But instead, time stopped. Their hands remained locked together, but not in a handshake. In a handhold like they hadn't had in years. Irvel held her breath, and then withdrew her hand fast, like she'd touched a hot stove. "Hank . . ."

His eyes told her he was feeling the same thing, but he acted like nothing had happened. "Irvel . . . you have to say yes. Go with me."

Irvel remembered to breathe. She turned and dried

her hands so he wouldn't see the feelings his touch had stirred in her. "Maybe I will." She kept her voice steady. "That's all I want. To help us win this war."

"So it's a deal? You'll go?" Hank was still asking the question when Sam entered the kitchen.

"Go where?" He flung his duffle bag on the kitchen table. Then he came to Irvel's side and kissed her cheek. He turned to Hank. "Did she tell you? We both gave blood."

"She didn't." Hank's eyes met hers and held for a single second longer than necessary. "You both should've told me. I would've gone, too."

"You . . . you can go tomorrow." Irvel nestled against Sam's side. She couldn't look in Hank's eyes now. Everything she'd ever wondered about his feelings for her these past few years had been spot-on. She knew it in that single handhold.

Suddenly a possibility hit. Was she the reason Hank had broken things off with Maggie? She forced the question from her mind and turned to Sam again. He looked deep in her eyes. "Go where? What were you and Hank saying?"

Irvel remembered. "Hank was just talking about a group of college kids heading to Indy later this week. The manufacturing plant is looking for volunteers."

"Oh." Sam turned to Hank. Something seemed instantly off between them. "Okay. Interesting."

"I have to help somehow." Hank crossed his arms, his eyes glued to his brother. "All I want is to go with you."

Whatever tension had built between them seemed to dissipate with those words. "I know." Sam pulled Hank into a long, hard hug. They both had tears when they stepped back.

Irvel did, too. How had life changed so drastically in a single day?

"It's not right." Hank clenched his jaw. "I should be with you on that bus tomorrow."

"No." Sam looked more in control now. "You need to be here. Volunteer at that manufacturing plant. Or somewhere." He returned to his spot next to Irvel, but his attention was completely on Hank. "Could you do me a favor?"

"Anything."

Irvel's heart broke. Hank had always looked up to Sam. The two were closer than any brothers she knew.

"I have to be at the fire station at nine tomorrow morning. So at seven, could you meet me here in the kitchen? I want to take you somewhere."

Hank nodded. He was still fighting tears, but he found the words. "I'll be here. Seven o'clock."

"Good." Sam exhaled. He checked the clock on the wall. "Mom's making dinner in an hour. I need to talk to Irvel. Alone. If you don't mind." His tone was kind, gentle. He didn't seem threatened by Hank's friendship with Irvel. Not whatsoever. And of course he wasn't. Hank would never do anything to harm his brother.

Especially not when it came to Irvel Holland.

Hank glanced at Irvel and then back at Sam. "Sure." He nodded. "I'll be out back."

Irvel had no idea what Sam wanted to talk about. They'd just spent two hours together between the walk and giving blood.

Sam took her hand. "Come on." He walked her out to the living room and they sat side by side on the sofa. "Irvel." He turned so he was facing her.

What was happening? Was this when he was going to ask her to marry him? Irvel's heart fluttered and then pounded. What would she tell him? That she wasn't ready, didn't know her own mind on the matter? How could she turn him down now, when he would be on a bus off to war in the morning?

"You look nervous." Sam chuckled. "You okay?"

"I am. I just . . . I don't want you to go." Their knees were touching. Irvel could feel hers shaking.

Sam took both her hands in his. "Something's not quite right between us, Irvel. Do you sense that?"

This was a curveball. Irvel blinked. "Of course things aren't right, Sam. We're at war. You're leaving tomorrow. All of life is upside down."

"No." His voice was calm. "I mean with us." He searched her eyes. "I don't know what it is . . . so, I thought I'd ask." He didn't look away. "What's on your mind?"

Irvel tried to breathe, but her words stuck in her throat. What was she supposed to tell him? "Sam . . . I just . . . nothing. Nothing's wrong."

He didn't look quite like he believed her. While their faces were still close, Sam said something Irvel had never expected him to say. "I'm not sure if we're going to make it, Irvel. You and me. I keep waiting for you to look at me like . . ."

Was he going to say it? Was he going to point out the obvious? That Irvel looked differently at Hank than she did at Sam? She held her breath.

But Sam didn't go there. "Like I want you to look at me. That's why I haven't bought a ring yet. I don't think you're sure."

Irvel could breathe again. She exhaled and nodded. "I want to look at you that way, Sam. Really." Irvel sat straighter. This was the last conversation she had expected to have this late afternoon. "I feel like I will one day. I just need . . . I need more time."

His smile was the most compassionate she had ever known. "And time you shall have." He studied her face, her eyes. "I'd like to take a break, Irvel. You and me."

"A break? What?" Irvel felt her heart sink. "I love you. I wouldn't say it if I didn't mean it."

"I know." He kept hold of her hands. "I love you, too. And maybe we'll find our way back together. But for now . . . with me at war . . . I'm setting you free, Irvel. God alone knows if I'll even come home again."

"Don't say that." She squeezed his hands. "Please, Sam."

His voice dropped to a whisper. "I have to." He waited until he had more control. "Whether I make it back or not, I want you to find love. I want it for both of us. The right love, Irvel. Whoever that might be."

"No." Her tears were coming harder. Was he really breaking up with her? "Don't do this, Sam."

"Look at me." Peace saturated his every word. "Please."

Irvel's nose was running, and she could barely see through her tears. A box of tissues sat on the edge of the side table, so she took one. Anything to delay the point of this conversation. "Sam . . ."

He waited until she was more composed. "I mean it." He released her hands and took gentle hold of her face instead. Their eyes locked and held. "If it's not me—and I have a feeling it isn't—then find the right one." He hesitated. "Even if that guy is . . . someone I know."

And there it was. Proof that Sam had been paying attention all along.

"If you're talking about Hank, there's nothing between us. We've been friends, that's all. All this time, Sam, we've only been friends." Irvel was talking so fast, her words ran together.

"Irvel." Sam gently placed his thumb over her lips. "I'm not worried about you and Hank. I love you . . . and you love me, I know that. Maybe I'll come home and we'll find something better than what we've had this past year." He looked even deeper, all the way to her soul. "I'm just saying . . . I'm ending things for now. So, if it's not me, you can find the right love. You get that chance just once. Does that make sense?"

She squeezed her eyes shut and took on another rush of tears. "I still feel like it could be you, Sam. But . . . I don't know what I want." She grabbed another tissue and this time she put her arms around his neck and held on. Like all she wanted was to stay that way forever. Holding

Sam and trying to find a way to love him the way she still loved Hank. She sniffed. "You do believe me . . . Hank and I are just friends."

"I know." But Sam's sad smile told the truth. How he had probably thought for a long time that Hank and Irvel had feelings for each other. Feelings neither of them had admitted or were willing to admit. "I want you to be free to follow your heart."

Sobs shook her body, and her tears wouldn't stop. "I didn't ask to be set free, Sam. You're leaving and I might never see you again. And I hate that."

He wasn't letting up. "If Hank ends up being the one you love, Irvel, then I'll be okay with that. I'd have to be okay with it. I love you both." He kissed two tears from her cheeks. "One day, we'll all find our way back to normal."

"But . . ." She could barely speak. Here in this moment, she was utterly confused. "What if it's still you, Sam? I fell for you, remember? We wouldn't be having this conversation if that weren't true."

He held her close, his hand gentle on the back of her head. For a minute, they stayed that way, him calming her. When their eyes met again, he nodded. "It might be us. But it might not. That's why I want this break. It's something I had to say. So you'd know however things end up, I'm okay." He kissed her on her forehead one last time. "That's all."

The conversation was so hard. Irvel dried her eyes once more. "How long have you felt like this?"

"Just lately." He studied her face. "I kept waiting for

your eyes to tell me you were in love with me . . . only me. And with Hank home, with the war breaking out, a few times I saw it. The look I'd been waiting for. But you weren't looking at me, Irvel." He hesitated. "You were looking at my brother. And that's when it hit me. The reason you could never love me like I wanted you to love me. The reason we had to break up." He helped Irvel to her feet and faced her. "It's because you never quite let go of Hank."

He was right about all of it. "I never meant for things to be like this." She buried her face in his shoulder. "Hank doesn't love me like that."

"You never know." His breath was warm against her cheek, her hair. Then he found her eyes again. "I guess we'll have to see." He hesitated. "Just know that every day I'm fighting in this war—wherever I'm fighting it—I'll be thinking of you." He smiled, and he looked all right. Like he really could handle whatever happened from here. "But I'll also be thinking of my kid brother. God will make it clear."

Irvel nodded. "He will." She hugged him again, clung to him. "I'll miss you so much, Sam."

"I'll miss you, too."

They heard the voices of his parents, home with the groceries for Sam's send-off dinner. Over the meal, Irvel was quiet. They'd all been crying at one time or another today, so no one thought anything of her tearstained cheeks. Sam made no announcement, and she didn't either. No one would've known the two had just broken up.

Sam walked her home after dinner. He needed a good night's sleep, and he had to be up early for that chat he'd scheduled with Hank.

At her front doorstep, Irvel dabbed her eyes. "I'll be there tomorrow morning at nine . . . to see you off." There was nothing she could do to stop the tears. "I wouldn't miss it."

"Okay." He slipped his hands in his pockets. Already things were different between them. More distant. "I guess I'll see you then."

"Yes."

"There's one more thing." Sam moved a section of Irvel's blond hair off her shoulder, his eyes searching hers. "Would you consider teaching my high school math classes? Please? The kids need someone." The air was colder now, but Sam wasn't shivering. She'd never seen him more stoic. "I can't think of a person better than you to teach them."

"Sam . . . I don't know. I don't have my credential yet."

"I don't think that really matters at this point. Right?" He laughed. A sad sort of brevity for the moment. "You can't waste that mind of yours in a manufacturing plant, Irvel." His eyes pleaded with her. "Just think about it, okay?"

"I will." There was so much to figure out, so many details that needed attention. "Will you write to me?"

"I will." Sam hugged her close. "I'm still your friend."

"I'll do the same." Irvel lifted her face to his. She still couldn't believe this, the breakup, the fact that Sam was leaving in the morning. Like the whole thing was a dream.

He hugged her goodbye a final time, and Irvel stood there watching him go until he reached the corner. He looked back and waved, his smile glistening in the glow of the streetlight. Then he turned the corner and walked out of sight. Sam was kind and strong and good, and Irvel was the most blessed girl to have had the chance to date him this past year.

When he was gone, when she wasn't sure she could survive the heartache and confusion racking her body, Irvel dropped slowly to her top porch step and closed her eyes. *Please, God, bring him home again.* Whatever happened after that, they could figure it out later.

Irvel's tears consumed her as she dragged herself back into the house. She'd see Sam tomorrow, but there would be lots of people. Sam's whole family, and Hank. This was their own private goodbye and it left her with the one question that consumed her. The same one heavy on the hearts of a hundred women across Bloomington that night.

What if she never saw Sam Myers again?

DECEMBER 9, 1941

9

Hank was in the kitchen five minutes early looking for his favorite Michigan sweatshirt. He couldn't stop shivering. Not that an extra layer of clothing would help. The cold feeling wasn't from the weather.

Today his big brother, his best friend was going off to fight in World War II.

Sam met him near the front door. His things were sitting in the entryway. One duffle bag, one backpack. Everything that mattered had to fit in those.

"You're all packed up?" Hank looked at the bags. "Not much, huh?"

"I got what matters. A few changes of clothes, a toothbrush and deodorant." He paused. "And my Bible. That most of all."

Hank nodded. How had this happened so fast? "Feels like it's all a dream."

"We had a few years to get ready."

"I guess we did." Hank thought about that. "Days and weeks to talk about the war and Hitler and Japan. I just never really thought it would happen, I guess."

Sam smiled. "Come on. I'll drive." Sam had his own

car—a used Plymouth. It did the job getting him to and from his teaching job at Bloomington High each day.

All night, Hank had been looking forward to this morning and dreading it at the same time. Once they were in the car, he turned to Sam. "Where are we going?"

"You'll see." Sam's sad smile never really left his face. As if he was going to enjoy the next few hours, before he left. No telling if they'd have a morning like this again.

A few minutes later, Hank had his answer. Sam pulled the old Plymouth into the parking lot at Bloomington High. Classes were out for the rest of the week, so the place was deserted. "You and I played a lot of games here." Sam drove around to the back of the school and parked near the baseball fields. "A lot of contests."

"We did." Because Hank was just two years younger than Sam, they shared just about every athletic experience.

"You know what my favorite sport was, here at Bloomington?" Sam gazed across the ball field.

"Wrestling? You were the best wrestler this school has ever seen. Before or since."

Sam laughed, soft and quiet. "Thanks." He turned to Hank. "But no, that wasn't it."

"Okay." Hank shifted in his seat. "So, what was it? Track? The shot put?"

"Follow me." Sam got out of the car and Hank tagged along beside him.

They walked to the edge of the baseball outfield and Sam's eyes narrowed. Like he was seeing senior year, hitting that solo shot home run over the right-field wall to beat Indy's Center Grove High all over again.

Hank moved the toe of his shoe around in the grass. He wasn't sure where this was going.

His brother leaned his shoulder into the fence and turned to Hank. "Baseball. That was my favorite. Because it was the only one we played together."

"You only played your junior and senior years."

"I played because of you. Those were your freshman and sophomore years." Sam's smile remained, and he motioned to Hank. "Let's take a seat."

It was still cold, but Hank wasn't shivering anymore. The memories of a thousand hours on this ball field were keeping him warm.

They sat side by side and Sam took a deep breath. "How many times did Couch Calhoun make us run those bases?"

"I lost track." Hank chuckled. "It was all so important back then."

"That's what I want to remember." Sam's attention was still on the diamond. "What it felt like to be that boy, back when the real world was a million miles away and all that mattered was stealing second."

For the next half hour, they talked about high school, everything they remembered about baseball and wrestling and track. "Funny how four years is nothing." Sam sighed. "But in high school it sets the trajectory for your whole life."

Hank had thought about that before. "Best days of my life."

"Mine, too." Sam turned to Hank. "That's why I brought you out here. So, we could talk about high school."

"I'm glad." Hank pulled his jacket more tightly around his ribs. "I'll always remember this." He didn't want to sound too maudlin, so he laughed and poked Sam in the shoulder. "We should make it a tradition. When you get back from the war."

"Sure. Okay." Sam's smile faded some. For a while he looked out across the field again, then he took a long breath. "But it's the other part of high school and junior high I want to talk about."

"The other part?" Hank sat up straighter. There was only one other part of his school days, as far as he was concerned. But his brother couldn't be talking about—

"Irvel Holland." After a few seconds, Sam turned to him again. "That part."

Where was he going with this? "She's your girl, Sam. That was a long time ago."

"I want to know." There was no accusation, no confrontation here. "You still had two years at both schools after I moved on. So . . . how was it . . . between you two?"

This was the last thing Hank wanted to talk about this morning. "Can we get back to baseball?"

Sam sighed. "The thing is, I asked you a question a year ago before Thanksgiving. About Irvel . . . about whether you two were just friends and—"

"We were." Hank's voice rose a little. "That's all we've ever been."

"So, you're telling me you never—not for a minute—thought one day you'd be more than friends with that pretty blond girl who was always at your side?"

Hank started to open his mouth, thought about denying he'd ever felt something more, but there was a problem. He couldn't lie to his brother, hours before he left. A long breath came from Hank, like he'd been holding it for ten minutes.

After a moment, Sam nodded. "That's what I thought." Again, he didn't sound upset. More like someone who finally understood a puzzle he'd been trying to solve.

"The timing was never right for Irvel and me." Hank stood and paced the length of the bleachers and back. "You asked me if you could take her to dinner?" His voice was choked with emotion. "You're the best guy I know, Sam. My best friend . . . my older brother." He was breathing hard, trying to make sense of this. "What was I supposed to say to you?"

"I get it. It wasn't your fault." Sam slipped his hands in the pockets of his jacket. He still wasn't shivering. "It was mine."

Hank dropped to the bench beside Sam. "What?" He shook his head. "How could it be your fault?"

"Because." He put his hand on Hank's shoulder. "You were my little brother. I should've seen you were in love with Irvel. I should've known you better than that." A single laugh came from him. "Of course you wouldn't hang out with Irvel Holland every day since sixth grade if you only ever wanted to be her friend."

"The timing . . . it was always wrong for us." Hank gritted his teeth. He wanted a way out of this conversation, but there was none. "A year ago, I had Maggie Wright with me and Irvel was single. Something I didn't know when I invited Maggie to join us. And of course, I thought she was spending Thanksgiving with her aunt's family."

"Gary Walsh saw to that." This time Sam's laugh came more easily. "Telling me Irvel's family would be gone to Kentucky. So I'd tell you . . . and you'd bring Maggie." He paused. "A girl you never really loved." He raised his brow at Hank. "Right?"

"I wanted to love her." How did things become such a mess? "I tried, Sam. After you and Irvel became a thing." Hank could feel his emotions rising with every word. "Once I saw how happy you were with Irvel, that's all I wanted. To forget about Irvel and move on with Maggie. I swear it, Sam. I figured it was you and Irvel, together forever." He made a fist and hit his knee. "Because by then it was too late for me and her."

Sam was beyond calm. He nodded again, like he could finally see after a year of foggy vision. "And that's why you want to move to the West Coast. When you graduate. So you won't have to watch the two of us."

"Dangit, Sam, don't." Angry tears stung Hank's eyes. "Don't do this. Irvel is *your* girl."

Quiet filled the space between them for a few beats. "The funny thing is . . . I kept praying one day she would give me that look, you know?" Sam stared straight at him.

"The one a girl gives you when you're her whole world . . . and she wants to spend the rest of her life with you."

Hank knew the look. Irvel had given him that look yesterday. He hung his head and said nothing.

"I thought, maybe when she graduated in May, then she'd have more time and a clearer mind. Like I told you, I figured by then she'd be ready. And she'd have that look in her eyes, the one I kept hoping to see." His single laugh sounded more ironic than sad. "And the whole time . . . the whole time, you know what I think?"

Hank lifted his head. "What?"

"I think she's been in love with you." Sam took a deep breath and flung his arm around Hank's shoulders. "And you know what? I'm okay with that."

"It's not like that. She and I never—"

"Shhh. Hank . . . don't." Sam had that smile again, the one that said he was at peace with God and everyone else. "I told Irvel I could see it. The way she looked at you." He stood and stared at the baseball field once more. "We broke up last night." He looked back at Hank. "Maybe we'll find our way back together." The corners of his lips lifted. "Probably not."

Hank's heart was reeling. Sam and Irvel had broken up? He stood now. "Irvel can just stay single until you come home. Then the answers will be clear. They will be. For all of us."

"Until then . . ." Sam put his arm around Hank's shoulders again. "You take care of our girl, okay? She's going to need you."

Once more Hank wanted to shout at his brother and tell him not to say something like that. "You're coming home."

"I know." He grinned. "And we'll see who gets the girl. Whoever it is, this . . . you and me . . . this comes first."

"Always." Hank pulled his brother close and the two stayed that way for half a minute.

Sam stepped back first. "I gotta get going." He pointed out to the field. "Remember that practice game? You were pitching and I was up to bat? Count was full and Coach called a ball?"

The memory made Hank shake his head. A laugh built in his heart and it caused the world to feel right again. "I swore it was a strike. You and me, we argued about that for a week."

Sam winked at him. "You were right. Coach was testing your cool." He laughed, like the memory was clear as day. "Best strike you threw all year."

"Are you kidding me?" Hank grabbed Sam in a headlock and rubbed his knuckles on his brother's scalp. "How could you keep that from me? All this time?"

They wrestled and laughed and after a few minutes more of remembering, they stared at the baseball field, breathless. Then they headed back to Sam's car. When they were both inside, Sam raised the keys. "Drive her for me while I'm gone. Ol' girl hates sitting in the driveway."

Hank wanted to tell his brother no. Sam would be back before any of them knew it, so there was no point in anyone else driving the Plymouth. But the look in Sam's eyes allowed no debate.

"Okay." Hank leaned back in his seat. "I'll take good care of her."

When they pulled into the driveway, Sam shot him the most serious look of the morning. "Don't you try to push your way into this war. One brother, that's what they said." He gave Hank a light shove in the shoulder. "You got it?"

"Got it." Hank didn't remind Sam that he could still be drafted. There were enough uncertainties without bringing up the obvious.

Inside, their mother had made eggs and bacon—Sam's favorite—and after a quiet breakfast, they loaded up their father's Ford sedan and headed for the fire station. When they parked, their father turned to the backseat, where Sam and Hank were sitting side by side.

Like when they were kids growing up.

"I'd like to pray, before you go, Son." Their dad's voice was thick. Like he was trying not to cry. "God's got you. He has all of us."

They climbed out of the truck and formed a tight circle. The way they'd always been. They put their arms around each other, but before their father could start to pray, they heard feet running toward them.

"Wait." Hank looked over his shoulder. It was Irvel, in a dress and long fur-lined coat. "Please . . . can I pray with you?"

Their mom smiled. "Of course, dear. Come on."

Irvel positioned herself between their mother and Sam. Hank forced himself to keep his eyes closed as their father began.

"Dear God, we come to You asking for protection over our boy Sam." There was a crack in his voice and after a few seconds, Mom took over.

"Please, Lord, put an army of angels around Sam as he leaves home. Every day, no matter the situation, remind him that he is not alone. Wherever he goes, You will be there, also. Joshua 1:9 says that, and we believe it to be Your word. The truth."

She must've given their dad a look, because he started up again. "War is a terrible thing. It was never part of Your plan, Father. But there are times in the life of a man when he must stand up for what is right." Mr. Myers sniffed a few times. "Together, let us conquer this terrible darkness, that light might reign once more in this world. Thank You, for allowing our son the chance to make a difference in the battle. Guard him, guide him, and bring him home safe. In Jesus' name, amen."

Around the circle came a chorus of amens. Hank stepped back and looked at the bus across the street. Already guys were climbing on board. It was time for Sam to go. No final words or lingering hugs could stop the fact that in five minutes, the bus was pulling out.

With Irvel standing close by, Sam hugged their father, and then their mother, who was already crying. When it was Hank's turn, he pulled Sam into a final embrace, and spoke close to Sam's ear. "Thanks for this morning. You're the best brother a guy could ever have."

"You, too." Sam held out both hands. When they were kids, they had invented a special handshake. One that involved their wrists and elbows and thumbs. It was something only the two of them knew, and they both agreed a long time ago that it looked ridiculous.

But they did it here, anyway.

Finally, Sam turned to Irvel. Hank didn't want to see the two say goodbye. Not after his talk with Sam this morning at the high school. Sam was right. Whatever happened, happened. Irvel was no longer Sam's girl, but the two of them still loved each other. Hank wasn't about to let his mind wander beyond that.

"One minute!" Across the street someone in charge yelled at the guys not yet on the bus.

"Gotta go. Love you all!" Sam stepped away from them. "I'll write!"

Hank and his parents and Irvel watched while Sam climbed on the bus and took a seat at the back. Sam was still waving as the bus drove down the street and turned left, out of sight.

And like that, the four of them came together in a hug—much like the other families and friends who had come here this morning to see the bus off. War had come to the United States, and that could only mean one thing. It was time for American boys to take the war to their enemy. Hank could only second his father's prayer.

Please God . . . guard him, guide him, and bring him home safe.

DECEMBER 15, 1941

10

That Monday, a week after Sam left, Irvel found herself sitting in Principal Jay Faust's office. She was keeping the promise she'd made to Sam. If the administration found her fit, Irvel was willing to take Sam's place teaching math at Bloomington High. Eighteen months before she had planned to apply.

Last week, Irvel had gathered her transcripts from her nearly four years at Indiana University, including the marks she was currently making in each of her classes. Given the fact that the nation was at war, her professors agreed to waive her final exams.

"Based on your scores, you would have aced every test, anyway," one of her professors told her. "You'll do just fine teaching math, Miss Holland."

His words brought her comfort now.

Principal Faust was a tall, thin man in his fifties with little hair and a creative way of styling it across his bald head. He seemed sincere and dedicated to his work, even here as he pored over her Indiana grades. After a few minutes, he set her application packet down. "Very nice." The man sat on the edge of his desk. "Sam told us about you.

The administration already had a spot in mind for next fall. Even while you earned your teaching certificate. But I believe you're ready now."

He pulled a set of stapled pages from the top of his file cabinet and nodded. "First, though, every teacher must take this math test. It covers all facets of mathematics from simple multiplication and division to advanced calculus." The principal grabbed a pencil and handed it to her, along with the document. "Before we bring you onto our staff, we like to see your limitations." He smiled. "All teachers have them."

"Yes, sir." She took the packet and the pencil. An excited energy ran from Irvel's spine to her feet. She tapped the toes of her shoes quietly, so the principal wouldn't notice. Tests like this were her favorite. She lifted her eyes to the principal. "Would you like me to take it now?"

"Yes." The man checked the clock on the wall. Ten-fifteen. "You have one hour, Irvel. I'll come get you at that time. Don't worry if you can't finish it. No one does. Just complete what you can." He moved toward the door. "I'll be in the next office if you have any questions." He paused on his way out. "Oh. And good luck."

"Thank you, sir." Irvel loved a challenge, and this figured to be one of the biggest. The test contained six pages of problems, with room to show work. Fifty questions in all, including an entire page of word problems. She raced through the first two pages and took her time when she hit page three.

Even still she made great time—at least it seemed like

it. There was nothing in the last three pages that tripped her up. Irvel set her pencil down and laid the finished packet on her desk. She looked at the clock on the wall. What time had she started the test? Surely it had been more than an hour ago. Principal Faust must have forgotten about her.

After a few minutes, Irvel gathered the pencil and packet and moved for the door. She walked into the next office, where Principal Faust was working at his desk. He looked up. "Miss Holland? Did you have a question?"

"No, sir." She hesitated. "I finished the test. I wondered if . . . maybe you forgot about the time."

Principal Faust stared at his watch, and then at her. "No, Miss Holland. I did not forget."

That did it. Now Irvel had been rude. The man was probably going to send her packing back to Indiana University, and later tonight she'd have to write to Sam and tell him she'd failed. Insubordination. Right off the bat.

She was about to apologize, when the man stood and took a step toward her.

"You *finished* the test?"

"I did." Irvel stood stone-still. Any minute he would tell her to get her handbag and leave.

Instead, he squinted, like she was some rare type of oddity. "Miss Holland . . . you still have seven minutes left."

"Oh." She blinked. "Okay . . . is that allowed?"

"Allowed? Yes, but . . . I hope you didn't rush your answers." A dazed laugh came from him. "Please. Bring me the test. Then you can wait back in the other room while I grade it."

Irvel did as he asked. Once she was alone and back at the desk where she had taken the test, she stared out the window. A boy and girl walked across the yard, probably headed to class. Just a couple of teenagers.

The boy had dark hair and broad shoulders . . . the girl was blond.

And suddenly Irvel wasn't sitting here trying to figure out how to take over Sam's class. She was seventeen again, walking beside Hank Myers, headed to English class. Right there on that very courtyard.

She and Hank hadn't talked about Sam breaking up with her, and with Sam gone, she didn't feel right stopping in at the Myerses' house. She knew about Sam's time with Hank the morning he left, but she had no idea what they had talked about or whether Hank knew Sam and Irvel were no longer together. It was hardly something Irvel was going to bring up. Her allegiance was still to Sam, even if they were no longer officially in a relationship. It had only been a week, after all.

Irvel's heart sank at the thought of her kind Sam. For now, all she wanted was for Sam to come home safe. So they could figure everything out. Even so, her heart was back in the fall of 1937, fall of her senior year here at Bloomington, when she heard the door open. She turned and rose to her feet. Principal Faust was standing there, her test in his hand. "You missed one, Miss Holland."

"I did?" That wasn't too bad, right? She nodded. "Which one?"

"A calculus problem on the fifth page." He stared at her. "You got a ninety-eight. No one hired here at Bloomington has ever finished this test anywhere near that score." He came closer and raised the test. "Would you mind if I keep this?"

"Not at all." Hope surged. Maybe she was going to get the job, after all.

The principal stopped five feet from her, still studying her. "You have an extraordinary gift. Do you know that?"

Irvel hadn't ever really thought about it that way. "I love math." She smiled. "If that's what you mean."

"That much is obvious." He took a deep breath. "We would very much like you to take over Sam Myers's classroom. Starting tomorrow, if you're available. The substitute in his room now doesn't know simple algebra."

"Yes, sir." Irvel could already see herself writing to Sam and telling him the good news.

"You're very young. Twenty-one, right?"

Irvel nodded.

Principal Faust sized her up in a fatherly way. "Does it worry you, teaching students so close to your age?"

She took her time with that one. The thought had crossed her mind. "I promised Sam I would try."

"Yes." Principal Faust's expression grew somber. "Sam wrote me a letter to that effect. Before he left."

"I figured I might be working here part-time next school year, anyway." Irvel felt short next to the man.

"While I got my teaching certificate. I wouldn't be much older then."

"True." He still looked concerned. "We're all praying for Sam. Ten of our teachers were on that bus headed to war last week. The whole world feels like it's upside down."

"Yes, sir." Tears stung Irvel's eyes, but she held them back. This was not the time or place. "Everyone needs to do something."

"Even you." He held out his hand and shook hers. "Miss Holland, I'd like to welcome you to our staff. We'll see you tomorrow morning."

A swell of emotion rose in Irvel. She was doing the one thing Sam had asked of her. "Thank you, sir. I'll be here."

He crossed the room and grabbed two math books. "You'll be teaching the freshmen and sophomores. I've marked the spot in each text where Sam left off."

"Very good. I'll be ready."

"I'm sure you will be." He chuckled and walked her to the school's exit. "Good day, Miss Holland."

"Good day."

She lived just five blocks from the school, so she would walk back and forth each day. Irvel didn't mind. She had spent the past nearly four years walking to Indiana University. But as she crossed the parking lot, she saw Hank step out of Sam's Plymouth. He wore long trousers and a dress shirt.

Irvel stopped and stared. What could Hank possibly be doing here?

He spotted her at the same time, and for a few seconds, neither of them moved. Then he slipped into his dress jacket, closed the car door and walked to her. "Hey."

"Hi." She looked over her shoulder at the sign that hung above the school's entrance. Wasn't it just yesterday the two of them were here? She turned to Hank. "Familiar, huh?"

Hank looked at the sign and nodded, deep, like he had a dozen things he wanted to say. "Like yesterday."

Their eyes met, and Irvel pulled her long coat tighter around her. "Why are you here?"

Hank shrugged. "Doing my part." He had never looked so handsome. "The principal called. He wants me to take over the government classes. The former teacher left on the bus with Sam."

"Of course." She didn't look away. "I guess that means the other kids can go to Indy to work the manufacturing plant."

The slightest smile played at the corners of Hank's lips. "Exactly."

Neither of them seemed ready to talk about Sam. Hank slipped his hands into his pockets. "I have to go."

"Okay." They never stood close. Like neither of them would dare do anything here that they wouldn't do with Sam beside them.

Hank looked like he might head inside the building. But then he stopped, and his eyes held hers . . . just for a few seconds. "My mom's making dinner tonight. Maybe you could join us?" He shaded his eyes against the chilly midmorning sun. "I'd like to talk. If that's okay."

"Yeah. I'd like that." Not for a minute did she want to betray Sam. Broken up or not. "Maybe we can write to him. Together."

"Great." Hank nodded. "I'd like that. See you at five?"

"I'll be there." They didn't hug or linger or look at each other longer than it took to say their goodbyes. But even so, Irvel felt guilty as she walked home. How was she supposed to handle this new life? War had given them no choice, so here they were. Hank and her. Forced to navigate new territory with Sam soon to be a world away.

Irvel had no idea how it was going to work, but they had to try. They couldn't avoid each other until Sam came home. He wouldn't want that for them, either. It was the reason he had ended things with her.

Dinner that night was one long conversation about the developments overseas. On Thursday, Germany and Italy had declared war on the United States. Then on Saturday, Bulgaria and Hungary had made their own declarations.

As if things weren't bad enough.

Meanwhile the Japanese were sinking British warships in the South China Sea.

Irvel poked her fork through Mrs. Myers's spaghetti. Fear stirred within her. Not the panic she'd battled months ago, but a feeling that bordered on terror, all the same. "How does something like this ever end?" She looked from Hank to his parents. "How does it get worked out?"

It must've been a good question, because no one had an answer. "Something of this scope," Mr. Myers said, setting his napkin down, "we've never seen anything like it before. Only God knows how it'll all end."

"This much is true . . ." Hank's mother didn't seem to have touched her food. "The loss of a generation of young men can't possibly be the answer."

Across from her, Hank looked frustrated. He stared at his mother. "Are you saying Sam's involvement in this war doesn't matter? That he isn't making a difference?"

Irvel kept quiet. She'd never felt tensions so high in the Myers home.

"No." His mom's answer was swift. "I'm saying the leaders of these countries need to figure things out without involving hundreds of thousands of troops." She lowered her voice. "I just hate it." Her eyes locked on Hank's. "Do you understand?"

Hank hesitated. But then his shoulders sank. "Yes." His expression softened. "I'm sorry . . . it's just, we have to fight back. We have to."

"We all hate it." Hank's father took his wife's hand. "But Hank's right. Japan left us no choice."

The conversation continued through dinner and warm chocolate cake and coffee. They talked about the efforts in Europe and which countries might fall next and the Jewish camps increasing in size and number. Reports said Hitler was sending the Jews to places more dangerous than ghetto neighborhoods.

Every moment of their talk was heavy and discouraging and futile. But what else would they talk about? Irvel guessed the war was all anyone was discussing, everywhere across the nation. Finally, Hank's mother pushed back from the table. "I'll go do the dishes."

"I'll help." His dad was on his feet, also, and the two disappeared into the kitchen.

Hank looked at Irvel. "My mom doesn't like talking about it."

"Me, either." She crossed her arms tight in front of her. "It makes me sad and sick . . . thinking about what might be happening. Even now."

Sam wasn't set to leave for the war theater until the third week of January. After that, he could be in the Pacific or fighting somewhere in Europe. The thought terrified her.

Hank stood and moved toward the living room. "I'm going to make a fire." He nodded to her. "Join me?"

"Yes." Irvel followed him. They had to hash things out at some point. Figure a path from here to whenever Sam came home. This silence, the conversations they weren't having, it wasn't like them.

She sat on the sofa while Hank stacked logs in the fireplace. She could hear his parents doing the dishes in the kitchen, their voices low and muffled.

When the flame caught, Hank took the spot on the other end of the sofa. It felt like miles of space between them. Irvel turned and leaned against the armrest, her back to the flames. "None of this is easy, Hank. For either of us." She gave the slightest shrug. "But it's okay for you and me to be friends."

"I know." His answer was quick. He turned to face her, too. "Sam told me the two of you . . . that you're on a break. It's just . . . I don't know how to be around you . . . how to honor Sam in all this."

She nodded. The sound of the crackling fire was easy on her spirit. "Remember what you said to me a year ago Thanksgiving? When we talked out back for those few minutes?"

His expression softened. "I told you I'd be your friend forever."

"I said the same thing." Irvel smiled at him. "We've been friends for so long, Hank. I think Sam wants that for us. At least that."

For a long time, Hank stared at the fire, like he was considering how much he should tell her. When he turned his eyes to her, the walls he'd kept up for so long were gone. "Sam knows."

Irvel didn't have to ask what he meant. She took her time. Once they talked about this, there would be no going back. "He told you?"

"At the ball field." Hank leaned over his knees and stared at the floor for a beat. "He said he thought that all this time, the whole time you two have been dating, that really you were always in love with . . ." He looked at her, defeated. "In love with me."

With everything in her, Irvel wanted to deny it. But she couldn't.

"I get it." Hank sat straight again, his eyes on hers. "We have a history."

Irvel blinked back tears. "Sam can never be the one who walked me home from the creek when we were twelve, dripping wet." She laughed so she wouldn't cry.

"No." He laughed, too, and it was like a dam of ice had broken. "Sam wouldn't have let you fall in."

They both smiled at the memory. Irvel pulled one knee up. The fire was warm on her shoulders. "I told Sam I loved him. Even though we're broken up. And that nothing would change that."

"Good." Genuine peace flooded Hank's eyes. "That's what I told him, too. That he had to get back here so the two of you could figure out whether you have something or not."

Irvel tried to read Hank's heart. What was he saying? That he had never been romantically interested in her? She let the questions pass. Because being this close to Hank only reminded her what she had tried to forget since she and Sam began dating. She still loved Hank Myers. Even if she never told him or Sam or anyone ever.

She loved him still.

Hank's parents must've turned in early, because there were no longer any sounds coming from the kitchen. The fire was dying down, so Hank stood and stoked it for a minute or so, before throwing on another log.

Without meaning to, Irvel turned and let her eyes follow him. For that one moment, Irvel gave herself permission to watch him, to really look at Hank. At the man he had become in the last year. Neither of them were kids now, and spending time together in the coming season would be telling.

So, it was important to clarify things now. When Hank was back on his half of the sofa, when they were facing each other again, Irvel let the truth come. "I care very much for you, Hank. Things are changing so fast, but let's do more of this. We can talk and laugh and work together. We can write letters to Sam and trust God that he will come home." She locked eyes with him, the way she had longed to do for far too long.

Hank didn't look away. "And we can figure out the rest in time."

She smiled, even though she could feel it stop short of her eyes. "Right."

Hank looked all the way to her soul, the way only he could. After a few seconds, he took a deep breath and smiled. He held her gaze again. "I miss being your friend, Irvel. I missed it the whole time you and Sam were dating." He paused. "But you two have only been apart for a week. So for now, we'll go back to life before you and Sam. You and me, best friends. Nothing more. I promise."

And with that, the air between them changed and the uncertainties fell away. They were going to be okay. They'd never dated, after all. They could be friends now.

Hank pulled his mother's card table from the corner and set it in front of the sofa. From the slim drawer, he pulled a few pieces of stationery and a couple pens. "You wanted to write letters to Sam?" He grinned at her. "Let's write."

For the next half hour, that's what they did. They wrote Sam everything they were feeling and asked him everything they were wondering. Irvel asked him about basic training and what they were being taught, and she told him that she'd had dinner at his family's house that night. Best of all she told him that she'd been hired to fill his spot in the classroom.

But only until you come home.

She studied her letter and added something else.

Tomorrow I'll tell your students what a brave hero you are. I love you, Sam. I miss you.

She read those lines again. They were true. She did love him and she certainly missed him. They had been almost inseparable for more than a year. She smiled and finished.

Until next time, your friend, Irvel.

Irvel wondered if Hank had written anything in his letter about their conversation tonight, how they had made a promise to remain friends only. For now, anyway. And how they both wanted Sam to come home so he and Irvel could figure things out. If she had to guess, that's just what Hank would've written. Because he wouldn't do anything to hurt his brother. No matter what it cost him.

And Irvel wouldn't, either.

JANUARY 1942

11

Christmas came and went and the pact Hank had made with Irvel that night remained. No matter how difficult, or how much Hank longed for her, the breakup with Sam was too recent. And Sam would come first. He would always come first.

But with their renewed friendship, Hank and Irvel walked to Bloomington High together each morning, and Hank walked her home each day when school let out. The transition from college student to high school teacher proved to be fairly easy for both of them.

"I'm not sure I want to be a teacher forever," he told Irvel on their way home from school one day. "But I could get used to this. I feel like we're making a difference."

"We are." Irvel smiled at him. "Not a day goes by when one of my students doesn't ask about Sam. It's like by talking about his days overseas they can somehow keep him from harm."

"That would make Sam so happy." Hank took his time. The walks with Irvel were too special to rush.

Each day, their conversations grew easier until by mid-January they felt like they'd never been apart. Keeping things on a friendship-only level was not easy for Hank. But it would be a long time before he could take things to another level. He would honor his brother in all this. It was that simple.

Yes, he thought about her for hours after they said goodbye each day, and true, sometimes he saw Irvel's face in his dreams. But he would settle for Irvel's friendship. At least he had her in his life, at least he could look into her eyes on their walks to and from school.

And at school each day, the teens seemed to understand that listening and learning and making life easier for their new teachers was their way of helping with the war effort. Irvel had dinner with Hank and his parents several times a week, and together they'd share letters from Sam and compare notes on what they'd heard on the radio, how bad the war was getting.

In early February, Hank and Irvel both got letters from Sam. So did Hank's parents. Sam had been assigned to the Army's 34th Infantry Division, along with more than four thousand troops. They had set sail from New York Harbor on January 15, on a number of warships, and had traveled across the Atlantic Ocean to the British Isles.

They tell us it could be a while before we see any fighting. In the meantime, we are helping Europe build reinforcements. Everyone here feels we're a welcome sight. Please don't worry about me. I'll keep writing!

The certainty that Sam was safe and not about to see action in the war for some time made Hank and Irvel and their families relax a little. Hank and Irvel kept to their deal, respecting Sam and the situation. But the two friends were getting closer. There was no way around that.

By then, the Japanese were on the move in the Pacific, taking a new island every day or so. They also took prisoners, mostly British troops. Hank couldn't imagine how terrible that experience must've been.

That Saturday night, Hank and Irvel graded papers on his family's sofa again at the card table. A snowstorm had hit, and it was raging outside, so Hank kept the fire going. They had the radio on, listening to music from the Grand Ole Opry—Irvel's favorite. By then everyone in America was used to programs being interrupted with the latest from the war.

Which is what happened just after eight o'clock.

"We interrupt this program with a special announcement." The reporter's voice was serious. They were always serious. "We have learned that Chancellor Hitler of the Third Reich spoke last month, on the thirtieth of January, at an indoor arena in Berlin. In his speech, Hitler blamed the failure of the effort to take over the Soviet Union on weather. He also threatened the entire Jewish population in Europe . . . with annihilation."

The man continued, with more bad news, how American forces were now advancing in the Pacific. When the report was over, the singing returned. As if the most horrible things had not just been said.

"The annihilation of the entire population of Jews?" Irvel stood and walked a few steps toward the fire. She turned and faced Hank. "He can't do that, can he?"

Hank didn't know the answer. "He needs to be stopped. That's why we're fighting. To stop a handful of evil men."

"But the Jews." She started shaking, trembling from the horror of Hitler's intentions. Like maybe she was about to have one of the panic attacks she used to get. Her teeth chattered. "We . . . we have to do something more, Hank. How are we making a difference here? Teaching math and government?"

"Hey, hey." Hank was on his feet. "We're making a difference, Irvel. We are."

But still she was shaking, tears welling in her eyes. "Hank . . . what's going to happen?"

He came to her and for the first time since Sam left, Hank did something he had promised himself he wouldn't do. He took Irvel into his arms and held her, rocked her until she wasn't trembling. The whole time he tried not to think about the way her body felt against his, how he could barely breathe with the faint scent of her perfume consuming him. After a minute, he could feel her heart beating hard against his chest.

He stepped back. That was enough. Even then he had to work so she wouldn't see the effect the embrace had on him.

Irvel straightened her dress and pulled her sweater tight. "My former classmate Ruth Cohen and I had dinner yesterday. She told me about her Jewish family members in Poland. They live in one of those ghettos we heard about." She sighed and returned to her spot on the couch.

Hank did the same.

"There's talk of Hitler creating a 'final solution' to the Jews across Europe." Irvel's face grew pale. "He wants to kill them, Hank. All of them." She shook her head. "Have you heard about that?"

"I have." Hank wanted to reach for her hand, anything to make her feel better. But he wouldn't cross that line again. "I heard about it today at a teachers' meeting for the government department."

"You remember how afraid this all used to make me?" Irvel set her jaw, as if her resolve was growing with every breath.

"Your panic attacks." Hank ached for her. "I remember."

She shook her head. "I don't feel that way anymore, Hank." She anchored her elbows on the stack of papers she'd been grading. "I'd go there myself if I could. Fight in the Pacific to help us win this thing and get our troops home."

Hank studied her, the fire in her eyes a reflection of the one in the hearth. His precious Irvel was growing up. "If they'd give you a chance, Irvel Holland, I believe you could stop the Japanese in their tracks."

"But for now, I have to pray someone else can do it." Irvel understood. Women were fighting the war on the home front. Same as the guys not yet drafted.

"I'll tell you this." Hank slid a little closer to her. He

wanted her to see that he felt the same way. "If I get a chance to fight in this war, I'll request the front lines. The place where the evil axis will feel it most."

That seemed to take Irvel out of her intense state of proclamations. "Not the front lines, Hank." She tilted her head. "You have to use your brains. Help break Japan's codes. Like we talked about that day. Now that . . ." She smiled, trying to find her way back to casual. "That's something that could make a difference."

The conversation shifted to life in the classroom, the students who had fathers shipped out to the war and the ones who wanted to lie about their age to join them. Irvel's parents owned a warehouse typically used for their paper supply business.

"Now they have a hundred people working there, all of them making parts for fighter jets." Irvel smiled. "I love that."

"Maybe we can help out next weekend. Or a few evenings a week."

"Yes! I like that." She looked down at the next student's paper. "And your parents are working a blood drive next weekend. Your mother told me. Looks like they'll be doing that every Saturday."

FDR had talked about implementing rationing. Putting limits on food so that surplus supplies could be shipped overseas. Irvel looked determined again. "We should definitely help with that. Maybe some of the food might make it to the Jewish ghettos or the troops in the Pacific islands."

"Maybe." Hank smiled at her.

Then—without hesitating—Irvel put her hand on his arm and gave him a slight squeeze. "Hank . . . I'm glad I have you to go through this with."

She moved her hand away just as quickly, like she had only just realized what she'd done. Clearly, she hadn't been thinking. Before Hank could respond, Irvel changed the subject. "I heard that Bloomington High is letting the kids have their Spring Formal dance. I think it's the right choice. The students need something normal."

They talked and graded papers for another hour, but through it all, Hank couldn't stop thinking of how—even though he had tried not to—with everything in him, he was falling more in love with Irvel. He would never act on his feelings, not for a long time. But his feelings were there, more intense all the time. He was sure of the fact. Because a day later he still remembered Irvel's words about being glad they were going through this together.

And he could still feel her touch against his skin.

• • •

IRVEL NEVER SHOULD'VE touched Hank.

She had promised herself she wouldn't, no matter how trying the days became or how taxing the news on the war grew. If they were going to stick to their promise to be only friends, then she must not do that again. Not ever. After all, she'd only done so out of habit for how they had been before.

The same went for the hug she and Hank had shared. The hug that had stayed with her even now, a week later. The sight of Hank, the nearness of him on their walks to and from school, the sound of his voice against her heart . . . all of it took her breath.

Sam had been so right about her feelings for Hank, and now that she was single and Sam was gone, Irvel sometimes wondered why it mattered so much that she and Hank keep such rigid boundaries. But then she would remember Sam's face, his loyalty and sincerity. She owed him much more time than this before she moved on.

If she moved on.

Her last class of the day had just ended, and she was collecting test papers from her second-year algebra students, putting them in her oversize bag when there was a knock at the door. Irvel turned and there, standing ten feet from her, were two men in black trench coats. They were dressed in dark pants and dress shirts.

Like they were on official business.

Irvel faced them. "Can I help you?"

"Yes." The shorter of the two gave a serious nod. "Are you Irvel Holland?"

A sick feeling turned her stomach. Was this . . . could they be here to tell her something had happened to—

"There's nothing wrong." The older, taller man seemed to relax a bit. "If that's what you're thinking."

Irvel sat down behind her desk. "That's good. And yes, I'm Irvel." She studied the men. Were they from the state's school board, checking to see that she was, indeed, capable of teaching six classes of high school math? Yes, that must be it. She prepared to defend herself.

"Do you mind if we talk for a moment?" The shorter one wore a smart-looking hat. He shut the door behind them. "We have permission from Principal Faust."

None of this made sense. She forced the worry from her mind. "Okay. Have a seat, gentlemen. Please."

The two men sat at a couple of student desks at the front of the room. Irvel folded her hands. "Please . . . what's this about?"

"I'm Staff Sergeant Don Maynard." The shorter of the two removed his hat and set it on the desk in front of him. He pointed to his companion. "This is Master Sergeant Alan Willis."

"Nice to meet you." Irvel's heart was racing. If this didn't involve Sam, why were they here? "How . . . how can I help you?"

Staff Sergeant Maynard leaned forward. "We work under General William Donovan, the newly appointed Coordinator of Information tasked by President Roosevelt to create a more strategic approach to intelligence gathering."

Willis took over. "General Donovan is now working in conjunction with the Joint Chiefs of Staff." He looked at Irvel, as if he wasn't sure she was comprehending this. "Previously, intelligence operations were carried out by the Department of State, the Office of Naval Intelligence, and the War Department's Military Intelligence Division."

Irvel was too stunned to speak.

"The president believes we will accomplish more in the field of intelligence if these groups work in a coordinated effort. General Donovan is overseeing those orders." Willis folded his hands on the desk. "Soon we expect FDR to instate the Office of Strategic Services, representing all of those divisions working together."

Anything Irvel might ask now would only show her ignorance. There must be a mistake. Irvel knew no one in any of those outfits. "How . . . does this involve me?"

"We're looking for mathematicians, Miss Holland." Maynard looked more serious now. "Civilians who can help us break enemy codes so we can win this war and get our boys home."

Willis released a long breath. "We're working with collegiate educators to identify our brightest young math minds." He paused. "A professor at Indiana University suggested we talk with you."

Irvel sat a little straighter. Her heart pounded hard within her, but not because she was afraid. Not this time.

"We spoke with Principal Faust, and he confirmed that you are the most adept at all levels of math of any teacher he's ever employed." Maynard crossed his arms. "Do you understand what we are saying, Miss Holland?"

"Not really." She wondered if at any moment, Hank would enter her classroom, as was their routine when school let out. But she saw no one at the door. "You think I have a keen mind for math." She nodded. "Yes, I believe I have that."

Maynard stood and came a few steps closer. "We want you to work for the U.S. government, Miss Holland. Directly under the two of us and General Donovan. This new department will be made up of thousands of civilians, many of them women. We think you can help."

"To put it more simply." Willis stood now, too. "Miss Holland, we would like to ask you to be a spy for the U.S. government, to employ your extraordinary skills in clandestine ways in an effort to help your country defeat the Axis powers."

A thrill of purpose and destiny crashed over Irvel. She breathed in deep. Far from afraid, she was suddenly excited about the future. "How would I do that?"

"First . . ." Maynard's expression grew deathly serious. He lowered his voice. "If you accept this mission, you must tell no one. Not your parents or Hank Myers. Not Sam in the British Isles."

Chills ran down Irvel's arms. They had clearly studied her from afar. They knew about both Hank and Sam. She gulped a bit of air. "I'm listening."

They went on to explain that Irvel would tell her family and friends she was going to work as a nurse for the Navy. Recruited because of her intelligence. "There are two more officers from our department in the hallway, guarding the door," Staff Sergeant Maynard continued. "You will have to explain this, and the nurse story is how you'll manage that."

Two guards? Irvel's excitement rose a notch. The whole school would be talking about this.

Willis explained that for the next several months, she would receive training. "A car will pick you up at your parents' house three nights a week and take you to our office in a country manor a few miles outside Bloomington." He hesitated. "We have also identified one of your former classmates who will undergo training with you. Should you agree."

Irvel could barely breathe. Could that be Ruth Cohen? Either way, the offer these men were making was absolutely serious. They had done their homework. She thought about Ruth, about the hardship she and her family had undergone immigrating to the United States in the early 1930s. How wonderful if it was her they were talking about. Or maybe it was Jackie Conrady? Whoever it was, she would not be doing the spy work alone!

There was more.

"After your training, when school lets out for the summer—sometime in May—we would send you and your cohort on a warship into the Pacific theater. We would cover your expenses and provide you with a stipend to live on." Maynard leaned forward. "Again, the men you'd come in contact with would believe you were a Navy nurse. But both of you would primarily work on breaking codes from the belly of the ship. Where timing would be most critical."

Willis took up the conversation. "From the ship, we would send you on other missions as well." The expression on his face told Irvel this was maybe the most dangerous part. "At times you would be asked to deliver sensitive documents to key points of contact behind enemy lines. Each day there might be a different assignment. All of them life-threatening."

Irvel felt like she was dreaming, like she would wake up and all of this would only be some wild fantasy. Her way of trying to save soldiers and rescue the Jewish people or the Pacific Islanders. The way she might help win the war. But this was not a dream. She looked from Willis to his partner. "If I accept this . . . I can't tell anyone?"

Both men stood.

"Yes, that's right." Maynard took a step toward the door. The meeting was over, apparently. "As we said, you'd tell everyone you were training to be a nurse. Willing to go to Europe or the Pacific to help in that capacity. No one can know the truth. Not a soul. Not even your other classmate from Indiana University. Not until and unless you both accept. At that point you could discuss this at your first training."

"I understand." She still had a dozen questions, but they could come later. "When do you need to know?"

"Tomorrow." Willis handed her a pink ribbon. "If you accept our offer, you will wear this pink ribbon in your hair when you come to school. We will have someone watching. In that case, on Wednesday we would have a car pick you up at home for your first night of training."

"Nursing training, if anyone asks. Don't forget." Maynard shook Irvel's hand. "We would very much like you to accept this offer, Miss Holland." He hesitated, his eyes locked on hers. "Your country needs you."

Irvel nodded. "Thank you. I understand."

The men exited the room, and through the window of her door, Irvel saw the two who had been guarding the entrance. The four of them left together. As soon as they were gone, Hank entered her classroom in a rush. "Irvel . . . what in the world?"

Her head was still spinning. "I know." *Act natural,* she told herself. *Don't say a word.* She took a quick breath and gathered her things. "Such a big deal. Guards and everything."

Hank approached her. Concern was written into his eyes and face. "Why were they here?"

"Recruiting." She did her best to look more whimsical than worried. "They're looking for women willing to be trained as naval nurses. For overseas work."

"Overseas?" Hank looked like he might faint. "You're a math teacher. You don't have any training as a nurse."

"They did their research." Irvel slipped into her coat and faced Hank. "They want women with good college marks, so we can learn quickly how to help the injured and dying."

That seemed to land on Hank. "Okay . . . so . . ." He nodded, slow and hesitant. "What are you going to do?"

"I'm not sure." She started for the door and Hank stayed at her side. "Maybe I should go, Hank." She cast him a sideways look. "You said it . . . we all have to do our part."

"You are. Working here . . . with the students."

"They told me I could finish out the semester." She shrugged. *Play it cool, Irvel. Play it cool.* "I'll talk to my parents and make my decision."

And that's just what she did. She told her parents about the opportunity, and how she could be trained in the next few months through night classes and be ready to help save the lives of men in the European and Pacific war theaters. As she spoke the words, Irvel realized something again. She truly was not afraid. She was excited. The U.S. government had recruited her to be a spy! Who would've believed it?

The next day, she talked in greater detail with Hank about the possibility of leaving—to work as a nurse. He mentioned that another of America's warships had been hit by the Japanese. "It would be very dangerous, Irvel . . . working as a nurse out at sea in the middle of the war."

"I know. I'm still thinking about it." She hated lying to him. "I'd be saving lives."

Just at that moment, she saw Ruth Cohen enter school from the other direction. The two looked at each other and—without Hank noticing—they shared a smile. A thrill worked its way through Irvel. Ruth was the other spy recruit and it was really happening, because in their hair that day was the same thing.

A single pink ribbon.

SPRING 1942

12

It wasn't only the world at war that spring of 1942. Hank felt like his entire world was spinning out of control. His brother was getting ready for action now. Sam's last letter said that he and his division were being trained in military conduct and doing various new drills to prepare them for combat.

We're working with all sorts of new weapons, Sam wrote. *Learning how to clean each one and how to load them. We're being trained on assembly and then we're practicing how to be accurate when we have to use them. And we will have to use them.*

Hank read and reread those words. They shouldn't have surprised him. Of course Sam was learning how to use military-grade weapons, and of course he would have to fire big guns—most likely the minute he stepped foot on a battlefield. But it had never hit Hank before what that actually meant. How Sam was going to have to fire on the enemy and actually kill people in order to help defeat the Axis powers.

And likewise, the enemy would be firing on Sam.

The reality was sobering, especially when Hank was

doing nothing to win the war by staying in Bloomington and teaching government classes to high school kids.

On top of that, Irvel had decided to accept the government's offer to work as a naval nurse on a warship come summer. Someone from the military was picking her up three evenings a week for training at someone's country house. Something Irvel had said was perfectly normal. He had tried five times to talk her out of the idea. Irvel had never wanted to be a nurse, so why now? Why in the middle of the war? But always her answer was the same.

"What if it was Sam out there who needed a nurse, someone to save his life?" Irvel's confidence took his breath. She was completely different than she'd been before Pearl Harbor. "I have to go, Hank. I'm ready. I want to do this."

At least tonight they could talk about something else. Tonight was the Spring Formal dance, the one the students had been looking forward to. Hank and Irvel were both signed up as chaperones. The theme was "Doing Our Part" and kids had been encouraged to get their suits and dresses at a secondhand store. Especially since there was still talk of rationing on just about every radio program.

Hank had found a suit from the early 1930s, navy trousers and an oversize navy jacket. He wore a white button-down shirt and a bowler hat over his dark blond hair. He adjusted his polka-dotted tie in the bathroom mirror.

Truly, all he wanted was for Sam to come home. But right now, he also wanted tonight to be four years ago, and this his senior dance, with Irvel as his date. If only he'd made her his girlfriend back then, the relationship between her and Sam never would've happened.

He held on to the edge of the sink and exhaled. That chance was gone.

Even still, twenty minutes later he was standing at Irvel's front door. Because it was the right thing to do, he had stopped to pick up a corsage of daisies and carnations for Irvel. Her favorite. It would've been wrong to take her to the dance—even as chaperones—and not get her flowers.

Hank would've done that if she were his sister.

But he wasn't ready for the way Irvel looked when she opened the door. Her red dress was longer than usual with a hundred little pleats at her waist. At the neckline was a bright white collar and tiny white buttons down the front. The skirt swished with every move as she stepped out on the porch. The same porch where he'd come to visit her a thousand times in their growing-up years.

"Hi." Her smile was shy, as if she were thinking the same thing he was. She looked down at her dress. "I found this old thing at the antique store near the campus."

"You look . . . beautiful." No matter how he tried to stop his feelings for her, he couldn't. It was like holding back the tide. Hank felt dizzy looking at the dress, being this close to her, but he gathered his senses. "Here." He held out the corsage. "I got this for you."

"Thanks." She looked genuinely surprised. Like she hadn't expected this. "Do you want to pin it on me?"

He nodded. "Yes. Definitely." He wasn't sure he could

do that and not faint from wanting her. But he had to try, had to right his wayward feelings before his heart capsized here on her front porch. He took a step closer and hoped she couldn't see his trembling fingers.

Careful not to let the pin prick her, he secured the flowers to the upper left part of her dress. Then he stood back and took her in, all of her. "You look so pretty."

Her eyes seemed to say everything neither of them would dare voice. "The corsage is beautiful." She angled her head, her eyes never leaving his. "So thoughtful, Hank."

Spring temperatures had arrived, but the nights were still chilly. Hank helped her with her coat and the two of them rode in Sam's Plymouth to the dance. The drive took only a few minutes, but Hank was intoxicated by the faint smell of Irvel's perfume. How could she be leaving in a few months on a warship?

All of it was too much to think about. On this night, he wanted to forget whatever was next for Sam . . . or where Irvel was headed. Tonight they had only this dance, and the job of keeping the kids in line.

The task turned out to be harder than Hank had imagined. He caught four of the senior boys pouring rum in the punch, and he had to dump the entire batch out behind the school. The cook had lots more in the cafeteria refrigerator, but Hank was disappointed.

He ordered the kids out back through a side door in the gym, and there he lined them up along the brick wall. "Is this who you want to be? Kids who break the rules and get in trouble?"

The boys were silent, staring at the toes of their shoes or off at the night sky. Hank felt his frustration grow. "Look at me. Right now." He might not have been much older than the boys, but he was in charge and what they'd done was serious.

Something in his tone must've gotten the kids' attention. They turned their eyes to him. Hank took a step closer. "Everywhere, everyone is talking about doing their part in this war effort." He looked down the line at each of the kids. "You know what that means for you?"

"Enlisting," one of the boys muttered. The others snickered.

"No." Hank raised his voice a notch. "Not enlisting. Not yet. It means setting an example. Letting this world know that American boys do things right." He paused, all eyes on him. "You spike the punch and some freshman drinks it . . . or a sophomore. And they crash their car on the way home. Someone could get killed." He let that sink in. "That isn't a joke, boys."

Gradually, the brashness left their eyes. Like they could see Hank was right. One of them looked like he was about to cry.

Hank held out his hand. "Give me the liquor. Now."

Not one, but two boys held out small bottles of alcohol. "Sorry, Mr. Myers. I . . . didn't think about that."

As Hank took the liquor, he remembered something. His classmates had tried to do this the year he was a senior here. But somehow, back then—even though Hank hadn't participated—the act had felt like harmless fun. Now, with Hank's brother and many of his former classmates at war, behavior like this felt practically traitorous.

Young people needed to be sober-minded. The war demanded it.

The group agreed and Hank walked them back inside. He dumped out the rum in a cafeteria sink and returned to the gym. Across the dance floor, Irvel spotted him. She made her way to him around the dancing couples and groups of kids. "I had to go after a wayward couple." She smiled at him. "They wanted to have a private dance, apparently. Out back by the baseball field. I gave them two options."

"Two?" There was an easiness between them now, more friendship than flirty, but Hank loved it. How he had missed this shared camaraderie with Irvel.

"Yes." She uttered a soft laugh. "We call their parents and send them home. Or they join the other dancers in the gym."

"I like it." He chuckled. "And on this end of the dance floor, we now have a fresh bowl of punch, compliments of the cafeteria. Otherwise, half the student body would've been drunk in an hour."

Just then, Principal Faust took the microphone at the front of the room. The band on the stage behind him stopped playing. "Students, this next number is something special. Please clear the floor."

The boys and girls did as they were asked.

"We have a highly trained dance teacher here at Bloomington. Most of you have been through her class as part of your physical education."

A low murmur of laughter came from the kids. Miss Bloom's dance class was notoriously dreaded by students who passed through Bloomington High. She was a former Broadway dancer who took the art very seriously. Hank always thought she was in the wrong job, since most teenagers didn't care about the samba or waltz.

But there were two kids Hank and Irvel's year who had cared. Yes, Hank and Irvel! They both laughed. They were maybe the only ones who had actually enjoyed their time with Miss Bloom.

Principal Faust was explaining what was next. "We're going to see what you've learned, students. And we'll start with . . . the slow fox-trot." He waved his arm to the band. "Let's get things started!"

The band started playing Glenn Miller's "Moonlight Serenade," and for ten seconds the floor remained empty. The slow fox-trot was one of the most difficult ballroom dances Miss Bloom taught. But Hank and Irvel had aced it the year they took dance here together.

"Well . . ." Hank looked at Irvel and raised his brow. "Should we show them?"

Her eyes sparkled. "I don't think we have a choice."

"I thought you'd say that." He held out his hand and she took it. Then with the confidence they'd found when they were juniors in high school, they took the center of the dance floor and faced each other. With his left hand, Hank took hold of Irvel's right one, and held it high over their heads. He placed his right hand gently below her shoulder.

Irvel arched her back and tilted her head away from Hank's. He spoke just loud enough to be heard over the melodious strains of the song. "Five, six, seven, eight."

Like they were gliding across ice, they began to dance. Irvel slid her feet back in long, graceful strides, and Hank moved forward, as if the two were connected at their waists. Irvel's smile was almost more of a laugh, the same way Hank felt. Like in the sparkling lights of the dance floor with the big band music playing, it was hard to believe this was really happening. But one thing was sure. In this routine they had learned long ago, neither of them had forgotten a single move.

Students gathered around the edge of the floor almost as soon as Hank and Irvel began dancing. By the time the two of them had made their way halfway around the room, the teens were cheering.

"Mr. Myers! Look at you!" The boys pumped their fists and clapped for their teacher.

The same was true for Irvel. Girls all over the gym squealed and cheered and jumped around, cheering her on. "Go, Miss Holland," they yelled.

Despite the years gone by, Hank could barely breathe for the way Irvel's body moved in time with his. It was as if they had danced this way every week. She anticipated his every move, and the students cheered at the sight of them.

Hank had expected a few other couples would join them, drawing from the training they had certainly gotten from Miss Bloom. But no one did. For more than three minutes, the song and the moment and the dance belonged to Hank and Irvel alone.

When the number ended, the two struck a final pose, their hands up, palm to palm. Classic fox-trot. Irvel straightened her back and looked into his eyes. They were still both laughing, both breathing hard, their bodies close as the students cheered. They stayed that way for what felt like a lifetime and a single moment.

And Hank knew that the feel of Irvel's hands on his would stay with him always.

Finally, he twirled her around so they could both face the high schoolers. Again the kids clapped and celebrated the way their two teachers had pulled off the routine. Hank took Irvel's hand and led her off the dance floor to a far wall. The band switched up the tempo and began to play a faster swing song.

After watching Hank and Irvel, the kids must've been ready to dance, because they packed the floor.

Hank leaned close to Irvel. "Looks like we cracked the ice." Only then did he realize he was still holding her hand. And suddenly, like springtime snow, gone was everything he'd promised himself about keeping his distance from Irvel. About not letting himself fall more in love with her.

They were both still catching their breath, and Hank saw in Irvel's eyes the same thing he was feeling. A longing that was impossible to deny. She couldn't stop smiling as she looked out at the dance floor. "I can't believe we remembered it."

"Miss Bloom would be proud."

They danced once more together, when the band played "I'll Be Seeing You." The two of them spent the entire number eyes locked on each other, as if the words were spilling from the band singer just for them. Toward the end of the song, they both sang along, their hearts keeping time. The lyrics spoke of finding each other in the morning sun and when the night was new.

Hank ran his thumb along her cheek as he sang the next line. "I'll be looking at the moon, but I'll be seeing you."

After that, they kept an appropriate distance between them, and they stayed clear of the dance floor. Three minutes was definitely enough to make Hank question how long he could remain only friends with Irvel.

Before the dance ended, a group of giggly teenage girls ran up to Hank and Irvel. One of them stepped forward. "We didn't know you two were dating!"

"You're the cutest couple ever." A brunette from the back grinned at them. "Of course, Peggy here was hoping Mr. Myers was single."

The girls laughed and ran off.

Hank was almost afraid to look at Irvel. Before he could, she gently pressed her elbow to his ribs. "It's okay. They don't know."

"Right." He dared look at her, allow his eyes to meet hers. "I'm sorry . . . if the dance was too much."

She shook her head. Her eyes caught the light and she looked like she had back when the high school dance was theirs. "It was fun." She didn't look away, her smile consuming him. "We're allowed to have a good time."

When the dance was over, Hank drove Irvel home. He parked out front and turned to her. Neither of them seemed in a hurry to leave the moment. She shifted in her seat so she could see him better. "That was fun."

"It was." The mood between them was light, easy. A lifetime of history had brought them to this place. "The kids were shocked."

"They think we're so old." Irvel laughed. "Except that pretty little redhead who hoped you were single. Better to let her think you're not. I think she's seventeen."

"True." Hank wanted to reach for her hand and tell her he couldn't pretend anymore. He was in love with her. But as soon as the thought took root, he could see Sam's face. He pressed himself back against the car door, putting a few more inches between them. "Tonight . . . felt like a day borrowed from the past."

"Yes." She let her eyes linger on his, but then he watched her walls go up. She took a deep breath. "I need to go. I want to write to Sam before I turn in."

"Sure." Hank opened his car door. "Me, too."

He walked her to the front porch and this time he kept his distance. He gave her a single nod. "Have a good night, Irvel."

"You, too, Hank." If she didn't care for him the way he cared for her, if she had a heart for Sam only, then Irvel should've looked away then. She should've turned and gone inside before the conversation could carry on a second longer.

Instead, she came to him, put her arms around his

neck, and held on to him as if maybe he could rescue her one more time. From the swirling waters of the future. Hank pulled her close and they stayed that way until Hank knew even another heartbeat with Irvel in his arms would be wrong.

She leaned back, their faces close, and she searched his eyes. "This is okay, Hank." The cold night air rustled the branches in the trees nearby. Irvel's voice was softer than the wind. "We're not doing anything wrong."

"I know. We can do this." He wanted to kiss her so badly. "Once in a while."

"Yes." She seemed to move closer to him. Her eyes never left his. "Once in a while."

He could feel her breath against his neck, sense her heartbeat in her chest. If he didn't take control of the situation now, he never would. And Sam would come home from the war to find Irvel, fully and completely, Hank's.

Which—despite their breakup—still seemed like betrayal. "Irvel . . ."

"I know." She brought her face close. Just when it seemed they might finally kiss, her cheek brushed against his. "Hank . . . what are we going to do?"

Hank had no answers for her, but he knew this much . . . if he didn't move away from her there would be no turning back. "You and Sam just broke up." His voice was nothing more than the barest whisper. He still had his hand on her waist, still held her in his arms. "I won't say it again. Just this one last time." His lips came ever so close to touching hers. "But I will love you, Irvel Holland, till the day I die."

She drew back just enough to look in his eyes. "I love you, too." And only then did he see that tears had filled her eyes. "It was always different with Sam." She blinked and tears slid down her cheeks. The walls in her heart were back down again. "No matter what happens from here, I love you."

For a minute or so, they stayed that way, neither of them wanting the moment to end. Then, with every bit of his resolve, Hank stepped back. "I'll be seeing you, Irvel."

"I'll be seeing you, Hank." She stepped inside, but she never looked away and neither did he. Not until the door was shut behind her.

Only then did Hank exhale. He bent at the waist and held on to his knees. When he could breathe again, he returned to his car and drove home. They would probably never again talk about this, the night they chaperoned the Spring Formal. The night they confessed their love—as if it wasn't obvious every time their eyes met.

The night they almost kissed.

But Hank knew one thing for sure. When Irvel shipped out to war, he would hold on to the way she felt in his arms, the way she had danced with him across the gym floor and the way her face had felt against his.

He would hold on to this night forever.

SPRING 1942

13

Irvel fell against the closed door and tried to catch her breath. What had just happened? Her sides heaved and she shook her head. She had almost lost complete control of herself. While Sam was four thousand miles away across the ocean, she was here dancing the night away with Hank. God help her.

It wasn't right, and Irvel felt terrible. So what if she was technically single? She needed to put time between Sam and Hank. But she also felt wonderful. More wonderful than she had ever felt in all the days she had dated Sam. *Dear God, what sort of woman am I?* She heard no answer in the still of her parents' house. Sam was good and kind and if she had stayed with him, he would have loved her and cared for her all their days.

But now she could see clearly . . . she was fully and completely in love with Hank.

So, Irvel did what she could. She spent every chance possible with Hank, grading papers, eating lunch together, and of course walking to and from school. After the spring dance, Irvel found herself walking more slowly with Hank, wanting to stretch their time together. They had a few months left at most.

If only they'd had a little longer. Because a night like the Spring Formal was once in a lifetime for Hank and her. She was leaving soon—a spy for the military. She would give her all to the job despite the reality—some spies never made it home. Which was why everything about these days with Hank felt final.

It was a spring that would not come again. Not ever.

She only wished that while they were still here together in Bloomington, while they were still walking side by side each morning and afternoon to teach the students, she could tell Hank the truth about her training with the Office of Strategic Services.

The government hadn't made the name formal yet, but she and Ruth would be part of the newly formed OSS. They had learned that at one of their nighttime training sessions, just like Sergeant Maynard had told her. Most of the members were being recruited from the enlisted troops. But the plan was to bring in some four thousand women, and to fill those positions, the federal government and military had spread into cities and states looking for just the right candidates.

Over the weekend, Irvel had dinner with Hank's family and the group played cards and listened to the radio. Everything they heard, Irvel already knew. And so much more. She and Ruth and the other five girls in their training group were being briefed on information no one knew.

The details were terrible, but Irvel, of course, kept them to herself. She didn't dare speak a word to Hank or his parents. If she was going to be a spy for the military, she would follow the rules. To speak about any of it, they'd been told, could get them killed.

When she left that night, Hank walked her home. But he didn't hug her or linger near her door. That hadn't happened again, no matter how they felt. "How's the nursing going?" he asked her before he said good night.

"I like it." Her answer was quick, practiced. "I think I'm going to be a very good nurse, Hank."

He smiled at her. "I think so, too."

It was just as well that she was heading off to war. If she stayed in Bloomington another few months, she would have to admit even to Sam that she had fallen head over heels for Hank.

At training the next day, Irvel and Ruth sat together at one of the tables for two set up in the living room of the grand estate where they were being educated on the work of a spy. There were eight of them in the class.

Apparently, the people who owned the place were cooperating with the government, happy to help in whatever way they could. Irvel had never seen the owners of the home. Ruth had told her that training for OSS members across the country was happening in estate homes like this one, far enough outside big cities and situated on large plots of land so as not to catch anyone's attention.

Maynard and Willis were the instructors most nights,

though at times they would bring in specialists in everything from how to look like a Navy nurse when getting supplies on a Pacific island to the correct body language so as not to gain attention from their enemies. One night a week they received an hour of actual nursing training, so they could apply tourniquets and administer morphine. Basic lifesaving skills.

That way, if it came down to it, they would seem like actual Navy nurses.

Tonight, Maynard was talking. He explained that the U.S. had learned that Hitler's plan to kill millions of Jews was not only true, but underway. The plan was called the "Final Solution to the Jewish Question."

Anxiety poked pins at Irvel's courage. Hitler had to be stopped. How could anyone be so evil?

"One of our targets at this time is Nazi official Reinhard Heydrich, entrusted by Hitler to enact the Final Solution plan." He paused and read from a page of notes. "We are aware of hundreds of thousands of Jews who have been killed at Belzec, and another hundred thousand or so at Sobibor, both death camps in Poland.

"Back in 1939, Heydrich was the brains behind a fake Polish attack that allowed Hitler to invade Poland. He uses wire transmissions brilliantly. One of the reasons we have you here is because we believe you can be instrumental in breaking Heydrich's codes. Until now, we haven't found a way to stop what's happening to the Jewish people."

Irvel wanted to stand up and scream. They couldn't let this mass homicide continue. She glanced at Ruth, but her friend was hanging her head, her eyes closed. It took a moment before she lifted her face to Maynard again.

"Understand . . ." Their teacher continued. "These are men, women and children being marched to their death. In addition to pushing back German forces and helping Poland regain autonomy, we are looking to destroy the Nazis' efforts to carry out their terrible plan. And that's just in the European theater. We expect to use you primarily in the Pacific."

The details were overwhelming. Maynard must have seen that on their faces because he gave them a twenty-minute coffee break.

Already some had left for secret missions, missions the other girls knew nothing about. One day soon, Irvel and Ruth would leave for theirs, also. The two poured coffee from a pitcher in the kitchen and found a spot in the parlor, where they could talk. Maynard had given them the run of the downstairs during training hours.

Tonight's talk about the Jews was the most graphic they'd received so far. Irvel wasn't sure how she could bring up the subject, but she wanted to hear from Ruth. Once they were sitting in opposite chairs, Irvel leaned in. "You've never talked about it . . . what it was like living in Germany."

Ruth sipped her coffee. A faraway look came over her and she stared out the dark estate windows to the lit covered porch on the other side. "It was early 1935. I was young. Just fourteen." She turned to Irvel. "But I remember. I remember it all."

Irvel cupped her hand around her hot cup. "Since the first day I met you at school, I've wanted to ask. So, things were bad for your family . . . for the Jewish people? Even back then?"

For a moment, Ruth looked like she had returned to that time, like she was living through whatever had been the beginning of Hitler's hatred toward her people. She exhaled. "It was awful."

Ruth was twenty-one now, just like Irvel. Only Irvel's days as a young teenager were happy, spent with her family and Hank, discovering her math skills and taking dance lessons. She waited, in case Ruth might want to share more.

Her friend set her coffee down on the end table between them. "Hitler came into power in January 1933. In his speeches we heard about his suspicions of the Jews. But I don't think my parents thought he was going to start acting on his statements. Not at first, anyway."

The details of the story poured out over the next ten minutes. The first concentration camps opened in March that year, and by the first of April, Hitler called for a boycott of Jewish businesses. "My parents ran a tailoring shop." Ruth shook her head. "We couldn't survive with our neighbors boycotting us."

Next came a ban on Jewish people holding certain state positions or university jobs and by the end of April, the Gestapo was established.

"I guess I didn't realize he was working on this so long ago." Irvel was gripped by the terrible details. "Someone should have stopped him."

"Who?" Ruth took another sip of her coffee. "By May they were burning books written by Jews, and by July, Hitler had stripped us Jewish people of our German citizenship."

All in just over four months? What Irvel couldn't believe when she first heard about Hitler, and what she still couldn't believe now, was that people supported the murderous leader. How could a nation be so blind, so unable to see the truth?

"Just last week in church we talked about how people can become deceived. Our pastor read a verse about that . . . from the Bible." Irvel took her time. She had gone home that day and memorized the Scripture. Because it reminded her of Hitler.

"Tell me. What did it say?"

Irvel closed her eyes, recalling what she had committed to memory. "The Spirit clearly says that in later times some will abandon the faith and follow deceiving spirits and things taught by demons. Such teachings come through hypocritical liars, whose consciences have been seared as with a hot iron."

"Hmm." Ruth nodded. "Sounds like Hitler. And I'm impressed you remembered that."

"Scripture has become my greatest strength. It cured me of my panic and fear."

"I like that." Ruth smiled. "HaShem, our great God, is my Comforter, too."

Irvel still wanted to hear the rest of Ruth's story. "So how were things when you moved?"

"Getting worse." Ruth stood. Their break was nearly over. "My grandfather lived here, and he helped us leave Germany. Of course, I have lots of family members who were unable to leave. It was terrible, saying goodbye." She paused. "We set sail on a cargo ship along with dozens of families and we arrived in New York City with nothing but the clothes in our suitcases." She smiled at Irvel. "We moved to Indiana and tried to make a life for ourselves."

Irvel had so many questions. How were Ruth's family members still in Germany? And had her father been able to start a new business here in the United States? But Ruth was right. They had to get back to the meeting room.

Bit by bit through the rest of March and all of April, Ruth shared more of her story. How difficult life was in the U.S. at first, and how the family members still in Germany were suffering. Two sets of aunts and uncles and eight cousins—all Germans who were now living in Polish ghettos. Ruth still wrote to them.

"It was one of the reasons I agreed to be a spy." She held her head a bit higher, as if she were proud of the chance to help her family back in Europe. "Because maybe I can help save them. Before it's too late."

Irvel's friendship with Ruth made the reality of their impending departure easier. As the day drew near, Irvel kept writing letters to Sam, kept waiting for him to tell her he was moving out with his fellow soldiers to fight the Germans. But in his latest letter he told her, that wasn't possible.

The only way to counterattack at this point is . . . Sam

had written recently. Words were missing, clearly redacted by Sam's superiors for security. Irvel kept reading. *We're helping with that effort, whatever we can do from this side of enemy lines. I can't say much more than that. I believe it could still be . . . before we take part in . . .*

I hope you're enjoying teaching my class. Tell the kids I miss them. And I just know you're going to be the best nurse the Navy ever had. Please, Irvel. Tell me where they'll be sending you as soon as you know. I pray for us all. Give my baby brother a hug for me. Love, Sam.

Maybe it was the redacted words or the fact that she wasn't able to tell him the truth about her training, but Irvel felt herself growing distant from Sam. As her departure date neared, her mind was on Hank, and Hank alone. Not that she didn't care for Sam. She did. But life was changing, and she was changing with it. And her time with Hank in Bloomington was running out.

In late April one night, Master Sergeant Willis told them that big developments were happening in the effort to get the women of the OSS out into the Pacific war theater.

They had identified a cargo ship and hollowed out the hull to accommodate eleven hundred troops—including the women from Indiana. Some spies, some code breakers. Some both, Willis told them. "The ship will set sail in May from Boston's Port of Embarkation. You will travel with the troops to North Africa, where you may or may not stay for a season—depending on the work we have for you to do."

And all Irvel could see was Hank's face.

Ruth had a boyfriend, a business major at Indiana University. A few times that month, the two of them went to dinner with Hank and Irvel. Ruth asked her later about Hank. "He's in love with you . . . you can see that, right?"

"Yes." And Irvel told Ruth about Sam, and how wrong it would be to fall for Hank this soon after their breakup. Especially with Sam at war. Irvel felt sad about it all. "I pray every night that God will help us all figure it out . . . when the war ends."

They didn't talk much about Hank and Irvel after that, but Ruth understood. The next time they were all together, Ruth caught Irvel's eyes and the knowing was there. It wasn't only Hank in love with Irvel, her friend's expression seemed to say. Irvel was in love with him, too.

Finally, their departure on what was being called the USAHS *Acadia* Army Hospital Ship was only a day away. Irvel's parents still couldn't quite understand. "You were making a difference here, Irvel." Her mother put her hand on the side of Irvel's face. "You're gifted at math. Teaching those kids . . . what more could God want from you?"

Irvel gave her mother a sad smile. If only she knew.

Her parents held a going-away dinner for Irvel that night, and Hank and his parents joined. They prayed over Irvel, the way they had prayed over Sam back in December. When Hank's parents had gone home and hers were in bed, Hank remained. He opened the windows behind her parents' sofa and the two sat together, their knees touching.

And all Irvel could hope was that somehow this night would never end.

MAY 1942

14

A spring breeze played in Irvel's hair.

"I don't want you to leave." Hank turned to her. He brushed her blond bangs back from her face.

Irvel had wondered how tonight would go, whether they would give themselves permission to feel . . . just this one night. Now she had her answer. She reached for his hand and slipped her fingers between his. They had never done this, never held hands this way.

Hank took hold of her other hand, too. "I've wanted to do this ever since that fox-trot. Palm to palm that night . . . I still remember how that felt."

She wanted to ask him, what about Sam? She should've felt badly for this, for enjoying Hank's fingers between hers. But all she felt was wonderful.

"Can we have this?" She was dizzy, breathless, so near to Hank, with neither of them trying to pretend. At least not in this moment. "Can we have tonight?"

"Yes." Hank lifted her hand to his lips and kissed it. "Tonight is ours, Irvel. How can it not be?"

All she wanted was to fall in his arms and kiss him, but they couldn't do that. It was one thing to hold hands, but kissing would be forbidden. Not while she was so recently Sam's girlfriend.

"So . . . tell me about this ship." He looked deep into her eyes. "Will it be safe?"

Safe. A sad laugh slipped between her lips. "Nothing is safe in war, Hank. You know that."

"No." He looked at her. "Nothing."

"What about you?" She'd been sensing lately that Hank was restless. Maybe because school was out, and he wouldn't be needed in the classroom until mid-August. Or maybe because she was leaving. "Will you teach again in the fall?"

Hank didn't answer, and in the silence Irvel had all she needed to know. "You can't. You promised." She ran her thumbs over his. "Sam told you not to enlist. Not to fight."

"I have to join in. How can I not?" He clenched his jaw. "I can't stay here forever. Things are only getting worse." A whisper of wind came through the window and drifted between them. "I'm thinking about signing up. Of course I am."

His admission only made this moment worse. If they were all separated, fighting their own battles in the war, then what? And how would they ever all make it home safe again?

Hank released her hands. He stood and turned on the radio. Glenn Miller was playing a new song. "At Last." Hank returned to her and helped her to her feet. "Please, Irvel . . . dance with me."

There was nowhere else she wanted to be than here, in

her family's living room, dancing with Hank Myers. She came to him, and he slipped his arm around her waist. The words to the song felt written for the moment. *At last . . . my love has come along.*

Irvel closed her eyes and laid her head on Hank's chest. She could hear his heartbeat. *Please, God, don't let this be the last time*. She looked up at him, and suddenly his face was so close, his lips nearly touching hers. They danced like that for what felt like forever, the whole time, Irvel knowing she could never kiss him now, and yet wanting his kiss with everything in her.

The song ended, and "Moonlight Serenade" came on. "Hey . . ." His eyes held hers. "Our song."

And with that he held her hand high, and they danced the fox-trot on the living room rug. Halfway through, Hank held up his palms and she did the same, letting hers meld into his. And in a rush of music and memories and missed opportunities they could never get back, she stopped dancing and looked up at him, their faces a breath apart.

"Irvel . . ." The melody continued to play, but it was as if their hearts had a will of their own. Before he could finish the sentence, his lips were on hers. Slow and warm and full.

She slid her hands into his hair and all of life was only this moment, this kiss and the way it built and became them. It was a moment when she should have felt terrible. The worst, most awful former girlfriend to Sam.

But all she could feel was Hank's lips on hers. If she'd known it would be like this, she never would've dated

Gary Walsh, never would've lost the chance to be Hank's . . . forever and only his. She returned his kiss, and their lips fit together perfectly. Like they were made for each other.

So, this was what she had missed out on? The kiss they had never shared in high school or college, the one they had never experienced until now. Time stopped, but the song kept playing. Their song.

Finally, Hank drew back. He framed her face with his hands, his eyes smoky. "Irvel . . . I'm . . . I'm sorry." His breath came faster than before. "We shouldn't . . ."

Irvel put her finger to his lips. "Shhh." She ran her thumb along his cheek, his chin. "Tonight is ours."

And so it was. A car was picking her up before dawn. But here, for the next half hour, they danced to Glenn Miller. Again and again their lips found each other and Irvel wanted the feeling to last forever.

Even as they moved to the door and Hank said goodbye, they couldn't stop. Hank held her and kissed her and Irvel wished the hands on the clock would stop turning.

Hank held her close for a very long time, and then his lips found hers once more. "I don't know what happens next." He kissed her forehead and pressed the side of his face against hers. "I just know . . . I can't live without you."

"I'll leave tomorrow . . . but you'll have my heart. You always will."

"And you will have mine. Wherever you go, Irvel."

Tears welled in her eyes. She felt terrible about Sam,

but there was nothing either of them could do about that. Not tonight.

Hank kissed her a final time, and then he left. When he looked back, Irvel could see that he had tears on his face, too. He held up his hand, the one that had held her so close just a moment ago.

As he turned the corner, Irvel was sure about something. After tonight she would never be the same again. As soon as she had the chance, she had to tell her ex-boyfriend Sam the truth. That he had been right to break up with her. That it had been over between them from the beginning.

Because Irvel would always and always and forever only be in love with Hank Myers. She would pray every day, every hour that God would bring Hank and her back home safely someday.

So she could spend the rest of her life showing him.

• • •

HANK WOKE UP sick to his stomach for two reasons.

First, Irvel was gone. She was picked up by some car that by now would've taken her to a train, which would take her to a ship that would leave from New York Harbor. And then she'd be off into the Atlantic headed for the war. From there, most likely she would ship out to the Pacific. Hank felt like his heart had gone with her, so even climbing out of bed was an effort.

Also, something about it didn't add up. Hank had been too distracted by the closeness of Irvel to ask the questions that had been plaguing him since she told him about her opportunity. So his questions remained. Why would they take a math teacher and train her as a nurse? Weren't there enough other people signing up to do nursing work?

Irvel had been afraid of blood most of her life, after all.

Hank had heard of other women, friends of theirs, signing up for nursing duties and being dropped off at the train station to leave for the Pacific or European theaters. But Irvel had been picked up by someone in the service. Was that normal? Were other nurses headed to war having that same sort of experience?

Now it was too late to find his answers. Irvel was gone. And there was the other reason he felt sick to his stomach today.

He had betrayed his older brother. His best friend. The one who had been there for him at every turn. Sam would be shocked if he could've known what had happened between Hank and Irvel last night. Or would he?

Hadn't Sam basically given Hank permission to pursue Irvel? If that was the right thing for Hank?

Once up, Hank skipped breakfast. He made his way to the backyard and tore out the crabgrass that had taken root across his parents' lawn. His dad was always going to get to it, but with the war at hand, his factory was working seven days a week making parts for planes and ships. Most days his father worked well into the night.

Hank wore jeans and a white T-shirt. He started near the back door, ripping at the noxious weeds and collecting them in a basket. Another, then another, and another.

Clawing his fingers into the ground, grabbing at the root and pulling the chunk of crabgrass from the ground. An hour later, his fingers were bleeding, but he kept pulling, kept digging through the dirt with his bare hands, tearing out everything that didn't belong there.

The way he wanted to pull the weeds from his heart. Should he feel guilty? Would Sam be angry with him if he knew what had happened between Hank and Irvel?

Just before dinner, his mother came home from her work at the local blood bank. She stepped out back and stared at him. By then, Hank had worked his way almost to the back fence. "Hank?" She took a few steps closer and surveyed the hundreds of holes scattered throughout the yard. "What in the world are you doing?"

Only then did Hank realize how he must've looked. Sweat running down his face, shirt drenched. Sides heaving from the effort in the hot and humid midday sun. "Fixing the yard." He wiped his bare arm over his forehead so he could see her better. "It needed help."

For a moment his mother only stared at him, like she must've known something else was wrong with Hank. But then she smiled. "Thank you. Your father will appreciate it."

Hank nodded and got back to work. When he finished, he dumped the basket in the trash bin and what wouldn't fit, he piled up beside it. Then he returned to the house. He was about to take a shower when he saw a letter on the kitchen counter, a letter from Sam to him. Hank felt the sting of tears in his eyes.

Sam, would you hate me if you knew?

He grabbed the envelope and took it to the bedroom. There, on the edge of his bed, he stared at the empty place across from him, the spot where Sam had slept before leaving for the war. After a minute, Hank opened the letter and began to read.

Hey there, Hank,

Sorry I haven't written in a few days, we've been doing training exercises. We keep hearing word that they'll be sending us north into the theater, but we're still waiting. Still getting ready, I guess. It makes me wish I'd signed up for the Marines. At least then I'd be fighting the Japanese.

I just wish they'd let us fight. More of us would mean a quicker victory for the Allied forces. That's how we all feel. In the meantime, the guys in my division are getting to know the locals, hitting up the bars and making friends with the women. If you know what I mean.

But not me. I go home after a hard day of training and read my Bible in my barracks. Because one of these days they'll let us fight and then we'll finish this thing and they'll send us home.

I was thinking the other day about you

and Irvel, about how you're probably spending a lot of your time together. Hank, don't feel guilty if you fall in love with her. Everything is crazy now. You won't hurt my feelings if you and her become a thing. I sort of feel like you already have.

Streams of slow, steady tears made their way down Hank's cheeks. He ran his fist over them, rough and angry. Even from across the world, Sam had known. Of course he would know, what with Hank and Irvel here in Bloomington working together. Still, how could he have kissed Irvel? What was he thinking? He blinked a few times so he could see his brother's letter again.

Hank, remember when we were little? We'd play war games in the backyard and pretend to capture the enemy? Then we'd laugh and head inside for a ham sandwich and a nap? I was thinking the other day how much I miss those days.

Miss you, also. You better not enlist. Mom and Dad need one of us to hold down the home front. Love you, Hank.

Your brother, Sam

Hank sniffed and set the letter down on the dresser that lay between their twin beds. Sam was right when it came to just about everything. But he was wrong about one thing. Their parents did not need him to help at home. He'd pulled out a year's worth of crabgrass. How much more could he help them?

He took a shower, and when he was cleaned up and in a fresh pair of jeans, Hank knew exactly what he was going to do. Pulling weeds and helping around the house could never right the way things were in the world, or the distance between him and his brother.

Without telling his mom, Hank walked to the local police station and enlisted. Not for the Army. He didn't want to wait around for someone to okay the fight against Hitler in Europe. No, he enlisted with the Marines. That way he could go where it mattered—to the Pacific and the fight against the Japanese.

His mother cried when she heard the news, but his dad only pulled him into his arms and held him. For a long time. "I don't blame you." He kissed the side of Hank's head, a desperate sort of gruff kiss. "I'd do the same thing if I were your age."

Hank notified his principal at the high school and a week later he was on a train to Parris Island, South Carolina, and six weeks of basic. Every hour of pushing through mud and under rope courses and over towering walls, Hank kept one thought in mind.

He was about to give a little payback to the people who destroyed Pearl Harbor.

When his training was complete—the little training the guys were getting at the time—Hank boarded another train to San Diego and a week later he was on a ship headed across the Pacific. With everything in him, he tried not to think about Irvel, where she was and what she was doing and whether she was safe wherever they'd stationed her. He prayed for her safety and for Sam's and for the day when they might all be back home together.

Along the way, every day the men heard reports. Sometimes whispered one to another, and sometimes from their commanders. The losses in the Pacific were staggering. The Allied forces were doing everything in their power to establish control of the Solomon Islands, to protect Australia from being the next target.

"Privates, when it's your turn to take the beach, you will see things a man should never have to see. Death will be all around, and it may come to you. Do not be afraid," their sergeant told them on deck one day after training exercises. "Rather, remember this. War is only won at a very great cost. And we *will* win this war."

Hank tried to hang on to that single hope. Whatever their losses, and despite the fact that a great number of the men sharing his bunk room would probably not make it home, they were still going to win this war. The sergeant had said so.

Not only that, but Hank was begging God it might be so.

That evil would be thwarted and freedom and light would win. Even if it meant he spent his final days out here on this ship or fighting on a foreign beachhead. Still, sometimes at night, stacked like sardines in the bowels of the ship sailing across the Pacific and with their vessel dodging enemy torpedoes, Hank would think about his brother. He had made a plan, by then. When the war was over, Hank would tell Sam the truth about what had happened between him and Irvel, and how sorry he was. How it had happened too soon, and he hated himself for that.

He would tell Sam everything and ask for his forgiveness. Otherwise, Hank couldn't live with himself.

If only he made it back home and had the chance.

JUNE 1, 1942

15

From the bow of the USS *Solace*, the deep and murky waters of the Pacific Ocean were quiet that night. Irvel stood at the railing and stared out. The decision to take them from Europe here to the islands had been a quick one. They needed code breakers on ships in the Pacific. So here they were.

Stars dotted the sky, twinkling and casting diamonds of light on the waves. No storms on the horizon. Not from the heavens, anyway.

Keep me safe, my God, for in You I take refuge. The words were from Psalm 16. Irvel's latest section of memorized Scripture. She closed her eyes and silently ran her way through the next nine verses. *You make known to me the path of life; You will fill me with joy in Your presence, with eternal pleasures at Your right hand*.

The words circled her and filled her soul, like a very real shield about her. The ship pitched and yawed and Irvel let the words run through her heart and mind again. She was used to the sway of the ship by now. She and Ruth Cohen had been transferred to the *Solace* two weeks ago, doing what they had been trained to do. Breaking codes. The work was tedious, but it was saving lives. Irvel and Ruth had been assured of that.

Other code breakers worked on the ship, some of them intercepting Japanese chatter, translating it and helping make sense of the enemy's plans in real time. This was different from the code breaking happening in Washington, D.C., and at various military bases. Here on the ship, codes needed to be broken for urgent decisions. And quickly Irvel and Ruth had become the military's favorites for that type of work. In addition, Irvel and Ruth created new codes for U.S. troops in the Pacific theater. Codes that could not be broken, no matter how hard the Japanese might try.

Of course, the two friends dressed as Navy nurses. And they had received enough preliminary nursing training to pass as naval nurses to the other crew on board.

Irvel breathed in deep, the night air cool and damp in her lungs. Her mind was still spinning from the task at hand. Something big was brewing. Code breakers stationed in a windowless basement in the heart of Pearl Harbor had figured out how to decode Japanese intelligence. The team of U.S. code breakers in Hawaii were cracking the broad-strokes plans. But the enemy was constantly changing their codes, even minutes before an attack. Which was the reason so many teams of code breakers were needed. Irvel and Ruth handled codes that dealt with last-minute timing.

From everything they were gathering, it looked like the Japanese Imperial Army was about to attack U.S. forces on the island of Midway.

Irvel and Ruth were tasked with gathering intel on any codes that might be changing as the impending attack drew near.

Irvel heard someone come up beside her and turned to see her friend. "I thought you'd be here." Ruth took hold of the railing and stared out at the ocean. "So much is riding on this."

"It is." Irvel narrowed her eyes, searching the horizon for signs of enemy submarines. As a hospital ship, the *Solace* should've been safe from Japanese attack. But anything was possible in this war. They'd learned that much. "I needed to breathe."

"Me, too." Ruth stood a bit straighter. "Joe wrote to me."

Joe was Ruth's boyfriend. He was fighting in the Pacific somewhere, probably aboard one of the ships getting ready to stage an assault on a Japanese-held island. There were many. Irvel turned to her friend. "Did he say much?"

"Just that they were getting ready. They expect to be sent onshore soon. The fight will be fierce."

"Yes. The enemy won't give up easily." Irvel sighed. Everything about this war was fierce.

They still had fifteen minutes on their break, but Irvel motioned to Ruth. "Let's get back. Every minute counts."

Ruth fell in beside her, and the two made their way across the deck and down several flights of stairs. A few of the doctors on board and a number of privates turned and smiled at them as they walked by.

None of them would've guessed the truth. That Irvel and Ruth were not nurses on board to help injured men they might collect from various islands. They were spies and code breakers, intent on preventing the loss of tens of thousands in a Midway battle that would likely happen in the next few days.

Back at their stations in the belly of the ship, Irvel and Ruth worked alongside one of the leaders of the Office of Strategic Services. Using advanced mathematical codes, they transmitted messages to the office back in Pearl Harbor. The goal was simple.

Create a code even that team couldn't break. If they couldn't break it, neither could their enemies.

When Irvel and Ruth finally found a code that was unbreakable, it was time to set a plan in motion. By then the Pearl Harbor code breakers had proven to their commanders that they were right about the impending attack. They had broken the Japanese code—something no one else had ever done.

Now it was time to protect the U.S. from the enemy doing the same thing.

"You must create a message and send it out to our fleet at Midway," their sergeant told them. "The message is this: Get your aircraft carriers out of Midway. Place them in a new spot, three hundred miles north of Midway. We're giving the location a new name," he told them. "Call it 'Point Luck.'"

For the next twelve hours straight, using the formulas they had developed the day before, Irvel and Ruth created a message no enemy could break, one designed to instruct the fleet about this new plan.

That night Irvel sat up in her bunk and watched the weary nurses return to their sleeping quarters all around her and Ruth. The ship could care for six hundred wounded soldiers, and apparently in the past few months it had needed to care for far fewer than that.

But their day was coming. Everyone on board knew that. When the time came to storm the beaches of the Solomon Islands, there would be casualties. The USS *Solace* was currently near Midway Island, ready to help. Because of their training, Irvel and Ruth were ready to help, should the day come when they were needed.

Irvel's one prayer was that the need wouldn't happen at Midway, that the codes they had created would help move U.S. troops out of harm's way without the Japanese learning the plan.

She pulled her thin sheet over her legs and reached for a bag beneath her bunk. In it was a box of stationery and a number of pens. She had written many letters to her parents since leaving home. But in the past few weeks, she hadn't written to Sam or Hank. She didn't know what to say.

It seemed wrong to confess to Sam her feelings for Hank, and until she did, it seemed unthinkable to confess her love in letters to Hank. So Irvel prayed for them instead.

Hank's was the last face she saw every night when she fell asleep and the first each morning when she woke up.

She still had a feeling he had enlisted and that he was somewhere out here in foreign waters in the Pacific. If that were true, Irvel couldn't bear the thought. Not for either of the Myers brothers. She had a hundred things she wanted to tell Hank, but she wouldn't let herself until she wrote to Sam.

And finally, that night, late in the hours of June 2, having done all she could do to prepare the U.S. troops for Midway, Irvel pulled out a piece of stationery and began to write.

Dear Sam,

I hope this finds you safe and well. I know you're anxious to get fighting, to push Hitler back to Germany. But even so I like to picture you in London, helping the locals and training for the day when you ship out. Safe. Whole. Well. That's how I see you.

Sam, I never wanted to write this letter . . . but I have no choice. I cannot live with myself if I don't tell you what happened after you left. For the longest time, Hank and I worked together at the high school and shared meals and talked about the war. We tried not to think about the past.

Our past.

Because, Sam, you must remember that Hank and I have a past. From our days in junior high. At first, the two of us never talked about it, never hinted at anything more than a friendship between us. But the feelings I had for Hank were always there. Just like you said.

I saw that more clearly after you left.

You were right. I couldn't be sure about the future . . . I wasn't ready for a ring . . . all because of my feelings for Hank.

Irvel read what she had written and she reminded herself to breathe. She would not blame this on Hank. No matter what happened in the months and years ahead, whether the three of them made it home or not, she couldn't stand the thought of Sam thinking what had happened was Hank's doing.

It was hers. She would take the blame. There was more to say so she found her spot and kept writing.

If this is hard to read, just know it is even harder to write. But I had to tell you where things are at. First, I'm a nurse now, working in the Pacific theater. I know, I should've told you sooner. I'm sure you've written, and I've asked my mom to hold your letters. I'll read them someday. But right now everything is upside down, Sam. I'm surviving out here only because of

God's promises. His words. I carry them like a sword.

She paused again. Sooner or later she needed to get to the point.

Anyway, all I want is for this war to end, for the Allied troops to win and for the three of us to be home again in Bloomington, safe and whole. I want life to go back to how it was. But I can't control that. None of us can. So I had to tell you.

I will always care about you, always cherish the friend you've been to me, Sam. If I had understood my feelings for Hank a year ago, I never would've agreed to take that first date with you. But I didn't know. Not until you were gone and I had time with Hank. The two of us.

So, if by some stroke of heaven, God allows us all to come home, I must tell you that I am in love with Hank. I can't help it. I think I've always been in love with him. Please, Sam, try to understand. Hank would never want to hurt you. He'd probably leave for a life overseas if it meant protecting you.

But you said it yourself, Sam. Before you left. You said you wanted me to look at you the way I looked at Hank. You knew even before I fully did, before my feelings for Hank were completely clear to me.

I know that's why you ended things with me before you left. But you probably thought it would take a year or two before anything developed between Hank and me. If it ever did. But it's happened much more quickly. When I left, it was with the knowledge that I am truly in love with Hank. I had to tell you. I had to be honest.

So that when we see each other again, we can find the friendship we had before this past year.

A single tear fell onto the stationery sheet. Irvel wiped it off with her fingertip, and a few of the words smeared. She sniffed. She was almost finished.

I have this most beautiful feeling you'll understand what I'm saying, and that wherever you are when you read this, you will smile. Maybe through tears-like mine right now. But still, you'll understand. Because you are and always will be one of the best guys I know. Praying for you. Thinking of you fondly.

Love, Irvel

Before she could rip it up or change her mind, Irvel folded the single sheet, slipped it into an envelope and addressed it to Sam. Then she took it to the mail bin and dropped it inside. She waited until she was back under the covers before letting the tears come in earnest. Why hadn't she turned Sam down from the beginning? That first date? At least until she knew Hank's heart.

So what if he had been dating Maggie? If she would've had a deep conversation with him, he would've broken up with Maggie and Irvel would've known from that moment on that her heart would only belong to Hank.

But this was where they were, and now she had done it. She had told Sam the truth. He would understand, and maybe some far-off day they would laugh fondly at this time in their lives. When the lines of love and friendship blurred and none of them could grasp the seriousness of what the future held.

Irvel's heart hurt for having to write the letter. But now that she had, she could do something she'd been wanting to do since she and Hank said goodbye on her parents' porch the night before she left.

She could write to the man of her dreams: Hank Myers.

• • •

A FEW HOURS later, Irvel was woken in the dark of night by the head nurse on the ship. In the bunk next to her, Ruth got the same awakening. No words were needed. The head nurse was also a member of the OSS, charged primarily with getting Irvel and Ruth onshore for various spy missions, and overseeing the other nurses so no one asked questions about the activities of Irvel and Ruth. The expression on the woman's face now was enough to tell them this was not a drill.

In utter silence, Irvel and Ruth slipped into their nurses' uniforms and followed their leader out of the bunk room, up a series of ladders and to a ramp connected to a dock that led to what looked like a village. Irvel had no idea where they were. It didn't matter.

"You will take this." The woman handed a nurse's bag to Irvel. "Travel together into the village to a two-story building on the main street. The building will have a red-painted door. You will go inside, asking about more medical supplies. A man will be waiting for you, and he will give you a bundle of bandages and medications."

Irvel didn't dare glance at Ruth. She already knew that her friend was taking in the details as quickly as Irvel was. Memorizing them. Something else they were both good at, and another reason they were brought into the OSS.

The woman was still talking. "The man will put these things in a new identical bag, and you will leave this one behind."

No way Irvel would ask what was in the bag she was holding. That didn't matter. What did was getting it into the right hands. She nodded and beside her, Ruth did the same thing.

"You must be back before sunup."

They wasted no time. Once they had reached the end

of the dock and headed into the village, Irvel realized they were behind enemy lines. Armed Japanese fighters stood at every corner, one at a time glaring at Irvel and Ruth. "Keep walking," Irvel said. "They won't harm us."

Rules of war stated that medical ships and personnel were off-limits, but the work was still dangerous. Of course, the Japanese didn't have to follow the rules, but it was dishonorable to break them.

Shadows fell across the road, and Irvel could feel that they were being watched at every turn. She kept her breathing steady. They would be fine. The two of them had to believe that. Had to be confident as they walked past dozens of Japanese military men. If the Japanese thought they looked shifty or afraid, they could be captured.

And that would be that.

The night was so dark, but finally Irvel could see the red painted door a block ahead. She tightened her hold on the medical bag and picked up her pace. Irvel smiled at Ruth, like this were any other ordinary outing and the two were happy to be on solid ground, thankful to have a way to get more supplies. As if they weren't spies carrying top-secret messages to secret allies.

Suddenly from the shadows, two men lurched in front of them and aimed semiautomatic pistols straight at their faces. Irvel was learning Japanese as quickly as she could, but as the men began yelling at the same time, she had no idea what they were saying.

She said the thing she was trained to say, and she said

it in Japanese. "Have honor, fine gentlemen. We are nurses in need of supplies."

Both men lowered their guns. They looked at each other and then at Irvel and Ruth again. Finally, the older of the two stepped aside and motioned toward the building with the red door. "Go," he said in English. "Hurry."

The men with the guns were not happy about the presence of American women in the village, but they seemed to have responded well to one word: *honor*. Which was exactly what their OSS training had taught Irvel and Ruth about the Japanese.

And so, out of honor, they allowed Irvel and Ruth to pass through and a few minutes later, as Irvel carried a much fuller identical bag, the men stood at bay, scrutinizing them, glaring at them. Irvel resisted the urge to run, and fifteen minutes later—just before sunup—they were back on the ship and setting out to sea.

Four hours later, Irvel and Ruth were in their recognizance room interpreting code when they received word. The Japanese had been caught off guard at Point Luck. In a matter of minutes, the United States had sunk three Japanese aircraft carriers and shot down more than a hundred planes. A battle had ensued, but it appeared that Midway would be a tremendous victory for the U.S. forces.

Casualties and injured members of the Navy and Marine Corps were shuttled to safe island harbors, where other hospital ships helped get them to field hospitals. The *Solace* took some of those, and Irvel and Ruth were called to help with initial intake of the wounded.

Despite the victory, the destruction of human life in the Battle of Midway was horrific, like nothing Irvel could've imagined. Men missing limbs, and with gaping wounds and burns that spanned most of their faces and bodies. Irvel and Ruth deftly worked alongside actual nurses applying tourniquets and shooting men with morphine to keep them from feeling the worst of their injuries.

That day, dozens of men did not make it, and when the remaining victims were stable, again Irvel and Ruth found their way to the deck. Both of them were blood-smeared and in shock over what they had seen.

Ruth grabbed tight to the railing and lifted her face to the sky. "What must God think of all this?"

"It is horrendous. More than I can take in. But still . . ." The idea had consumed Irvel's mind, too. "But still . . . we won today, Ruth. We have much to be thankful for."

Ruth nodded. "I know. It's just . . . every face, every man today, I could see my Joe. I fear that at the end of all this they will each merely go down as a number. A casualty. One in a list of a hundred thousand lost people."

Irvel lifted her face to the night sky. "When in reality, each one is somebody's son. Someone's brother or boyfriend."

"Or husband." Ruth breathed in sharp through her nose. "I think I know what was in the bag this morning."

Irvel turned to her. They rarely knew the details behind a delivery like the one they'd done earlier today. "How?"

"I heard the sergeants talking." Ruth lowered her voice. "It was instructions for the dive bombers. Radar had exact coordinates for where the Japanese ships were. It was too sensitive to send by code. Even our codes."

The news took a moment to make its way from Irvel's mind to her heart. "Otherwise . . ."

"Right." Ruth faced the ocean again. "Otherwise, we might've lost today."

Ruth had just finished her sentence when something caught Irvel's eye. Something long and silvery, speeding their way through the dark waters. In a rush of motion, what looked like a Japanese torpedo seemed to brush against the *Solace* and continue on through the ocean.

Neither of them said anything for a few minutes.

"We're a hospital ship." Ruth finally broke the silence. "How dare they?"

"Anything can happen out here." Irvel steadied herself. Had the torpedo hit with them on the upper deck, they might have both been killed. Mid-conversation.

That night in her bunk, the weight of her work lay heavy on Irvel, like an iron vise she couldn't escape. Not that she wanted to escape it. She was just exhausted, that's all. She tossed and turned until finally, as nurses all around her slept, there was something Irvel had to do.

She pulled out a piece of stationery, found her pen and began to write.

Dear Hank,

I hope this finds you at home, helping your parents and getting ready for another year of teaching our favorite high school students. But I have a feeling it won't find you there. Wherever you are, I'm sorry I haven't written sooner. Though I'm busy out here in the Pacific, and though I believe I'm making a difference in my nurse's uniform, in many ways I'm still standing on my front porch.

Waving goodbye to you.

I thought you should know, I wrote to Sam. I told him he was right about breaking up with me, and that I had already fallen in love with you, Hank. I explained that it was my fault, not yours, but that there was only one Myers brother I'd ever love. The one I had given my heart to when I was just a kid. I believe he'll understand. I'm praying for that.

Now that I've been honest with Sam, I can finally write to you and tell you that though I love you with every breath, I don't want you to hold out hope for us. Our hospital ship was nearly hit tonight by a stray Japanese torpedo, Hank. Don't spend your hours thinking about me or about us. That's a million years away from this.

Just stay alive. Please, Hank, could you do that one thing for me? Just stay alive.

Until next time, with all my love, with every heartbeat,

Love, Irvel.

She dropped the letter in the mail bin and fell asleep picturing Hank and someone else. The Japanese fighter, his gun aimed straight at Irvel's face.

In the weeks to follow there was more of the same. More bag drops and lies and finding a way to survive while helping her country. Until finally Irvel rarely thought about Hank at all, but only about something critical to every member of the OSS.

Survival.

AUGUST 1, 1942

16

They were headed for the Guadalcanal, the Island of Death, and everyone on board knew it. Hank felt a nudge on his shoulder as a voice rang out through the hull of the *Queen Mary*.

"Get up. Next shift." Those in command made their way through the bunk area waking up the privates. "Everyone up!"

Hank was on his feet and dressed in two minutes flat. Something he'd learned in his training on Parris Island. Whatever else you do, be ready to move. With thousands of marines on board the troop transport, sleep came in shifts. And when they weren't sleeping, the marines stood shoulder to shoulder getting food, eating it, and waiting to sleep again.

In two more minutes, Hank and his division were on the deck, breathing fresh air and sunshine and waiting for their turn to eat. Only then did he lift his face to the sky and close his eyes. *God, wherever she is, please keep her safe. Help her to help others, help her save lives, but please . . . save hers. And please be with my brother, Sam. Protect him, Father. We all need You.*

He opened his eyes and tried to imagine how many men surrounded him. Far more than his initial division that had sailed from San Diego to Pearl Harbor, and then transferred to this troop ship for the journey into the war raging in the Pacific.

The ship zigzagged across the ocean toward Guadalcanal, keeping speeds that would protect it from enemy torpedoes. Hank made eye contact with the guy beside him. They had learned to keep their footing as the ship maneuvered its way closer to the fight. Being out here at sea wasn't what any of the men on board were concerned about.

It was the landing. The one expected to come in a week at Guadalcanal.

"You write home to your family?" The guy had red hair and a skinny face. He was shivering in the morning ocean air. "We land in a week."

"Yeah. I wrote home." Hank thought about the pack with his belongings, the one under the bunk he shared with two other marines. He had written to Irvel, too, but he didn't say so. "What about you?"

"I did. Not sure . . . if we'll get another ch-ch-chance." He shrugged. His bony shoulders made him look like a high school freshman. "There's a reason they call it Death Island."

"Best not to think about that." Hank patted the guy on the back. "We'll be okay."

The redhead didn't look so sure. The ship pitched and ten guys crashed into each other before righting themselves. When they were steady again, the guy looked at Hank. “Can I be honest?”

“Sure.” Hank felt for the guy.

“I’m scared to death.” He held out his hand. “I’m Bill. Bill Bailey.”

“Bill.” Hank shook the private’s hand. “I’m Hank Myers.” He looked a little deeper. “You still in high school, Bill?”

The guy looked over his shoulder, like he didn’t want to be caught saying whatever he was about to say. “I am. Junior from Asheville, North Carolina.”

“You lied about your age, huh?”

“Had no choice.” Bill wasn’t shaking as bad now. “My daddy signed up. I’m the oldest of three boys.” He raised his bony shoulders again. “Had to make him proud.”

Once more the ship pitched, but this time the cluster of men that included Hank and Bill held their ground. Hank studied the kid. “You a praying man, Bill?”

“Not really.” Bill crossed his arms. He was shivering again. “I seen you praying with a few of the guys yesterday. I thought maybe . . . maybe you could pray for me. Everyone’s calling you Preacher.”

Hank felt the most complete sense of peace wash over him. *You have me here for a reason, Lord. I believe that.* He took a deep breath. “I like that.” He grinned at the kid. “Let’s get one thing straight first.” All around them, guys were in a hundred quiet conversations as they inched closer to the front of the food line. “Jesus. He’s the Savior, the one who came to earth and died for your sins and mine. You want God to hear your prayers, you gotta get things right with Jesus."

Bill was shivering harder again, despite the rising sun on their faces. "I gotta lot of sins, Hank."

"That's okay." Hank put his arm around Bill's shoulders. He thought about Irvel and the night before she left. "I do, too." With that, right there in a crowd of a thousand early morning marines, Hank prayed for Bill. That God would forgive him for his sins, and that Jesus would make His home in Bill's heart for all time. When the prayer ended, Hank gave Bill a light slap on the back. "How does that feel?"

For a few seconds, Bill said nothing. Then he straightened and looked around. He wasn't shivering at all. "It . . . it's wonderful." He put his hand over his heart. "He's right here. I can feel Him. Jesus."

"I'll have the chaplain get you a Bible. Read it, Bill. God's love letter to us."

"I will." The line moved then, and Bill shifted with his group farther up. Bill held his hand up as he left Hank. "Thanks, Preacher Man."

Hank waved. The grin didn't leave his face all day. No telling what lay ahead, but for now the only way to be ready was to make things right with Jesus. Later that day four more guys approached Hank, and by the fourth of August, a few dozen privates each day were wanting to pray with Hank.

Finally, it was August 6, and word went through the

troops. They would make landfall in the morning. "August seventh will go down in history as the day we moved the Japanese Imperial Navy out of the Pacific," their sergeant told them. "Be ready, men." He looked over the group, thousands of them altogether. "Be ready."

Across the sea of faces, Hank spotted Bill again. The redhead gave Hank a thumbs-up, as if to say, *I'm ready, Hank. Because of Jesus, I'm ready.*

Hank gave him a thumbs-up, too.

Their leader explained the situation in the simplest of terms. "You will take the beach at Guadalcanal, and you will eliminate the enemy. We will take back the airstrip and turn the Japanese away. We will stop their aggressive efforts from tomorrow forward."

Hank felt a thrill of hope. After Midway, the Japanese had stopped going on the offensive. But the enemy troops had taken control of a number of islands in the Pacific. It was time to send their troops home.

"Otherwise"—their sergeant's voice was somber—"the Japanese will take Australia. And life as we know it will change." He paused. "It's up to us to make sure that doesn't happen. Say your prayers tonight, men. Many of you will not get to do so tomorrow night. But every one of you must know this . . . the sacrifice is worth it. You are defending Australia, but you are defending every free person in the world. Including your own families and loved ones. Take pride. This world needs you."

No matter how much passion filled the man's voice, the

speech was chilling. That night before he fell asleep, Hank did what he'd done almost every evening since he enlisted.

He wrote to Irvel.

He expected her letters to get to her, since he had an address for her with the U.S. Navy. But if his notes were reaching her, he had no proof. In all this time, he hadn't received one letter from her in response. And last night came the worst news of all. A letter from her mother. The message was short, but it clearly came straight from her heart.

Hank pulled it from his bag and read it again.

Dear Hank,

I know you'd rather this letter be from Irvel. But I am sorry to report I've heard nothing from her since she left. Letters to Irvel from us, and from you and Sam, have all been returned to our home address. I didn't want you to think it was only your letters, or that she was responding to us and not you.

Please, don't let this cripple you with fear and worry. God knows where Irvel is and what she's doing. I believe there must be a reason why she hasn't responded, and why our letters are being returned. One day soon we will all know.

Be safe, Hank. I remain in daily prayer for you, Sam, and Irvel.

Love,
Mrs. Holland.

He wouldn't have the strength to storm the beaches of Guadalcanal tomorrow if he believed for one minute that something had happened to Irvel. That she had been working as a nurse on a ship and somehow lost her life helping others. No, that wasn't possible. Like her mother said, there was a reason her mail wasn't getting through. Something they could talk about later when the war was over.

For now, he could only do what he had done every night since he left. He pulled out a V-mail form and began to write.

Dear Irvel,

Your mother says your letters are not going through. That makes me sad, not because I believe something has happened to you, but because you're not feeling my love from here to there. Wherever you are.

Tomorrow, my love, we will leave our ship and make our way onto a beach I can't talk about. Our leaders expect it will be dangerous. But I know this . . . Jesus is with me, and I am with you. And because of that, I am not afraid.

If you should read this before I see you again, just know that I don't want you to be afraid, either. God has a plan in all this, no matter what. One way or another, we will see each other again.

Hank could only hope that this letter would get through, that whatever the problem or mix-up, the Navy would figure it out and she would start to receive his mail. He kept writing.

Oh, and I am writing to Sam each day, too. I know he will understand the situation between us. After all, you were mine way before you were ever his. He'll see that. He's my best friend.

I love you with every breath, every heartbeat.

Love, Hank

He slipped her letter in the mail bin and fell asleep.

In the morning, he woke to a rush of activity. They were preparing to land. Hank donned his uniform and checked his M1 Garand .30 caliber rifle. He took a deep breath and closed his eyes. *God, be with me, bring us victory against evil today.* Whatever lay ahead he was ready.

Two hours later, Hank and thousands of marines seemed to have caught the Japanese entirely off guard. The next day, with almost no resistance, the marines had taken back Henderson Field, effectively preventing the Japanese from using Guadalcanal as an air base.

But twenty-four hours later, under the cover of bad weather and late night, the Japanese struck back. Hank wondered if the sound of enemy fire would ever stop. Before morning hit, they took losses they had never expected, and there were dead marines everywhere, including one whose face Hank would never forget.

The face of Bill Bailey.

• • •

THE WAR ON Guadalcanal had been raging for more than two months and somehow Hank was still alive. He hunkered in a hole with twenty other marines, all of them waiting for daybreak. If only they hadn't taken the Japanese Navy for granted.

Here on Guadalcanal, the battle had become something of a grudge match, and morale was low. Even for Hank. So much death, so much dying. And more than that were the marines passing from sickness and starvation.

Finally, early in October, members of the U.S. Army began arriving on the island and gradually the U.S. took the offensive. It was four days into the resurgence of help from the Army that Hank was moving from one position to another when he heard a familiar voice just ahead.

"Hank! Over here!"

Hank kept running toward safety. To stand in the open field was to get yourself killed. But as he neared a thicket of trees he saw where the voice was coming from and just under cover he stopped. "Sam?"

The soldier stepped out enough to be seen. Yes! It was Sam! Hank ran to him and the two grabbed hold of each other, locked in an embrace as fierce as the fighting all around them. After a while, Hank stepped back. "I thought you were in Europe."

"They sent some of us here." Sam grinned at him, and once more the two hugged. "We heard you needed backup."

"Of course." Hank was laughing and crying at the same time. "My big brother to the rescue."

One of their sergeants waved at them. "Quiet."

Immediately the brothers lowered their voices. By some miracle, Hank and Sam were now both part of a group trying to take over a supply shed of ammunition a hundred yards ahead. It was a strategic move, important to defeating the enemy on this small Pacific Island.

"And you!" Sam kept his voice down. "The bigger question is what are you doing here? You said you weren't going to enlist."

Hank didn't say anything. He just let his eyes lock onto those of his brother. Sam hesitated, and then nodded. "I get it. I couldn't stay home. You couldn't, either. Of course."

The mission ahead involved waiting till nightfall, several hours. Then they would take the supply shed and seize the Japanese weapon stash. In that time, Hank listened while Sam told him about the war in Europe. "We're making strides. The Allied forces are strong. Right now the concern is for the countries Hitler is taking over. And for the Jewish people." He hesitated. "Lately it's been for you marines out here in the Pacific."

Hank nodded. "We needed you."

They caught up about the war and the awful things they'd seen and Hank told him about Bill Bailey. An hour before dark, something caught Hank's eyes. A pair of nurses on bikes heading up a nearby road. He blinked a few times and stared at the women. One of them was blond, and if Hank didn't know better, he would've thought she was Irvel.

But that wasn't possible. She was in the European theater. Or was she?

Suddenly Hank wasn't sure about anything but the most obvious. Sam was alive and he was here. And for now—in the midst of this battle—that was all that mattered.

Their sergeant gave orders to stay lower than before. When Hank glanced that way again, the women were gone. But it reminded him of something that had to be said. Because he wouldn't face another minute of danger without telling his brother the truth.

Hank turned to Sam. "Sam . . . about Irvel."

Sam looked away for a long moment. "I miss her." He turned to Hank again. "I'm sure you do, too."

A sinking feeling came over Hank. Clearly, Sam had not heard from Irvel about how things had gone after he left for the war.

Hank's heart began to pound. "I do. I miss her." He swallowed. This wasn't the time, but he couldn't go another minute without telling Sam the truth. "After you left . . . the two of us, we tried to be friends, Sam. We did."

A gradual dawning came over Sam. His eyes narrowed and he faced Hank. "What's that supposed to mean?"

"It means . . . we tried." Hank could barely breathe. "But in the end, we couldn't manage it. She's a nurse now, on a Navy ship. Did you know that?"

"Her letters stopped coming." Sam looked like he might throw up from the shock of all this. "I . . . I thought she was busy teaching."

Hank explained how Irvel got recruited to work on a naval ship because of her intelligence. But it was what happened before she left that he was dreading telling his brother now.

"Where is she?" Sam's face looked pale, gaunt. "Has anyone heard from her?"

"No. Her mother wrote and said all letters to her had been returned to her parents' home."

"Is that what you were going to tell me?" Sam sounded suspicious.

All around them, men were in semi-sleeping positions, quiet, waiting for their call to action. Hank kept his voice to a whisper. "No. It isn't."

Sam worked the muscles in his jaw. "So tell me."

He put his hand on Sam's shoulder. "The night before she left, I kissed her. I tried not to, Sam, but I couldn't help it. I love her." He wouldn't blame this on Irvel. Never mind that they both had feelings for each other, this was his burden to bear, his truth to tell.

For a long moment Sam only stared at him. Then he hung his head. Like hearing this news had made a part of his heart die. Even if she was no longer Sam's girl.

Finally, Hank took hold of Sam's shoulder and helped him to his feet. For a few seconds it seemed Sam might punch him in the face. But then his older brother's expression eased. "Man, that hurts."

Hank wasn't sure what to say. "I'm sorry."

"I know. It's not your fault." Sam ran his hands through his dirty hair. "I could tell she was in love with you. Every time you came home from U of M."

"I should've told you so that night, when you asked if you could take her on a dinner date." Hank hated this, hated seeing his brother hurting. "It's just that . . . the two of us . . ." He stopped short. They were on the battlefield. This was no time for excuses. "I'm sorry, Sam. That's all."

It took Sam a minute, but after a while he seemed in control again. He exhaled hard. "I get it. She was your friend since junior high." Sam's voice trembled. "I said I wouldn't get in the way of her loving someone else. Even if that someone was you. And I won't."

Hank had no words.

They were still low to the ground, still following their commander's orders. But Sam was still able to put his arm around Hank's neck. Defeat colored Sam's expression. "I always wanted her to look at me the way she looked at you. And I was never going to get that because she loved you first, little brother. She always loved you."

Hank wasn't sure what to say. "She loves you, too."

"As a friend." Sam wasn't upset anymore. His peace was palpable. "I hope you'll ask me to be your best man. When we're all home again."

Mud encrusted Hank's boots and flies crawled over his skin. Like most of the men, he'd taken shrapnel more than once. Surface damage. His uniform was a stiff mass of blood and open wounds and body odor. It was hard to imagine ever being home in Bloomington. But he never looked away from his older brother. "I'll do that, Sam. I'll ask you." He hugged his brother again, as close to a full embrace as he could give him from their position on the ground. "I'm sorry, Sam. I'm so sorry."

After a beat, Sam gave Hank a sad grin. "It's okay. Someday I'll find a girl, and she'll look at me the way Irvel . . . looks at you."

"Shhh." The sergeant turned around and scowled at them. "Don't give us away."

Hank linked arms with Sam and for the next hour they didn't say a word. They didn't have to. When their eyes met, Hank could see his older brother playing catch with him in the backyard when they were in grade school, and then Sam walking beside him in the halls of Bloomington High, and him catching that day on the baseball field. He could feel him sitting beside him on the bleachers the day before he left for the war.

And now this, here. God had brought them back together again. More than that, Sam wasn't angry with him. He understood about Irvel. All Hank could think was this had to be a sign that everything was going to be okay. Somehow, they would fight their way off this forsaken Island of Death and make it back home. So that one day in the not-so-distant future, they could all dress in their finest suits and gather at the local church where Irvel would say *I do* to Hank.

And Sam would be standing at his side, grinning and understanding and loving them both.

The battle started with a single word.

"Now!" the sergeant whispered and pointed.

And like that it was time to fight. Hank and Sam and the other men snapped to attention. They knew the task ahead. They would capture the ammunition shed and close out the battle here at Guadalcanal and then they would be on their way home. Hank stayed at Sam's side, crouched low, guns ready. Together with the other men on their team, they raced silently across an open field toward the shed, and Hank was remembering how they had played war on the school playground when they were kids. And always . . . always they made it safe to the other side because—

An explosion lit up the night, right in front of Hank. Bodies and limbs and mud and plants were flying through the air and Hank reached for Sam. But he wasn't there. He wasn't beside him or on the ground or anywhere in sight. "Sam!" Hank's voice rang out amidst the gunfire and explosions. "Sam!"

Nothing. No response. And no matter how hard he looked, the fact remained.

His brother wasn't there.

OCTOBER 1942

17

Hank opened his eyes and his sergeant was standing there, right beside him. "We got the target." He nodded. "We took the ammunition."

Ammunition? Hank opened his mouth to talk, but his head was throbbing. He couldn't swallow, and there was a ringing in his ears. But then he remembered what had happened and how he and Sam were making their way across the open field when—

He sat straight up. Never mind the pain. "Where . . . where's my brother?"

The sergeant dropped down and rocked back on his heels. He put his hand to his mouth and stared at the ground.

"No." Hank struggled to his feet. Whatever his injuries, he could still move. He still had his arms and legs. He took lurching steps toward the door.

"The field hospital is in the big tent across the field." The sergeant still couldn't make eye contact. "We have control of this area. You're safe to go."

Safe to go? What was happening? Where was Sam and why wouldn't the sergeant look at him? Hank picked up speed and dragged himself twenty feet across the broken dirt to the makeshift hospital. Troops gathered near the entrance, but Hank pushed his way past.

A doctor just inside looked at him. He held a clipboard. "Who are you looking for?"

"Sam Myers." Hank couldn't think, couldn't breathe. How could this be real? "Take me to him. Please."

The man checked his list and hesitated. A hesitation Hank would remember the rest of his life. "I'm sorry. I'm not sure. I don't believe he made it."

"No. That's . . . that's not possible." Hank moved past the man into the tent, down one row of injured men and then another until he saw him. His brother. "Sam!"

Sam was propped up on a cot, one leg gone. His face was pale, but his eyes flickered open. He spotted Hank at the same time. "Brother." His voice sounded different, weaker. But he managed a smile. "I took it pretty bad."

Hank rushed to the edge of the cot and pulled Sam into his arms. His mind was spinning, his world crashing. Shock and disbelief shook him to the core and he wondered if this were a nightmare. "Sam . . . where . . . where's your leg?" Hank looked down at his brother's lower body. "I'll go. I'll go find it." He started to get up, but Sam stopped him.

"It's gone." He put his hands on either side of Hank's face. "It's okay. Stay here. Stay."

"No! Please, God, no!" Hank lost the fight to run. Instead, he held his brother and wondered why the sergeant had told him Sam was gone. He wasn't. He was alive and he was here. Never mind the leg. They could find a prosthetic leg later. All that mattered was this . . . Sam was alive.

His brother pulled back and looked deeply at him. "I . . . lost a lot of blood."

Blood. Was that what Sam needed? Hank would go find some, but even as he started to stand, Sam stopped him again. "Don't leave me."

It was the first time in all his life Hank had heard his brother sound afraid. Hank shook his head. "You . . . you're going to be okay."

"I . . . want you to tell Mom and Dad . . . I love them."

No . . . Hank shook his head. "Don't talk like that, Sam. You're going to be all right." Hank raised his voice. "Someone help us over here!"

Sam shook his head. Gradually, he slid back down to the cot. His eyes rolled slightly and he struggled to focus. "You're gonna make it out of here, Hank. God told me." Sam smiled, but the light inside him was fading. "You go love our Irvel, little brother. You love her. That was . . . always the right thing."

Hank wanted to scream at someone, grab a doctor or a nurse and order them to fix Sam right now. He couldn't go through life without his big brother! But there was no one to call, nothing to do. "I'm here, Sam. I'm not going anywhere."

"Remember . . ." Sam was breathing harder now, struggling to get air. "Remember that Christmas. You got the blue . . . BB gun."

Hank could do nothing to help Sam, so he stayed in the moment—this final moment with his best friend. His older brother. Hank found his voice. "It was all I ever wanted. That blue BB gun."

Sam chuckled, the slightest, saddest gurgling sound came from his throat. "Mom and Dad forgot. They . . . they gave me the blue one. So . . . before . . . before you came down on Christmas morning . . . we switched them."

Hank reached for Sam's hand and held it, squeezed it, as if by doing so he could keep his brother's body alive. "You . . . didn't have to do that."

"Nah . . . I . . . wanted the red one." Sam's eyes met Hank's and for a moment they were eight and six again, a couple of kids with the most golden life ahead of them. "I'll . . . wait for you, Hank. On the other side. I'll never be far."

"Don't go." Hank whispered the words. Tears choked his voice and his heart pounded inside him. Again he took Sam in his arms and held him close one last time. "I love you, Sam. You always were the best brother."

But for the first time ever, there was no response, nothing.

His brother Sam was gone.

• • •

IT WAS EARLY December, and Irvel and Ruth had completed four deliveries that week and Irvel was exhausted. She had been asleep for a few hours when her sergeant shook her awake. Another mission, that had to be it. Irvel was used to being woken up in the middle of the night.

Instead, the sergeant leaned close, his voice barely audible. "Get up, Irvel. We have news for you in the office."

No need to ask what office, Irvel already knew. The secret office where the OSS operated. Their leaders simply called it the office. Irvel dressed in her nurse's uniform and squinted in the dark.

Her heart beat so loud, she wondered if every woman in the bunk area could hear it.

What kind of news would require her sergeant to wake her in the dead of night? She followed her sergeant to the hidden room at the bottom of the ship. And there was the ship's commander, sitting on the desk, a piece of paper in his hand.

"I'm sorry, Irvel. This news came across a few minutes ago." He handed her the piece of paper.

The message was short and to the point. Army platoon leader Sam Myers had been killed in action at Guadalcanal. His brother, Hank, was with him, but Hank was missing and presumed dead.

"No! Please . . . God, no!" This had to be a terrible dream, it had to be. She sucked in a quick breath and steadied herself. Spots filled her vision and she felt herself starting to pass out.

Someone put smelling salts beneath her nose and she shook her head a few times. What was happening? She looked at the note in her hand. It wasn't a dream. How could this be? Sam was dead? And Hank was missing?

The sergeant attempted to hand Irvel a cup of water, but she shook her head. She wasn't sure she would survive the next few minutes. Water was the least of her concerns. She looked at the note again.

She was getting this news because both Sam and Hank had been writing letters to Irvel, letters that had been returned to Irvel's home address due to her work as a spy.

"Since you are a member of the OSS, their names showed up on our intel reports. You knew these brothers well?" Her commander stared at her.

"Yes." Irvel felt tears fill her eyes and spill onto her cheeks. "I loved them."

"Irvel." Her leader's voice was very serious. "Did Sam Myers or Hank Myers know about your work with the OSS?"

Irvel could barely make sense of the question. Her dear Sam was dead and her beloved Hank was missing. But all her leaders wanted to know was whether she'd broken protocol and told someone the truth about her spy work in the war? She shook her head. "No. I said nothing. Of course not."

Then she stared once more at the words on the paper. The note went on to say that most of the men had not survived this particular mission. Something about an ammunition shed.

And again, the letter stated, there was no word on Hank.

"No." Irvel stared at the sheet, and slowly she dropped to the nearest chair. Her voice was barely audible. "Why, God? Why them?" She let the piece of paper fall to the floor. "Why?"

"I'm sorry." The commander crossed his arms. "Sam was killed in battle. His body will be returned to his family. By now they may have identified Hank's body, as well. I'm sure they'll have a burial." For a moment, the man said nothing. Then he drew a sharp breath. "We have a few more missions for you and Ruth. Then we'd like you to go home, Irvel. You need some rest."

He apologized again, and then excused her. She took the paper from the floor before she left, and a few minutes later she was back in her bed. Just like that, as if Sam wasn't one of the most important people in her life. As if Hank wasn't the man she was in love with.

Irvel thought about Sam's students, the high schoolers in Bloomington who were earnestly waiting for their teacher to come home. Death was happening all around them, of course. This was war.

But Sam Myers? He was bigger than life. How could the enemy have killed him?

Her tears came hard then, and she wept herself to sleep. She cried for Sam, who never had the chance to find that girl who would look at him the way Irvel looked at Hank, and she cried for his parents, who would have to bury their older son.

But she cried most of all for Hank—because Hank might still be alive, out there somewhere. Because Hank had known his brother's love from his first day on earth. From his first breath. And now he would never have that here in this life again.

The next day, with eyes swollen from crying, Irvel

joined Ruth on a mission into a harbor town. Again, neither of them knew what island they were on. They followed instructions to the letter, even though Irvel's heart was breaking wide open. First, they purchased two dozen daisies along with several bags of medical supplies. Under very detailed orders, they walked past Japanese troops and appeared to wait for transport at the dock. As time passed, Irvel set her daisies down and drank water from her canteen. When no ship came, Irvel and Ruth returned through the city and to another harbor on the other side of the village, where the USS *Solace* was waiting for them.

No one suspected anything about the daisies Irvel left behind.

But that night when Irvel and Ruth were safely back aboard their ship, OSS troops on the ground blew up the land bridge where they had laid the daisies. Apparently, the move prevented Japanese soldiers from making landfall and giving support to an unnamed territory on the verge of falling to the United States.

Another day in the life of an American spy.

That night Irvel and Ruth again met up on the deck at their favorite spot. There, knowing her work for the day was over, Irvel told Ruth about Sam's death. "They say Hank may be gone, too." The tears came once more, and Irvel did nothing to stop them.

Ruth put her arm around Irvel's shoulders, and after a few minutes she admitted her own bad news. Her cousins had been taken to Buchenwald, one of Hitler's camps. "I have a bad feeling about this." She wiped tears from her own cheeks. "When is it ever going to end?"

"They told me I could go home. Take a break." Irvel sniffed and dried her face in the ocean wind. "But I don't want to go. This is all I have now. You and me, doing everything we can to defeat the enemy. That's the only thing that matters."

"I agree."

But Irvel knew this much. She wouldn't drop off a bag or leave flowers at the base of a bridge or design codes to protect American troops without seeing the kind face of Sam Myers. And without one very desperate prayer.

That somehow, some way, Hank was still alive.

• • •

THROUGH CHRISTMAS AND into the new year, Irvel and Ruth kept working. They kept their nursing cover, allowing them passage almost anywhere. They delivered secret documents wrapped inside rolls of bandages, and handed off messages in empty canteens to troops watching over prisoners of war.

The work was dangerous, but Irvel had long since stopped caring. Every mission meant that someone else's older brother might come home. That was all she needed to keep her going. She wouldn't need a break until the war was over.

That's how she felt right up until February 8, 1943.

On that day, there were no missions because the news

had reached the *Solace*. The battle at Guadalcanal was over. The United States had claimed victory, despite losing more than seven thousand men and seeing more than eight thousand injured.

Now that it was safe to anchor off Guadalcanal and collect the remaining wounded, Irvel and Ruth were busy around the clock giving morphine to wounded men. That's where she was when her sergeant found her again. "The commander wants to see you."

What this time? Irvel could barely feel her feet as she made her way to the small windowless office. Instead of a letter, the commander held a marine's uniform jacket. Stitched across the front was one name:

H. Myers.

"We believe this belongs to your friend, Hank Myers." The man handed the jacket to Irvel. "They found his body by the shoreline. He had wandered away from his division of men, and a rogue enemy soldier apparently gunned him down." He paused. "Irvel, I'm so sorry."

She dropped to the nearest chair.

"Irvel . . . it's time to go home." The commander raised his brow. "You need time with family. Ruth is going home, too. I'm arranging transportation first thing next week. It's time you both . . ."

His words blurred and faded. She pressed Hank's jacket to her face and closed her eyes. Hank was gone and Irvel could feel herself dying, too. No telling how long her heart would keep beating. Years or decades, it didn't matter. She might draw breath, but one thing would always be true after this.

Her life had ended here in this tiny office on the USS *Solace*.

Hank Myers's jacket clutched to her heart. Breathing in all that was left of him.

• • •

IRVEL TOOK A taxi from the train station to her parents' home. She had been able to send them a message that she was coming home, but they had no idea it would be today. With Sam and Hank gone, she really didn't care whether she came home or not. But she owed her parents this visit.

It was Sunday in early March, and both her parents answered the door. Her mother practically fainted, and her father didn't look much better. The three of them clung to each other for what felt like an hour.

No words were needed.

The next day her parents took her to the cemetery at the edge of town, and she saw the two small grave markers—one for Sam and one for Hank. Irvel had just one question for her mother. "How . . . how could God take them both?"

Her mother had no answers. None of them did. The war was still raging in Europe and in the Pacific, and questions like that were pointless. War was ugly and indiscriminate. It didn't care about how much a soldier was loved or wanted back home. Everyone had losses.

But only Irvel had lost Sam and Hank Myers. And now

the world would never remember them. They were only two in a list of lost men too long to comprehend. Too vast to believe.

Irvel spent the next three months helping her mother at the Red Cross, visiting with Sam and Hank's parents, and working at her parents' factory, building plane and ship parts. But then her contact at the OSS reached out. They needed her back in the Pacific theater. Victory was possible, but they still needed code breakers and clandestine nurses who could deftly carry out missions on behalf of the U.S. forces.

"Please, Irvel . . . stay." Her mother put her hand alongside Irvel's cheek. "You've done enough."

She let her eyes get lost in her mother's, in the way they represented her childhood and youth, the days of innocence. "I have to go. For Sam and Hank, Mother."

After a beat, her mom nodded. "Okay. Your father and I will be here."

Two weeks later Irvel was back with Ruth on the USS *Solace*. By then, Ruth had heard from another relative still in one of the Jewish ghettos. Her aunts and uncles had all presumably been killed at Buchenwald. In what was now being called a killing camp. Like many other concentration camps. All of them nothing more than extermination centers.

The truth was too horrifying to grasp.

The morning after being reunited, Irvel and Ruth intercepted coordinates from a Japanese bomber. Working more quickly than ever before, they decoded the messages and the commander moved a battleship out of harm's way with minutes to spare.

Instead, the U.S. was able to sink the aggressor.

That's for you, Sam and Hank, Irvel told herself. She fell asleep believing God had a plan in all this. Even now. The words of Psalm 23 filled her heart.

> *The Lord is my Shepherd, I shall not want. He makes me lie down in green pastures . . . He leads me beside still waters. He restores my soul. He guides my feet in paths of righteousness for His name's sake. Even though I walk through the valley of the shadow of death, I shall fear no evil, for You are with me, Your rod and Your staff they comfort me.*

There were hours when it was hard to believe, but she held tight to the truth. *You're still here, God. You won't ever leave me.* Irvel exhaled. Then she repeated the psalm.

Over and over and over again.

SEPTEMBER 1943

18

Hank woke up in a military cot on the third Friday of September. A nurse was at his side.

"Well, hey there." She sat on the side of his cot. "We wondered if you'd ever wake up."

The young woman was pretty and kind. She explained that he had been found without his tags, passed out on the shoreline of Guadalcanal. "You're in the military hospital at Honolulu. I'm Jane."

Hank groaned a few times. He could barely comprehend what she was saying and his head was killing him.

"You suffered a serious head injury." Nurse Jane felt his forehead. "You've been in a coma for almost a year and during that time you also battled pneumonia. Here at the military hospital in Honolulu."

Almost a year? He blinked a few times and tried to sit up. The movement hurt his head.

"The bigger question is . . . *who* are you?" The nurse stood and faced him. "Here's all we know." She looked at her chart and then back at him. "Nearly everyone had been moved off Guadalcanal. Leaders, wounded men, survivors. At the last minute, they found you and another soldier. He was dead . . . and you, well, you were beat up pretty bad. You were unrecognizable."

A memory was coming back to Hank but he couldn't form words to explain it.

"Why don't you get some rest? You can tell us later. You've been here a very long time, soldier."

And like that, he faded off to darkness again.

It took three weeks before Hank could tell Nurse Jane his name and what he thought had happened. "I'm . . . Hank Myers." He gave her other details about his identity.

She jotted down the information. "I'll be back."

The next hour felt like five, but finally the nurse returned. She sat beside Hank and studied him. "We don't believe you're Hank Myers." She checked his chart again. She seemed to know the details of the situation. "Hank was found dead, not far from you."

"No." He shook his head. "I'm Hank. I gave that soldier my jacket because he was cold."

Over the next week, Hank tried to tell Nurse Jane his story, the one that was becoming clearer with every passing hour. Finally, he was able to get through the whole thing. "The battle was over. We'd won, but I lost my brother." Tears stung his eyes just saying the words. "So I walked out to the shore to pray."

Jane took the chair beside Hank's bed. She seemed gripped by the story.

"There I met another soldier going through the same thing. Shaken by the death and loss all around us. He was also freezing. Sick with something." Hank paused to catch his breath. "I prayed for him and gave him my jacket."

"Then what?" The nurse was jotting notes in his file.

"Two lone Japanese soldiers came out of the brush. They were armed. They killed the other guy right in front of me. And ripped off his tags. Then they aimed the gun at me." Hank could barely talk, remembering the horror of the moment. He still had no idea why the men didn't shoot him, too. "One of the Japanese shouted something at me and pointed to my tags. I took them off and handed them over."

Hank closed his eyes, the details too vivid.

"Take your time." Jane's voice was kind. "We can continue tomorrow."

"Okay. I . . . I need to sleep." And again, Hank was out.

The next day, he told the nurse the rest of the story. "Once they had my tags, the two soldiers began punching me, kicking me. Finally, one of them hit my head with the butt of his rifle. That's the last thing I remember."

Nurse Jane raised her brow. "I'd say God was watching out for you."

"He was." But even now Hank couldn't understand something. Why wasn't God looking out for Sam? Hank still had a headache, but he felt remarkable considering how long he'd been here. "Tell me? What's happening with the war?"

"It's still going strong." The nurse gave Hank an update on the European and Pacific theaters. "I'm pretty sure you'll get a pass back home. As soon as you're well enough to travel."

It took several months for Hank to get his strength back. During that time, the nurse rarely left his side. When he could take four laps around the hospital, word came from above. Hank was ready to be discharged.

The head of the hospital visited and told Hank his recovery was a miracle. Hank agreed. But he still needed one more gift from God. The chance to connect with Irvel.

He was resting in bed later that day, when the nurse came back around. "Mr. Myers, is there anything I can do for you?" She checked his blood pressure.

Hank sat up a bit. "There is one thing. Could you get me a V-mail form. I have to write to someone."

"Sure." The nurse left and returned with a V-mail and a pen. As she handed it to Hank, she raised her brow. "Whoever she is, she's a lucky girl."

But Hank didn't hear her. He was already writing. Five words in, his head began to throb and he set the piece of paper and pen down on his table. The pain was so bad, he lay down and closed his eyes.

The nurse was still nearby, and now she seemed to have seen what happened. She came to his side. "It takes time to recover from a coma. Let's take things slow."

• • •

FEBRUARY 1944

IT TOOK ANOTHER month before Hank could write a letter without getting a headache or walk without feeling dizzy. But as soon as he could, he wrote to his parents to tell them he was alive. By then the military had already informed them of the good news, but Hank wanted to write to them, himself.

Next he wrote to Irvel. He told her what had happened and he begged her to respond. Week after week, he wrote to her, and week after week he heard nothing in return. In fact, Hank had heard nothing since the day she must've left Bloomington for the Navy. Finally, all Hank could assume was the worst.

That Irvel had been killed, too.

When Hank was finally, fully recovered, he was discharged by the Marines because of the severity of his injuries. That same day he went to the Army office in Honolulu and made an unusual request. He wanted to reenlist and take part in the Army's final war efforts against Nazi Germany. Because he was in such good shape by then, Hank's request was granted.

"It's unconventional," his commander told him. "But in war, the rules don't always apply." He studied Hank. "I have a feeling this is personal."

It was. Hank remembered Irvel telling him about her concern for the Jewish people. If he could make a difference for them, he would gladly take on the risk of war. One more time, for Irvel.

Through the winter of 1943 and into 1944, Hank stopped writing to Irvel. He fought alongside the division that had once been Sam's. The guys remembered Sam Myers, of course, and they took him on gladly. Proof of a brother's love, they all said. The bond between Hank and them was immediate and unbreakable.

Each day the fight grew less fierce, as the Germans began to retreat. One by one, they were regaining European territories from the Germans. Finally, late one spring night in his bunk, Hank decided to write to Irvel once more.

My love,

I don't know where you are. But I feel it in my heart that you are alive. I think about your friend, Ruth, and her Jewish family members, probably trapped in some death camp. I'm doing what I can to free them, Irvel. We have to fight back against the evil that is Hitler. But just know that every day, no matter what other battle I'm fighting, I am thinking of you, loving you, missing you. I beg God that one day I might hold you in my arms again. At last.

Until then, I love you with all my life.

Hank

And so it continued through the rest of 1944 and into another brutal winter, through the beginning of 1945 until finally . . . finally on April 11, 1945, at 3:15 p.m., Hank and his U.S. 9th Armored Infantry Battalion did the one thing he'd longed to do since he joined his brother's group of men.

They liberated Buchenwald concentration camp.

The things Hank saw that day would stay with him all his life, scarring him, burning his conscience and searing his soul with a sort of pain man was never meant to experience. Bodies stacked forever high, ravines filled with human ash, and mountains of shoes and jewelry. But also 28,000 living prisoners—most of them on the verge of succumbing to starvation.

The very air smelled of death.

Hank and his fellow troops could not comprehend that the human heart might be capable of such atrocities. But they worked around the clock to get the prisoners safely evacuated. It might be another month before the war in Europe was officially over. But evacuating those prisoners gave Hank the one thing he had longed for.

Victory.

• • •

APRIL 28, 1945

IN THE SPRING of 1945, Irvel and Ruth moved to the USS *Pinkney* to do additional code breaking. Their enemies were constantly forming new codes, so the work wouldn't end until the war did. They were there, working together, when word came that Buchenwald had been liberated, and 28,000 Jewish people had been set free.

"Irvel . . . I can't believe it." Ruth shook her head, her eyes wide. Then she dropped slowly to the ground and wept.

By then, Ruth had gotten word that her boyfriend, Joe,

had been killed on one of the U.S. destroyers. But even that news hadn't hit Ruth the way the news of Buchenwald's liberation hit her. There was no way to know if her family had been spared, but the demonic reign of Hitler was coming to an end.

Irvel and Ruth bowed their heads and thanked God for what He had done that day.

After that it was time to get back to work.

At the end of April, Ruth and Irvel worked with other code breakers to help underwater demolition teams and minesweepers clear a five-mile stretch of beach in Okinawa. This allowed the men of the U.S. Tenth Army Division to establish a beachhead there. It was another turning point, another reason to believe the war was eventually going to end.

And Irvel and Ruth were there in the middle of it.

Irvel had taught Ruth some of her favorite Bible verses from the New Testament. "You know what I think?" Ruth told her a few days after the success at Okinawa. "I think this Jewish girl is starting to believe in Jesus."

They began talking about life after the war, how Ruth would likely go to California, where some of her relatives lived, and Irvel would go home to Bloomington. At least for now. "I'll see the memory of Sam and Hank everywhere." Irvel's heart ached at the thought. "Maybe I'll join you in California. Find a new group of kids to teach."

It was April 28th, just after dinner. Ruth had to get something from her bag, so she returned to the bunk room. But Irvel wanted to go up on the deck. So she could pray for what was ahead. Whatever plans God might still have for her.

And that's where she was when suddenly from the sky she saw a low-flying Japanese plane. But not just any plane. The markings on the aircraft were distinct. "Kamikaze!" she yelled out. "Take cover!"

But it was too late. The suicide bomber tore through the upper deck, leaving a thirty-foot hole and a wall of flames in its path. The explosion shot Irvel into the air, over the railing of the ship and into the frigid waters below.

The force pushed her so deep, Irvel had to swim up before she could find her way around the debris and bodies and parts of the ship still falling from the sky. But finally she gasped for air. At the same time, she saw a life raft and climbed over the side and onto the rubber mat floor.

Fire burned on the water all around her and the *Pinkney* was listing badly. People were screaming, and bodies floated to the ocean's surface. But just ahead she saw men in a rowboat coming toward her.

She was going to be rescued!

Before she could call out to them, a piece of the ship's railing came sailing through the air. She tried to dodge it, tried to ask God for protection, but the metal object hit her in the back of the head.

Then there was nothing but the fading sound of screaming and the heat from the fire.

And the deepest, most terrible darkness.

• • •

MAY 22, 1945

FINALLY, AFTER LOSSES that would take all of time to fully calculate, victory was declared in the European theater. V-Day, everyone called it. Two weeks later, Hank joined thousands of troops headed home, but he noticed a difference on the ship back to New York Harbor. Despite the victory, small talk seemed to be a thing of the past. Men stared off, hollow-eyed, like there was no way to unsee what they'd experienced in the past forty-two months.

Hank made his way to the upper deck and gazed out at the sea. *Where is she, God? My Irvel? Could You please bring her home? Please?* For hours, he begged God that somehow Irvel might be making her way home, too. He knew from his parents that Irvel had come home for three months, but then she'd shipped out again.

And all that time, Hank had not received one letter from her.

He took the train from the harbor to Bloomington, but as he stepped off the platform everything looked different. It felt different. Like all that was once good and wholesome and innocent about his life was gone forever.

He had written to his parents telling them that he would be on this ship, headed home on this day. But when he stepped off the train, there was no one waiting for him. His hands began to shake. Had something happened to his parents, too?

Taxis were lined up, but Hank felt like walking.

He slung his bag over his shoulder and began the three-mile trek from the station to his parents' neighborhood. The walk took him past the high school, and there at the baseball field, Hank stopped and grabbed hold of the chain-link fence.

The war felt like some sort of bad dream, all of it. Because Sam should be here, standing beside him, telling him about that crazy pitch all those years ago. And Irvel should be on his other side, laughing about falling in the stream when they were in junior high.

Instead he was alone.

A crisp spring wind stirred up the dirt between home plate and first base. As if the ghosts of yesterday were still on the field, still playing the game. He wanted to sit down and let the tears come, let his heart break wide open for all he had lost. But his eyes were dry. He'd seen too much to cry now. He sniffed a few times and kept walking.

At his parents' house, he turned up the walk and stopped halfway. It looked the same, as if life had frozen and here at home, time had stopped as his house waited for his return. He picked up his pace, but before he could reach the door, it swung open.

"Hank?" His mother was pale as a bedsheet. Her voice was part cry, part shriek. "Hank, you're alive! You really are!"

She tried to come to him, but she stopped and bent at the waist. Like she might pass out from the shock of it. "I told your father I wouldn't believe it until I held you in my arms."

Hank reached her and pulled her close. "They told you, right? And you got my letters? Of course I'm alive. I'm here."

"Yes . . . they told me and I have your letters." She was catching her breath. "But we buried you, Hank. I couldn't believe it until . . . until this."

His father must've heard the commotion out front, because in seconds Hank saw him rush through the door. He came to Hank and wrapped him in a hug Hank would remember forever. "You're here! I can't believe it!"

Together they went in the house and settled on the living room sofa. Only then, when his parents were more stable, did Hank ask the question he had carried with him across the ocean.

"What . . . what about Irvel?" He looked from his mom to his dad. "I wrote to her the whole time. But . . . I heard nothing."

"We haven't either." His father sighed. "No one has. Not since she returned to the war."

An ache consumed Hank's soul. "I hate not knowing."

Heartache was in his father's eyes, too. "We keep praying."

"Yes." Hank nodded. "We have to do that. God knows where she is."

That night as he fell asleep he could see Sam, the way his brother looked in his arms those final minutes. And he could feel Irvel in his arms again the night she said goodbye. A hundred other images crowded those, men blown to pieces, barbaric images from Buchenwald. Finally, Hank let the tears come. He cried long and deep for the loss of Sam, and for how much he missed the love of his life. The girl who would most likely never come home again, never sing "Moonlight Serenade" with him or dance in his arms.

His precious Irvel Holland.

JUNE 1, 1945

19

Irvel was alive.

For nearly a month she had been living with a kind older couple, recovering in their beach house on the shores of Honolulu. Also, her parents had been notified that she was recovering from wounds she'd received at war.

That much she knew. But no matter what the couple told her, she had no actual knowledge of how she got here or why. For most of the past four weeks she had known just two things.

Her name was Irvel Holland. And she was in love with a boy named Hank.

But this was the third morning that Irvel could sense the pieces of her memory falling into place. Like the feeling of waking from a deep sleep, where maybe her brain had just needed time to find its bearings.

Irvel sat in a chair near an open window overlooking the ocean. A breeze off the Pacific filled the room with warm sea air. From the beginning she had remembered something else. Her beloved Scripture verses.

She breathed in the sweet smell of early summer and closed her eyes. *Do not be afraid, do not be discouraged. The*

Lord your God will be with you wherever you go. Yes, that was the truth she needed to hold on to. The Lord was with her. Even here, even when the fragments of yesterday were finally finding their way back together.

Footsteps broke the reverie, and Irvel turned to see the older woman, Nancy Williams, carrying two delicate china teacups perched on a pair of saucers. The smell reached Irvel before Nancy did.

Peppermint tea. Something Irvel had come to love while living here. Strange drink for a warm summer day at the shore, but Irvel couldn't get enough of it.

Nancy handed one cup to Irvel, then she settled into the seat opposite her. They had these conversations daily, all part of Irvel's recovery. Nancy smiled. "You look well, Irvel. Very beautiful."

"Thank you." Irvel had a surprise for Nancy. The details in her brain were becoming clearer with every passing day. In fact, she was pretty sure she could remember everything.

"All right, then." Nancy sipped her tea. "Let's try again."

"Yes." Irvel set her cup down. "I'm ready."

"Good to hear." Nancy leaned closer. "Take your time, dear." She paused. "We'll start with the things you already know. What's your name?

"Irvel." She smiled. "Irvel Holland."

Nancy looked satisfied. At least Irvel wasn't regressing. "Very nice. Wonderful." She tilted her head, studying Irvel. "Why don't we let you lead? Tell me what you know."

Irvel liked that better. She felt like a science experiment being asked things any other person would easily know. She took a deep breath. "My name is Irvel Holland. I'm twenty-five years old. The United States is in the middle of World War II, and we got involved in December 1941, when the Japanese bombed Pearl Harbor." Irvel felt her expression turn sad. "Not far from here."

"That's right." Nancy sat a little straighter, her eyes wide. "This is wonderful, Irvel. Go on."

Irvel nodded. "My world back home—in Bloomington, Indiana—revolved around two brothers. Sam, who I was dating when Pearl Harbor was attacked. And his younger brother, Hank. The one I was in love with."

Nancy waited, listening.

"Sam and I broke up before he left for the war first. He joined the Army and was sent to the European theater." This was the part Irvel wasn't sure about. She wasn't allowed to tell anyone about her work as a spy for the OSS. "Then . . . well, then I was recruited to join the war effort in the Pacific."

"Recruited?" There was a knowing in Nancy's eyes. But she did not expand on the question.

"Yes." Irvel reached for her tea. "Because of my math skills. I . . . I was asked to be a nurse."

"Irvel, do the letters OSS mean anything to you?" Nancy leaned over her knees, her eyes intent. She lowered her voice. "Tell me."

"Yes." Irvel still wasn't sure. "The OSS is . . . the Office of Strategic Services."

"It's okay." Nancy put her hand on Irvel's shoulder and smiled. "I work for them, too."

"You're . . ." This had never occurred to Irvel. "You're a spy?"

"My husband and I both are. We've been code breakers working out of Pearl Harbor since a few weeks after the attacks there. Obviously, no one in our circle knows about this."

It was like a scene from a movie. Irvel felt dizzy, shocked. How could Nancy and Robert be spies? She stared at her hands and let the truth land on her. But of course they were spies. The government wouldn't have let Irvel fall into the hands of just anyone. She could've accidentally spilled secrets about the military.

"So . . . you remember?" Nancy straightened in her chair and took another sip of her tea.

"Yes. I . . . I'm a spy with the OSS. Posing as a nurse. I've been running hand-offs and code breaking since my training in the spring of 1942."

"Very good." Nancy took her time. Patient. "Please. Continue your story."

Irvel easily remembered where she left off. Her recruitment to the OSS. "After I left, Hank enlisted with the Marines. These details I only know because at some point I went home for three months. Sam and Hank's parents filled me in on what they knew."

"I'm aware of your trip back home." Nancy's smile was kind. Same as her eyes.

Still, Irvel was shocked to think the woman already

knew most of the details she was sharing. The government had clearly kept close tabs on her. But then, that shouldn't really have surprised her. She was a spy, after all.

Irvel sipped her peppermint tea for a moment before continuing. "It seems, Hank was sent to Guadalcanal, where he fought for months before the Army sent in backup. That happened in October of 1942, I believe."

"Correct." Nancy waited.

"And his brother, Sam . . . was one of the soldiers who showed up to help." Tears filled Irvel's eyes, but she blinked them back. "Not long after he arrived on the island . . . Sam was killed in battle. He . . . he died on Guadalcanal, and his body was shipped back to his family."

"Yes. I read that." Nancy reached for her hand and held it for a moment. "I'm very sorry, Irvel."

She wiped at a few stray tears. "I hate this war."

"We do, too."

Irvel exhaled. She continued the story, telling how she was in the midst of more missions than she could count when she was called into the office and given Hank's marine uniform jacket. "They told me he had been killed, and that his body had been found near the shore of Guadalcanal."

"Terrible." Nancy didn't say anything to refute Irvel's knowledge about Hank.

The past was easy to remember, easy to see, like a clear stream of images in her mind. She told Nancy about her time at home and then returning to work with her friend Ruth, and how Ruth's family in Poland had been sent to Buchenwald at the hands of Hitler.

"And what about Ruth?" Nancy smiled. "Do you remember what happened to Ruth?"

"Only from what you've told me." Irvel pictured her friend, the two of them on the ship deck nearly every night. "She survived the kamikaze attack, and she's finished her work with the OSS and she's back in California with family."

"That's right." Nancy paused. "Let's go for a walk." She held her hand out to Irvel and helped her to her feet. "Are you feeling well enough?"

"Yes. My body is perfect, and my mind." Irvel stretched and turned to Nancy again. "It's my heart that won't ever be the same."

A while later the two of them set out on the beach. They were ten minutes in, when Irvel stopped and stared at Nancy. "What does the government want from me now?"

"Honestly? Nothing. You've worked very hard." Nancy smiled. The two began walking again. "The OSS believes you and your friend, Ruth Cohen, saved tens of thousands of lives over the course of your service."

"But no one can know." Irvel loved the way the sand felt on her feet. Like she was a teenager on summer vacation with her family and war was something that had never happened at all. She kept her eyes straight ahead at the shoreline. "I haven't told a single person. Not my family. Not Sam when he was alive, and not Hank."

She didn't tell Nancy this, but she couldn't believe Hank was really dead. Never mind that she'd been to his gravesite in Bloomington. She couldn't explain it but something deep in her heart held out hope. Like when she breathed, she felt he was breathing the same air. Here on earth. Or maybe that was just Irvel longing for heaven, where she and Hank would never again be apart.

When they were nearly finished with their walk, Irvel stopped again, and turned to Nancy. "When can I go home?"

"Soon." Even through her sunglasses, Irvel could see the warmth in Nancy's eyes. "The general wants to talk to you first."

The general? Irvel figured she should feel nervous about that, but she didn't. She'd faced death a hundred times since the war began. Certainly, she could face the general in charge of the OSS.

Days later, the famous General Donovan visited her at the house on the beach in Honolulu. He brought with him two of his top officials from the OSS. Nancy set them up at the dining room table. General Donovan folded his hands and leveled his gaze at Irvel. "Miss Holland, your parents know nothing of your work on the USS *Pinkney*, and they must not know. They have been told only that you were injured at war, helping soldiers, and that you are recovering in Hawaii." He paused. "It is very important that you keep your vow of silence in relation to your work as a spy for the U.S. military, Miss Holland. It is critical." He paused. "Do you understand?"

Irvel did. She hadn't told anyone before, and she certainly wouldn't say anything now. But she did have a question for the general. The same one she'd had for Nancy on the beach. "Please . . . when can I go home?"

The general smiled. "We have booked passage for you on a Navy ship, which will take you back to San Diego. It leaves in four days." He paused. "From there we will fly you on an Army transport plane back to Indiana. You should be home by Monday, June eleventh."

"That . . . would be wonderful." She thought for a moment. "Please . . . tell my parents I love them, and I'm on my way home."

"Will do." The general nodded. "I'm sure it will be the best news they've heard since the war began."

Irvel could barely breathe. A feeling of elation practically lifted her from her chair. All she wanted was to run up her front sidewalk and fall into the arms of her parents. To let them see for themselves that she was done with the war and home for good.

She ended her time in Hawaii walking the beach and talking to God. She had memorized dozens of Scripture verses. But now that she had survived, now that she was headed home, she spent the quiet hours on the shore silently asking God what was next.

And whether by some crazy miracle chance, Hank might still be alive.

On her last day in Honolulu, Irvel underwent a physical exam provided by the Navy. Irvel felt wonderful, so she expected the doctor's appointment to be nothing more than routine. Instead, the man finished his tests and asked Irvel into his office.

His face looked ominous. "You suffered quite a head injury, Miss Holland."

"Yes." That was one detail she still couldn't quite remember. She could see the horrifying image of the kamikaze plane flying straight for the deck of the USS *Pinkney*. But she couldn't remember flying over the railing and landing in the water. She had no idea how she had wound up in the life raft or why a piece of the ship's railing had slammed into the back of her skull. She also didn't remember being rescued by one of the navel crews in lifeboats launched from the *Pinkney*, or her transport to Hawaii.

Nancy had explained all of that, but Irvel didn't remember.

The doctor looked at her chart. "With a head injury like yours, it's possible to suffer dementia at some point, perhaps later in life." The doctor frowned. "Much sooner than what might be normal." He sighed. "That isn't always a side effect of a head injury like yours, but it's possible. You need to be aware."

Irvel felt herself relax. By the look on the doctor's face, she had thought it was something terrible. Something urgent and problematic for her life today. A risk for when she was old? How could that matter now? She looked straight at the man, the way she had looked boldly into the eyes of Japanese troops on many missions. "Sir." She heard the confidence in her voice. "I'm not worried about some far-off day. All I want is to be well now . . . and to get home."

"I understand." The man folded his hands on Irvel's file and smiled. "I'm clearing you to go."

She practically danced out of the office, and the next day after she thanked Nancy and her husband, she boarded the Navy ship bound for San Diego. All she could picture were her parents' faces when they would finally see each other again. She would find Sam and Hank's parents, too.

And somehow all of them would find their way back to life.

The trip across the Pacific was stormy and dangerous. At one point, Irvel was sure the ship was going to sink. *Please, God*. She turned her eyes to the sky. *You protected me through missions more dangerous than I ever actually knew. Please get us home.*

God answered and in the next few hours, the storm dissipated. Irvel had never flown before, but the Army flight from San Diego to Indianapolis was a thrill she hadn't expected. She sat near the window and stared at the upsides of the clouds. *This must be what heaven looks like,* she thought. Up there she felt close to God.

And close to Sam.

But even then, she refused to think of Hank in heaven. Something in her heart was convinced he was still alive, even if the thought was completely irrational. Her heart would always be connected to Hank. As if somewhere out there, he had to be breathing in. Because her lungs could feel his life inside her.

Halfway home, one of the officials on board the plane stopped at her seat. "Miss Irvel Holland?"

"Yes." She wasn't the only person flying home. Some forty troops were also aboard the plane.

"I don't know your story." He smiled at her. "I don't have that level clearance. Let's just say that."

"Yes, sir." Irvel could feel her heart pounding. Even now she absolutely would not admit to being in the OSS. She would keep her promise.

"Anyway," the man shook his head, "you might not get a medal or an award for your duty to this country." He raised his brow. "But whatever you've been doing these past three years, the United States government is eternally grateful. I was told I could tell you that."

Irvel beamed from her spot near the window and nodded. "Please tell them I appreciate that. And . . . if I had it to do over again, I most certainly would."

The man faced her straight on and saluted her. "I'll do that."

Irvel returned the salute. It was a moment she would always remember. Proof that what she had done mattered, and that even beyond General Donovan, people at the top—whoever they were—knew about her work as a spy. The way she and Ruth and thousands of others had risked their lives every day with the OSS to assure an Allied victory in World War II.

As Irvel stepped off the plane in Indiana, she was overcome with emotion. It wasn't that she saw her parents waiting for her, the way some on the plane did. No one was there with balloons and signs to meet her. General Donovan had explained that her travel back to Indiana was top secret, and that her family was expecting her to be dropped off at their family home. No, Irvel's tears were because she was less than an hour from Bloomington. Never mind the people watching her, Irvel let the tears come.

The OSS had arranged a serviceman and a private car to take Irvel the rest of the way home. When she finally stepped out of the vehicle in front of her home that Monday afternoon, Irvel's parents burst through the door and ran to her. They hugged and cried and hugged again before they returned to the house.

Once inside, her dad stepped back and took gentle hold of her face. "We couldn't believe it when they informed us you were alive." He looked her up and down. "Your injuries must have been serious."

"I was hit in the head after an explosion." She had been given permission to say that. "But I'm fine now. I'm so happy to be home, Daddy." She couldn't stop crying. She hugged her parents again and stayed that way for a long while.

"Wait till Hank sees you." Her mother spoke the words into Irvel's blond hair. "He still doesn't know."

And in that single moment, Irvel felt the blood rush from her face. She couldn't speak, couldn't breathe. She took two steps back and stared at her mother, then her father and back again. "Hank . . ."

"Yes." Her mom wiped her eyes. "He's doing summer training this week at the high school." She searched Irvel's face. "Honey . . . didn't you know?"

She held on to her father's arm so she wouldn't collapse. "Are . . . you saying Hank's alive?"

"Of course, sweetheart." Her dad shook his head. "He's been writing to you every day since he got home. The body they buried was a different soldier. Hank had given the man his jacket."

Irvel could barely focus, barely feel the ground. Her dad went on, explaining how the tags belonging to Hank and the other man had been taken by Japanese soldiers, and how he'd been injured so badly he wound up in a coma. For a very long time.

Irvel had to sit down midway through the story. Otherwise, she would have fainted from the news. Not one of his letters had reached her, but what did that matter? Hank was alive and he was here in Bloomington! No wonder she could feel him in her heart all this time. She stood and embraced her parents again and the three of them laughed and cried until finally they moved to the kitchen, where her mother had fixed pancakes and eggs.

After they ate, Irvel washed her face and touched up her hair. When Hank came home from school that day, she would be sitting on his front porch waiting for him.

The way she had waited all her life for this one single day.

JUNE 11, 1945

20

Hank was thrilled to be going through summer training this week at Bloomington High. He could hardly wait for fall, to be back with the students. They were different kids now, of course. The ones he'd been teaching before the war were all grown. A number of them had been killed in Europe or the Pacific.

He tried not to think about it.

Principal Faust was leading this afternoon's teacher training session in Hank's classroom because it was one of the largest. "We're hoping to be more interactive in every course this fall." He pointed to the chalkboard. "Let's take this history lesson for example." He grabbed a book from his desk. "As you can imagine, history has been happening faster than our textbooks can keep up. So there is greater need for discourse and oral history."

Hank was taking notes. Being home, being back with his fellow teachers, was wonderful in so many ways. The normalcy was like fresh blood in Hank's veins. This was the life he had fought for, the one Sam and—most likely—Irvel had died for. Coming generations of U.S. citizens would not have to speak German or Japanese because of the sacrifice of millions of American men and women.

In that sense, everything about these ordinary summer training days was actually extraordinary. A gift, and a reminder from God. Life would go on, and it would go on in freedom because of the war. Because they had won.

Hank waited while his fellow teachers finished jotting down notes. As he did, his eyes found the American flag standing in the corner. It had been a gift from his father. "So you don't for one minute forget the sacrifice that allows you to stand up there teaching those kids," his dad had told him.

In a conversation with his fellow teachers last week at lunch, one of them brought up an unthinkable possibility. "I wonder if—fifty or seventy years from now—students will understand what happened in this war. The price paid and the victory won. Or will it disappear from history books altogether."

Not possible, Hank told them. The world would forever remember the sacrifices of the Allied troops, particularly those made by the United States. Students would always understand the horrors of the Jewish concentration camps and the fact that the United States and its allies had been willing to take very deep and personal losses to go toe to toe with a couple of evil dictators. And come out victors on the other side.

Time couldn't touch the truth of that.

The hour passed slowly, and finally it was time to go

home. Maggie Wright had moved to Bloomington. She taught English at the high school now, and every so often Hank would walk her home. He saw her in the teachers' lunchroom as he gathered his things from his locker.

"How was your day?" Maggie's smile was always sweet, always full of hope for the possibilities between the two of them.

Hank smiled. "That last hour was interesting. Encouraging us to add more conversation to the classroom. I liked it." He could tell she was waiting for him, hoping he would offer to walk with her. At least that's what Maggie's eyes told him.

But Hank just wasn't ready. He had loved Irvel for most of his life. He figured it would take at least that long to move on. "Hey." He walked up to Maggie and nodded at her. "You have a good night, okay?"

She smiled to hide her disappointment, but Hank caught it anyway. "Sure." She took a step back. "See you tomorrow?"

"Yeah. Definitely. More training." Hank watched Maggie gather her things and leave. He hated hurting her. A part of him wished she'd fall for some other Bloomington High teacher. That way he wouldn't feel so bad saying no. Because his rejection wasn't her fault. He just didn't have it in himself to spend time with her.

Outside it was cold, dark gray clouds covering the city. Hank pulled his coat more tightly around his shoulders. A light rain started as soon as he crossed the street for the walk home. Hank didn't care. Days like this he almost felt like the war had never happened. Like there was still a chance Sam would be waiting for him back home.

Irvel, too.

It was raining harder now. He turned his eyes to the ground. He would have driven if he'd known it was going to rain. But this June had been unseasonably cold, more rain than usual.

As if God was still crying over the losses from the war.

Ten minutes later, the rain let up and the clouds parted. Sunshine burst through and the most brilliant sky stretched across Bloomington. Hank stopped and looked up. A smile caught him off guard. "You still have plans for me, don't You, God?" He spoke the question out loud. Because the Lord was always that close. Even now when he ached from the losses in his life.

Across the street from where he stood, he saw a burst of daisies growing in the field. It had been a while since he'd done this, but today felt like the perfect time. He crossed and gathered a handful of the wet blossoms. White and yellow. Irvel's favorite.

Then he cut through the field to the creek that still ran behind the houses there, the one he and Irvel had been forbidden to walk along back when they were kids. He took the path slowly, looking at the water and the bank and the maple trees. Things that hadn't changed.

He would know the spot no matter how much time passed, the spot where Irvel had fallen into the fast-moving water. Hank stopped and set the flowers down there, on the edge of the bank. "You're still with me, Irvel."

He looked up and searched the sky. Her blue eyes and pretty face were so close he could almost see her watching him. "I can feel you today. More than usual."

Maybe because of the sudden burst of blue overhead, or the way the sun cast diamonds on the drops of water that hung from every living thing. Whatever it was, he could feel her. Like she was right here beside him.

He waited another moment. If only he could go back to that long-ago day when they were just twelve years old. He never would've let Irvel Holland get away, no matter what. Hank filled his lungs with the fresh early summer air and kept walking. It would be quicker to make his way back to the sidewalk. But he didn't care about quick today.

Where the stream intersected with the street he lived on, Hank made his way back to the sidewalk. He had lesson books to read tonight, and he had promised his dad he'd help replace the furnace filters. Next year he would move out, find his own place somewhere near the school. But for now, he was glad he still lived at home.

After the losses they'd lived through, he and his parents needed each other.

Hank kept walking, his eyes straight ahead. But as he got closer, he could see someone sitting on the front porch of his parents' house. A girl, it looked like. She wore what appeared to be a white sweater and she had . . . blond hair.

Hank stopped. His heart skipped a beat and his breath came faster. Was it really her, and if so, how could she be there, at his house? Maybe his time at the stream had made him crazy for missing her. He took another few steps, and as he did, the young woman stood and faced him. His breathing came faster still and his heart began to race even before his feet did.

The woman was Irvel. He had no doubt. And if he was wrong, then he'd rather live in this dream. Because with every step he was more sure, until finally he was convinced. Because he could see something that made him completely certain.

Irvel's beautiful blond hair.

• • •

IRVEL HAD BEEN waiting on Hank's front porch for two hours. She didn't care about the cold weather or the rain that had come and gone. Twice, his mother had come out to see if she was okay, if she wanted something to eat or a cup of coffee.

"No thank you." Irvel had smiled at her. "I want just one thing. Hank beside me."

His mother had blinked back happy tears and nodded. "I'll be inside. If you need me."

Before she left home earlier today, Irvel's mother had let her wear the wristwatch her father had given her for Christmas last year. A reminder that time was not a guarantee, but a very great gift.

Irvel had looked at the watch face a hundred times since two o'clock. She knew what time teachers left school on training days, and she knew how long it took Hank to walk home. Twenty-two minutes. At this point, he was at least thirty minutes late, and Irvel began to wonder if maybe he had gone out with friends. It was still summer break, after all.

But then, a man turned the corner and began walking in her direction.

Irvel would know his tall frame, his athletic gait anywhere. She stood, her mouth dry, her heart pounding. She understood now that Hank thought she was dead. There hadn't been time to get him the news. So she would be the last person he would be expecting to see standing on his parents' porch that afternoon.

His pace slowed and suddenly Hank stopped. He was still three houses away, close enough that they could actually make out each other's faces. Hank picked up his pace and after a few steps, he started to run toward her.

Irvel walked down his front porch steps and waited for him. "Hank . . ." He couldn't hear her, but she had to call to him. Had to feel his name on her lips so she would know this wasn't a dream. He was here, and he was running to her!

The closer he got, the clearer his face and eyes became and Irvel could see he was laughing. Laughing and crying and blinking back tears all at the same time. "Irvel!" He dropped his bag and let his coat fall to the ground. His warm voice cut through the cool June air. "Irvel Holland . . . is it really you?"

"Hank, it's me." She ran the last few steps and in a rush of impossibility she was in his arms. The way they hadn't been since the night before she left for the war.

He ran his hand over her hair and her back, and then

he took gentle hold of her shoulders and looked deep into her eyes, all the way to the place in her heart that belonged to him alone. "You're home! For so long I thought you were . . . that you hadn't made it."

"I did. Everything is fine." She framed his face with her hands. "I thought you were gone, too. I cried at your tombstone."

In some ways, they were both back from the dead and they had a thousand stories and moments and memories to share. But all that mattered here and now was this: they were alive and they were together.

And nothing in all of time would ever separate them again.

Before Irvel could say another word, Hank's face brushed against her cheek and in the sweetest moment of her life, his lips were on hers. His kiss was tender and strong and passionate. "Irvel . . . I love you. I can't believe you're here."

"I love you, too." She kissed him this time. "I dreamed of this. Every day while I was gone I dreamed of this and prayed for it."

He held her close again, and she clung to him, as if the vision of him might vanish in the early summer air if she let go. "You're alive." She whispered the words against his neck and he held her for what felt like half an hour.

Finally, he led her inside, and standing there with sandwiches was Hank's mother. Her face was tearstained, but her eyes held the brightest joy. "I never thought I'd see the two of you together again."

Hank and Irvel sat on the sofa and she stayed locked in his embrace. She still didn't want to let go, in case this was only a dream.

Hank's mother had to go to the post office, so Irvel and Hank were alone over lunch, talking about their time at war and finding their way past the shock of being together.

"The best thing about the war," Hank set his sandwich down, "besides winning, was something I took part in right at the end." He looked straight at her, as if he knew how this next part would hit her. "I was part of the group that liberated Buchenwald, Irvel." His voice fell a notch. "It was the most terrible place. But we helped rescue more than twenty thousand prisoners. They were starving to death, skin and bones, all of them."

What was this? Irvel stared at him, chills running down her arms. "You helped liberate Buchenwald?" She put her hand on Hank's knee. "My friend Ruth, she had family there. It was the one thing we both wanted to see happen."

"A thousand prisoners were kids, some as young as four." Hank stared off, like he was seeing the death camp again. "And there was this one little girl. She was only two. Brown hair and the most brilliant blue eyes. She kept crying for her mama." He shook his head. "Both her parents were dead, poor little girl." He looked at Irvel again. "I'll never forget the look in her eyes, the sound of her voice as she cried for her mother."

Irvel put her hand alongside Hank's cheek. "You're a

hero, Hank. I wish Ruth could know that you were one of the soldiers who liberated Buchenwald."

Then he told her the rest of the story. "There's a reason I was there to help with that mission." He explained that he had signed up again—for the Army that time—all so he could have a chance to free Jewish people from the death camps. "I kept thinking that's what you would've wanted me to do."

This time Irvel kissed him. She had never loved him more. Now that they were sharing stories, holding hands and kissing, now that he was so close beside her, she knew this wasn't a dream. And she knew something else, too.

She was going to hold on to Hank Myers for the rest of her life.

• • •

OTHER THAN THE hours he spent training in the classroom, Hank didn't leave Irvel's side in the weeks that followed. He couldn't get enough of her. They went to the cemetery so she could see for herself. His tombstone was gone.

But Sam's wasn't.

They spent an hour there, praying and remembering Sam, his cheerful disposition and confident smile. He would've been fine with Irvel and Hank, if he'd come home from the war. He would've celebrated the love between them, and he would've found the right girl. Hank had no doubt. The four of them—whoever the girl might have been—would have gone on double dates and played cards and talked about anything except the war.

And over time they would all have grown old together.

But it wasn't meant to be. "God has him." Hank had his arm around Irvel. "He's okay. I believe that."

"Me, too." Irvel still had her eyes on the tombstone with Sam's name. "He was so quick to sign up. So sure he could make a difference."

"He did." Hank had told Irvel some of what he had experienced with Sam in Guadalcanal. "We wouldn't have made it if it wasn't for the Army troops arriving that October." He gently lifted Irvel's chin. "Sam saved my life."

She nodded and blinked back tears. "He would do it all over again, if he had a choice."

"He would." Hank kissed her and ran his thumb along her face. "He told me he'd be waiting for me. When it was my turn. And we'd have forever to be brothers . . . and best friends."

A tear slid down Irvel's cheek. "Sounds like Sam."

They were quiet again, and after a while Hank took her back to her house, where her mother had made dinner. That night when her parents were in bed, Hank turned on the radio and they listened to Glenn Miller again. As if the years that had passed since the last time they had done this, never happened.

Tonight was special for more than the music. From the moment her parents turned in for the night, Hank's heart had been beating hard. He couldn't take his eyes off Irvel, couldn't believe she was really here. He'd had time to do a little shopping in the days since Irvel had come back into his life and he'd made up his mind. He was about to do something he had only dreamed of doing.

This was the night.

After a few songs, "Moonlight Serenade" came on. Hank stood and took her hand. They were halfway through the dance, when Hank stopped. He studied her, their faces a breath apart. He could barely inhale.

His heart in his throat, he took a small velvet box from his pocket and dropped down to one knee. "Irvel, I have to ask you a question."

She gasped and put her hands to her face, her eyes glistening with unshed tears. "Hank . . ."

"Irvel, I've loved you since junior high. I loved you even when I was stupid enough to date someone else." He let himself get lost in her eyes. "I will never, ever let you go again. Irvel Holland, please . . . will you marry me?"

"Yes!" She helped him to his feet and threw herself in his arms. "Yes, Hank. This is all I want for the rest of my life. You and me!" She stepped back and her hand shook as he slipped the diamond solitaire on her finger.

"I love you. I will always love you." He kissed her and held her, and in the dim light of her parents' living room they danced like one being, one heart, one soul. And all Hank could think as he breathed in the sweet scent of her perfume and felt her face against his was the truth that would shape every day after this one.

Irvel Holland had said yes!

DECEMBER 1945

21

They decided on a Christmas wedding, something happy to ease the memories of Sam and Christmases gone by. Irvel crossed off the days while they planned their big moment. Some days she even counted down the hours.

She and her mom picked out a simple wedding dress, white satin with taffeta along the bodice and train. They found a matching veil, Irvel tried it on with her mother's help. As the two stepped out of the dressing room, they stared at the mirror.

"You look like a vision, Irvel." Her mom took Irvel's hand and for a moment neither of them said anything. "I still can't believe this is really happening."

"Me, either." Irvel kissed her mother's cheek. "Do you really like it, the dress?"

"No bride . . . in all of time . . . ever looked more beautiful than you, Irvel. Hank will need his friends to hold him up."

Three days before the wedding, two large boxes arrived at Hank's house. Irvel was there when they were delivered, the two of them going over last-minute wedding plans. Hank stepped outside and brought in first one, then the other. Military stamps covered both boxes.

"What in the world?" Irvel walked with him to the kitchen table. His parents joined them as Hank opened the first package.

Stacked inside were what looked like hundreds of letters and V-mails. Originals. Irvel picked up one from the top. The handwriting was hers. "These are the letters. The ones I sent you."

"Why . . . why didn't they make it to me?" A thin layer of sweat broke out across Hank's forehead. "All this time? Where have they been?"

Irvel had no answers for him.

The second box was also full of letters from Irvel. All the way back to 1942, when Irvel first joined the OSS. Something she still couldn't say. "Every letter you ever wrote me is in these two boxes." Hank turned to her. "I always wondered. I mean . . . I knew you loved me, and that you wanted to write. But I thought maybe with Sam . . ."

Hank's parents had gone to bed by then, so Hank and Irvel were alone at the kitchen table. "You thought I wouldn't write to you? Because Sam and I had just ended things?"

"I wondered." Hank set down a handful of her letters and looked at her. "But you didn't get my letters, either. That's strange, right? It's like everything you wrote or that was written to you, didn't exist."

The truth came over Irvel then, and she dropped slowly to the nearest chair. For a moment, she only stared at the boxes, and the letters spread out on the table. Suddenly she understood. Of course mail hadn't reached her, not until she got home for her three-month break. And no wonder hers hadn't reached him or anyone else, for that matter.

Her location had always been top secret.

She thought about a letter she had received a month ago, something from the Office of Strategic Services—though that's not what the envelope said. According to the information in the note, General Donovan had disbanded the OSS on September 20th . . . just more than three months after Irvel left Honolulu.

Suddenly Irvel knew it was time. She couldn't keep this secret from Hank, not when three days from now they would be married. And since the OSS was no longer an agency of the U.S. government, Irvel was ready to tell Hank everything. She would never tell anyone else, but she had to tell Hank. He was about to be her other half. She took a deep breath. "Can you please sit down, Hank?"

The tone of her voice must've told him this was serious. He set a handful of her letters back in the box and took the chair beside her. He took her hands in his. "Irvel, you look pale." He brushed his thumb along her fingers. "Is . . . everything okay?"

"Yes." She smiled at him. "It is now. It will be." She took a slow breath. "Hank, I have something to tell you." Her eyes caught the box of letters and then she turned to him again. "I wasn't a nurse during the war."

Hank's face went blank. He still had hold of her hands, but now he looked worried about her. Like maybe her head injury was still causing her trouble. "Irvel . . . you trained here in town. All those nights. You were definitely a nurse."

"No." She could feel the sadness in her smile. "Definitely not, Hank." She steadied herself. "Have you heard of the Office of Strategic Services?"

Hank blinked, but he didn't say a single word.

A sigh came from Irvel, from deep inside her soul. "The OSS was an intelligence agency set up to help the U.S. military and Allied forces win the war." She released one of his hands and touched his face. "I'm telling you the truth, Hank. My mind is perfectly fine."

"The OSS?" A hint of understanding dawned in his eyes. "Are you saying . . . ?"

"Yes." She held his hands again.

Hank waited. He searched her eyes as if he still couldn't wrap his mind around any of this.

Irvel did her best to cxplain. "The OSS recruited thirteen thousand people as the war started. People who would serve as spies to help secure a victory." She gave the slightest nod. "Four thousand of them were women and . . . I was one of them."

A breath caught in Hank's throat. "You . . . you were a spy, Irvel?"

"I was." She could see this wasn't sinking in, so she took her explanation to another level. "I dressed like a naval nurse, and I spent the first half of the war on the USS *Solace*, a hospital ship. I worked with Ruth. My classmate, remember?"

"Ruth Cohen. Yes." Hank stood and paced toward the

window. When he turned, she could see that the truth was only gradually hitting him. "How . . . why did they recruit you?"

"Math." Irvel stood and went to him. She put her hand on his arm and looked long at him. "They heard about my math scores when I started work at Bloomington High. Spies who helped with code breaking had to have the highest scores."

"I always knew you were a genius." It was the first time he had cracked a smile. And even then, it was one of disbelief. "So . . . so what did you do? Dressed like a nurse?"

Irvel led him back to the sofa, and then she told him the whole story. How she and Ruth would travel into town—often behind enemy lines—on a false quest for medical supplies. "But always there was a message to deliver. Instructions that would make their way to Americans in command. Sometimes we would drop a bouquet of flowers on a bridge meant for the Allied forces to detonate." She tried to imagine what he was thinking. "It was dangerous. But we did what we could to help save lives."

She told him then about her tireless days as a code breaker. "When we weren't running missions, our job was to create codes for the U.S. troops, codes the Japanese couldn't break." She explained the situation with Midway, and how the code breakers had been credited with saving the lives of thousands of troops by not only learning the plans of the Japanese. "But by sending out codes telling American naval forces where to lie in wait for the enemy."

Since Irvel began her story in earnest, Hank still hadn't

said a word. The two of them sat side by side, but now he pulled Irvel into his arms and swayed with her. Even with the radio off. Like the news was making its way through every part of him. When he eased back, he studied her eyes. "You never told me, all those nights of training?"

"I couldn't." She ran her thumb along his brow. "No one knows. Not my parents. Not my friends. No one. I took an oath. No one else can ever know."

"And now?" Hank slid his fingers up and into her hair. "Why are you telling me now, Irvel?"

"Because in three days we'll say, 'I do.'" Her voice fell and she could hear the passion in her tone. She kissed him in a way that hinted of what was to come. "I wanted to share my whole heart and soul with you. Before we share our bodies."

He kissed her, then, longer this time. After a few minutes, he made the right choice to slide a few inches away. A smile tugged at his lips. "Well, imagine that. I'm marrying a military spy." He laughed, but it didn't dim the fire in his eyes. "Just one more reason to love you, Irvel Holland." He traced her jaw and her lower lip. "I want to hear about every story, every mission."

"That could take time. We'd have to be alone every time we talk about it." She was playing with him now, enjoying the attention. She stood and helped him to his feet and for a moment they danced to the sound of their heartbeats. Irvel laid her head on his shoulder. His nearness filled her senses, and she savored the feeling. Finally, she whispered close to his ear. "Very alone, if you know what I mean."

"Good." He pulled her closer still. "Because that's all I want now, for the rest of my life. The two of us. Alone together. That's all I need."

Irvel smiled. That's all she needed, too. Never mind jobs or bank accounts or buying a house. He only wanted her, and she only wanted him. That and the one gift only God could give them from this day forward.

Sweet, precious time.

• • •

THE WEDDING WAS Saturday, December 22, one of the most beautiful days Irvel could have imagined. Her white dress was offset by the red ones her friends wore. The men were in black tie with red carnations, and Hank wore a tuxedo.

No man had ever looked more handsome.

More than a hundred of their friends and family filled the pews. All of them changed by the war, all of them grieving someone—a brother or uncle, a father or son. A husband. This generation would always be changed by it. But here, three days before Christmas, Irvel and Hank's wedding was giving all of them a reason to celebrate. A reason to believe in life again. A reason to hold tight to the truth that love was stronger than war. No matter how great the losses they had incurred these last four years.

Irvel took her time walking down the aisle. Her father leaned close. "Hard to imagine heaven will feel better than this." He winked at her. "You look so beautiful, Irvel."

"Thank you." She smiled at him. Then her attention was on Hank alone.

Their guests seemed to disappear, and Irvel was singly focused, the way she'd been trained to be while serving as a spy. The whole world could end, and she would keep walking toward Hank Myers.

"Who gives this woman to be married?" The pastor who had long ago baptized Irvel looked at her father.

"Her mother and I do." Her dad lifted her veil. "You'll always be my little girl, Irvel." He kissed her forehead, then he took her left hand and placed it in Hank's. He nodded at Hank and returned to sit with Irvel's mother.

It was just the two of them now. Irvel faced Hank, and he held tight to both her hands. The pastor talked about how at one time or another, the families and friends of Hank and Irvel had thought them dead. "Jesus rose from the grave to give us life eternal." The pastor's voice rang with sincerity. "But with Hank and Irvel, he gave them new life here, as well. As if even assumed death couldn't stop God from bringing them back together. Bringing them to this moment."

Their vows were sweet and simple. Irvel promised to be Hank's best friend, to tell him everything in her heart, and listen to everything in his. Only the two of them could've understood the depth of her promise.

Hank committed to pursue Irvel forever, to long for her and stay with her and make memories with her as long as he lived.

After they exchanged rings, she caught a glimpse of her parents and his in the front row. All of them were crying and she realized again how beautiful this moment was, how impossible. That two people who were supposed to be dead were instead as alive as they'd ever been.

Promising each other forever.

The reception was white cake and a Christmas figgy pudding, and before Irvel and Hank left for their honeymoon, the whole room sang "Silent Night." The words held more meaning after the war. *All is calm . . . all is bright.*

Irvel smiled at the friends and family gathered around her and Hank. *All is bright, indeed,* she thought.

After the wedding, Hank drove them to Nashville for their first night as husband and wife. The roads were clear, and Irvel kept stealing glances at Hank. *How could this be real?* she would ask herself. Hank beside her, the two of them married! After all the heartache and loss and hidden secrets of the war, God had brought them here.

Hank surprised her by driving to the famous Hermitage Hotel, a place Irvel had only heard about on the radio. Many politicians and musical guests had stayed here. After dinner, Hank took her to the hotel's grand ballroom, where Francis Craig led a full orchestra of strings and horns.

The music was beautiful, and at one point—while the famous orchestra leader was on a break, Hank excused himself. During his next set, between songs, Craig pointed at Hank and Irvel.

"I heard a little something on my break." He winked at Hank. "We have a pair of newlyweds in our midst tonight." He smiled at them. "Hank and Irvel, this one's for you."

And with that, the orchestra launched into "Moonlight Serenade." Irvel couldn't believe it. If someone had woken her up and told her this was merely a dream, she would've believed it. She felt like she was dancing on the most delicate clouds as Hank led her across the floor. And when the song was over, Francis Craig had another surprise for them.

"I've been working on a new song. I'd like to try it out now." He grinned at Irvel and Hank. "For my favorite newlyweds."

The song was called "Near You," and every word seemed to fit Irvel and Hank perfectly. As if he had written it just for them.

Hank twirled her and held her close and when they finally made their way back to their room, the dance continued. The way it would continue every day for the rest of their lives.

In the morning, Hank surprised her with the next part of their honeymoon. He drove another eight hours south to Panama City Beach, and a room overlooking the ocean. "We had enough bad memories out at sea." He put his arm around her and led her onto their room's balcony. "After this week, the beach will only make us think of this, my love."

And so it was. After a week of loving Hank, and walking the sand with him, swimming in the surf beside him, Irvel no longer felt the cold Pacific on her face at the thought of the ocean. The beach belonged to them, to their love.

To this place where it began in earnest.

NOVEMBER 1947

22

Nearly two years had passed since their wedding day, and as 1947 came to a close, Hank could hardly wait for the newest miracle God had given them. The gift of their first child. But there was one thing that concerned him.

Irvel had been sick throughout her pregnancy. She had lost weight and some days she couldn't get out of bed. The doctor had been to the house, and he'd told them both that she needed to rest. "Her blood pressure is lower than I like." He looked worried. "Be sure you're getting plenty of fluids, Irvel."

She was a terrific patient, listening to her body and resting whenever she felt tired or dizzy. But Hank didn't like it. Back when they first realized that Irvel was pregnant, Hank had no idea of the risks inherent in any pregnancy.

And now the baby was due in just a few weeks. On Thanksgiving Day.

But two weeks before her due date, late on a Friday night in mid-November, Irvel began having sharp pains. Pains that doubled her over and caused her to scream. By then, Hank knew all the stories of Irvel's days as a spy. He knew her courage and strength, the way she could deliver a message behind enemy lines in the morning and be wrapping tourniquets around dying marines hours later.

Irvel wouldn't scream like that unless something was terribly wrong.

They lived several miles from their parents by then, in a small house just perfect for their happy new life together. But there was no way to get advice at that hour, so Hank grabbed a bag of clothes for Irvel and the baby and helped her to the car. The pains were getting worse with every passing hour.

"Please . . . Hank . . . d-d-don't worry." Irvel was pale and clammy. She could hardly form words to speak. Her eyes rolled back in her head. "I'll be f-f-fine."

Something was wrong. Hank was convinced. He put all his attention on the road and drove as fast as he could to the hospital. He stopped at the red lights, but only long enough to check cross-traffic. His Irvel was in trouble. He would do whatever it took to save her.

Halfway to the hospital, he remembered what Irvel had said about her spy missions, how she had a weapon the enemy could never counter. The Sword of the Spirit. The Word of God.

And so he began to speak out loud, half praying, half reciting words that had lived in his heart since he was a little boy. "Lord, You are our Shepherd, we will not want. You make us lie down in green pastures, You lead us beside still waters, You restore our soul."

A piercing scream came from Irvel.

Hank gripped the wheel and kept driving. "Even though we walk through the valley of the shadow of death, we will fear no evil. For You are with us. Your rod and Your staff they comfort us."

He continued that way until he pulled up at the emergency room door of the hospital. The moment he was out of the car he shouted at a nurse standing nearby. "Please! Someone help us!"

Immediately, the hospital staff sprang into action. Fifteen minutes later the doctor on call determined Irvel was bleeding. Her blood pressure was dangerously low. "I'm going to have to ask you to wait in the hall, Mr. Myers."

Hank felt the room begin to spin. He took hold of Irvel's hand and kissed her forehead. "I'll be right outside this door, my love. God is with you."

He made it only ten feet into the hallway before he collapsed against the wall. *God, please . . . spare her life. I can't live without her. Please, Father.* He wasn't sure if he was praying the words silently or out loud. He could barely draw a breath.

But somehow the minutes became hours, until just before daybreak, the doctor returned with a small bundle in his arms. A bundle wrapped in a blue blanket.

"Meet your son, Mr. Myers." He smiled. "Your wife is doing just fine. We gave her two units of blood and that made all the difference. You can go see her now."

Hank held out his arms and took the baby. The child had Irvel's beautiful face and Hank's strong chin. He brought the baby close to his chest and closed his eyes. "Thank you, Jesus. Thank You. Thank You."

A moment later he was at Irvel's side. She looked stunning, her hair tucked behind her ears, her eyes and face filled with the most wonderful smile. "Isn't he just perfect, Hank?"

"He is." Hank was still holding the baby, still clutching him tight. "Almost as perfect as you."

They were visited by both sets of parents that day, and in the evening hours Hank and Irvel decided on a name for their baby son. They would call him Charles Samuel, for Hank's father and brother. "Little Charlie." Hank was sitting beside Irvel in the hospital.

"I love it." Charlie was in Irvel's arms now. She had color in her cheeks again, and soon they would all go home.

Another miracle for the memory book.

• • •

JANUARY 1955

THE YEARS FLEW, and Irvel could do nothing to slow them down. When Charlie was two years old, Irvel returned to her love of teaching math, but only as a tutor. She wanted to spend her days with her little boy. Students would come to Hank and Irvel's house after school, so she could work around her toddler's nap schedule.

Hank left teaching and became a lawyer. He was a very good one and had his own law firm by the time

Charlie was in first grade. Irvel's delivery had been too difficult for her to have more children, but that didn't cast even a shadow of sorrow on the life Irvel shared with her beloved Hank.

The three of them took trips to the park and the zoo and twice a year they made their way down to the Gulf Coast for more memories at the beach.

In 1955, on Irvel's thirty-fifth birthday, when Charlie was seven, there was a knock at the door. Hank was home that afternoon, and there was a sparkle in his eyes. Something Irvel had noticed earlier in the day, too.

"Why don't you get it, Irvel?" Hank grinned at her. "It's your birthday, after all."

She felt her heart skip a beat. What was Hank up to? She stood and brushed out the wrinkles in her dress. Then she went to the door and opened it.

A woman stood there, and a preteen girl with blue eyes.

"Irvel!" The woman on the porch held out her arms. "I can't believe I'm here!"

"Ruth?" Irvel's tears were instant. "Ruth, I didn't believe I'd ever . . ." Irvel hugged her friend tight. In all her life, she had never expected to see Ruth Cohen again. She dried her eyes. Then both women laughed.

Ruth put her arm around the girl's shoulders. "This is Chloe. My daughter."

The child seemed too old to be Ruth's daughter, but that didn't matter. Irvel opened the door wide. "Nice to meet you, Chloe. Please, both of you, come in."

Once they were all seated around the living room, with Charlie doing his reading homework at the kitchen table, and Chloe sitting beside her mother, details of the surprise spilled out—first from Hank, and then from Ruth. Hank had used his contacts through the law firm to locate Ruth in Los Angeles. And then he had arranged for her to fly to Indiana for Irvel's birthday.

Irvel couldn't stop smiling. She still talked often with Hank about her long-lost friend. This was the best birthday present she'd ever had. They talked awhile longer, and Hank brought them all iced tea.

"This visit wasn't just for you and me." Ruth set her glass down on the coffee table and turned to Hank. "I have contacts, too, Hank." Fresh tears welled in Ruth's eyes. "I know you were one of the soldiers who liberated Buchenwald."

Chloe put her head on Ruth's shoulder and Ruth held the girl close. "One of the children you rescued was only two years old. A child with brown hair and blue eyes."

Irvel shot a look at Hank. "You've talked about that little girl."

"Of course. I remember her. She was so sad, crying for her mama." Hank's eyes filled with sorrow. "I always wondered what became of her. Did . . . did you know the girl?"

Ruth slipped her arm around Chloe's shoulders. For a few seconds she seemed overcome by emotion. She drew a slow breath. "The little girl was my second cousin. The only one of my family who survived Buchenwald." Ruth searched for her voice. "This is her, Hank. Chloe." Ruth kissed the top of her head. "She's twelve now. I'm raising her as my daughter."

They were quiet for a long moment, the shock rippling through Irvel and of course, Hank. Tears formed in his eyes and he got on his knees before the girl. "Nice to meet you, Chloe." He shook her hand. "For the second time."

She grinned, the sadness from a decade ago gone. "Nice to meet you, too, Mr. Myers." Clearly Ruth had told the girl something about Hank and his role in liberating the concentration camp.

Ruth and Chloe stayed two days, and every minute of it, Irvel could not stop thinking about how God had intertwined their lives. All of them. How Hank had been one of the troops that had set her adopted daughter free, and how God had allowed Hank to find Ruth and bring her here for a visit.

It was a gift that stayed with Irvel every day after that. And twice more in the coming decade Ruth made the trip to see Irvel and Hank in Bloomington. Each time she brought Chloe, and at their last get-together, Chloe was twenty. Over dinner, she personally thanked Hank for saving her life.

There were other moments, more than Irvel and Hank ever could've imagined. The celebration of Charlie's graduation from high school, and in 1965, the joy of seeing him off to college at Indiana University.

With their house far too quiet, a few times each week Hank would leave work early and take Irvel fishing at

Lake Monroe. Fishing was his new hobby. He bought a boat, and on those long warm afternoons, he and Irvel would spend the day on the water.

Always when they were together, they talked about days gone by and the goodness of God. Years passed, and Irvel's parents grew ill, Hank helped her take care of them, and often he and Charlie and Charlie's friends would fish together. The boys, Irvel called them.

In 1977, a few years after earning his MBA, Charlie married his college sweetheart, Peggy Landers. Six months later Charlie took a job with Warner Bros. Studios in Los Angeles.

Irvel waited until Charlie and Peggy had driven out of sight before turning and collapsing in Hank's arms. Their son had grown up and moved away. Now it was only the two of them. "I couldn't handle watching him leave without you, Hank."

He kissed her and wrapped his arms around her. "And I couldn't do it without you, my love."

Charlie and Peggy visited twice a year and in 1980, they welcomed their daughter, Audra Anne. The child was eight when Irvel first forgot her way home from the market.

That was one year ago.

Irvel wrote it off, that first time. "It's nothing," she told Hank. "Take me out on the lake. I just need to clear my head."

So Hank had done just that. He took her fishing and laughed with her, reminding her of a million happy moments.

A few months later, Charlie and Peggy brought Audra for another visit. The child loved her grandma Irvel and grandpa Hank. But when their son and his family left for home again, Irvel had the most terrifying thought in all her life.

She couldn't remember Audra's name.

It took her two days before she told Hank, and when she did it was through the most fearful tears. "I don't like this, Hank." She came to him and he put his arms around her. "Play me 'Moonlight Serenade.'"

Hank slipped a cassette tape in their stereo. The familiar tune filled the air, and Hank danced her around the living room. *There,* she told herself. Everything was going to be okay. And just in case, when the music ended, Hank brought out the big guns. Her Scripture verses.

The weapon Irvel had relied on all her adult life. He held Irvel and whispered over her the words from Joshua 1:9. "Do not be terrified, do not be discouraged. For the Lord your God will be with you wherever you go."

And so He was and so He would be, no matter what was happening to Irvel's memory.

God had gotten them through the wrong decisions to date other people during their college years and He had brought them home from the war.

God alone would get them through whatever was ahead.

• • •

HANK TURNED OFF the camera.

This was their third straight morning at the park, and

every day Irvel had worn the same red dress. She remembered that much. Red was the last color. He packed the camera up and folded his chair.

Then he helped Irvel to her feet. "We did it. We captured it all."

Her eyes grew shiny. Despite her smile, she shook her head. "Oh, Hank. We could never capture it all."

He looked at the bag, at the five tapes collected there. "But we have what we need." His eyes found hers again. "Our story, Irvel. So you always remember."

"Will you play the tapes for me, Hank?" Fear tried to find a place in her expression, but Irvel seemed to refuse it. "Whenever I forget?"

"Yes. I will play it forever." Hank couldn't ease the ache in his heart, the thought that times like this were limited now because of Irvel's diagnosis. "Do you hear it, my love?" It was a question he had asked her before. Even on days like this when no music was playing.

"I hear it." She played along, and in her eyes their lifetime of love was vibrant and alive. As if her memory had never been clearer. "*Moonlight Serenade*?"

He smiled. "Yes. That's it." He kissed her cheek and brushed his face against hers. "You've never looked more beautiful, my love. Dance with me, will you, Irvel?"

And there, with autumn leaves falling around them, with their story safe for all time in Hank's camera bag, they began to dance. Hank hummed the tune, the one etched on their hearts from the beginning.

The sound of children laughing came from the nearby

swings and in a far corner of the park, a football coach barked out orders to a dozen high school kids doing drills. Life was happening all around them.

But Hank and Irvel were in a world all their own.

Here, near this picnic table at the park, it was just the two of them, the way it would be for all time, dancing to Glenn Miller's "Moonlight Serenade." The couple whose love through the years often made others stop and smile in awe.

Irvel and Hank Myers. A love story for the ages.

The World War II spy . . . and the marine who would love her more than life.

Even long after the music stopped playing.

23

Audra closed the book and set it on the table beside her. Only then did she realize she'd been crying. No matter how many times she read the book, she never felt like she wrote it.

Only God and her grandparents could've done that.

She stared out the window. Snow was still falling outside, so it might be a few days before they got out of Washington, D.C. But it was worth the trip, however long it took to get home. Her grandma Irvel deserved her recognition.

The room was colder than before, so Audra turned up the heat. Then she sat back down and pulled the blanket more tightly around her. The rest of the story was in a postscript at the back of the book. Because Audra knew people would want to read about what happened to Irvel and Hank after her diagnosis.

She picked up the book and turned to the back section. With fresh tears making their way down her face, Audra began to read.

• • •

1989–2015

JUST ONCE—A POSTSCRIPT

HANK KEPT HIS promise to Irvel, the way he had kept every promise he ever made to her. He played one of the five videotapes for her every morning to start their day. He also found old photos from their decades together, and he framed them and hung them on the wall.

Framed them in red.

A photo of him and Irvel on their wedding day, and one of them in the ballroom at the Heritage Hotel in Nashville on their honeymoon. Achingly young and so in love. There was the photo the day they brought Charlie home from the hospital, and photos of their family vacations on the Gulf Coast.

Hank and Irvel with Charlie at his high school graduation, and the two of them dancing at their twenty-fifth wedding anniversary.

When Charlie and Peggy and Audra came to visit a few weeks later, Charlie was caught off guard by the number of framed photos on the wall. But after Hank explained it to their son, Charlie understood.

Red was the last color.

The doctor had been wrong about the time Irvel had left before her memory died. Hank liked to think he loved Irvel into keeping her memory a little longer. But three years later, he had to bring in nursing help so Irvel could continue living at home.

Irvel was always the kindest, most pleasant Alzheimer's patient. When she didn't recognize Charlie or Peggy or Audra, she still invited them to stay for dinner and asked about their lives. After dinner, she would ask for just one thing.

Peppermint tea.

"Dad, you need to get her into a facility. She's too much for you," Charlie told Hank on that visit. "It's too sad, having her here."

But Hank only smiled and shook his head. "I'll stay by her as long as I'm breathing." He patted their son on the shoulder. "She's my girl, son. No matter what words come out of her mouth, she remembers me. I can see it in her eyes."

Hank could especially see it when he played the videos for her, the pieces of their love story. Irvel would sit beside him smiling and nodding. "This is such a nice movie. It reminds me of something beautiful."

"Yes." And Hank would allow himself to get lost in her eyes again. "Something very beautiful."

But gradually Irvel grew more distant, less aware of life around her. The videotapes began to make her uncomfortable, reminding her that she was missing something. Forgetting something.

So, one winter day, Hank packed the tapes in a box, nailed the lid shut, and wrote across the top: *The story of Hank and Irvel . . . a love that could only happen just once.*

A year later, in 1995, on a hot summer day when Charlie and his family were visiting, Hank took their son fishing. A nurse stayed back at the house with Irvel and

Peggy and Audra. They spent most of the afternoon on the lake fishing, but when they were pulling the boat back up onto shore, Hank collapsed.

Charlie flagged down a police officer, and then gave his father CPR for ten minutes while an ambulance was dispatched. Paramedics did what they could, but Hank was gone.

Off to the place Sam had saved for him all those years earlier.

Charlie was crushed at the loss of his father. He thought about finding a way to bring his mother to his father's memorial service, but mentally, she was in no shape for such an outing. "Something's wrong," she kept saying. "Something's very wrong."

And of course, Charlie never knew about the box of tapes tucked away in the attic. Audra guessed her grandfather always planned to tell his family, but he was worried that bringing the tapes down too soon might upset Irvel. And then Hank ran out of time.

By then, Irvel didn't seem to know Audra or her parents, and she only asked about Hank in the late afternoons. "Hank's out fishing," she would say. "I'll sip some peppermint tea and wait for him to come home."

The situation was heartbreaking.

With no choice, Charlie and Peggy searched Bloomington for the perfect place for his mother. They settled on a small, warm facility called Sunset Hills Adult Care Home.

Charlie took two weeks off work, stayed at his parents' house and spent days with his mother at Sunset Hills, making sure she was comfortable and at ease. Even if she didn't remember him. There were only a handful of residents, and the staff seemed kind enough. On Charlie's second to last day there, his mother found him in the living room.

"I was thinking," she smiled at him. "This would be a lovely day for some peppermint tea."

The moment marked the most coherent thing Charlie's mother had said in a long time. Charlie had always known about his mother's love for peppermint tea, and how her fondness for the hot drink had come about during the war. Nothing more. Only Hank knew that a couple of spies had nursed Irvel back to health all while serving her the tea.

That day, Charlie hurried to the store and brought back ten boxes of peppermint tea for his mother. He was sipping a cup of it in a chair across from her when she nodded toward the window. "Sir . . ." She looked at Charlie. "Do you know when I should expect him?"

Charlie lowered his cup. It only confused her when he called her mother, so he chose his words carefully. "Who are you expecting?"

His mother smiled. "Hank, of course." She looked out the window again. "He's fishing today. With our son and his friends." Her eyes looked clear.

For a moment, Charlie sat there, not sure what to say. He cleared his throat. "Yes, Irvel . . . I think he'll be back very soon."

"Good." His mother took another sip. "I like it better when Hank is here."

Charlie stared at his mother. After a moment, he hurried off for her nurse. "She's remembering," he told her. "Something's changing in her brain."

The nurse contacted the on-call doctor, a man who came in and performed a quick test on Charlie's mother. All the while, Charlie prayed and hoped and waited for the good news. She was coming back to them, that had to be it.

But the doctor's exam proved nothing of the sort. "There's a cold, hard truth with Alzheimer's disease, Charlie," the man told him. "The brain might remember one thing, but only one thing. And not for long. This disease follows no rules."

Even so, his mother asked about his dad again the next day, just before Charlie left for Los Angeles. After that, he made a point of coming to see his mother every few months. Always she was happy and pleasant.

She drank peppermint tea each afternoon, and then she waited for her marine. Her Hank.

Around the turn of the century, Sunset Hills Adult Care underwent a staff change. One of the managers had been found to be cruel, denying the residents their favorite things and speaking to them in harsh tones.

Charlie did his part to get the woman fired, and about that time they brought in a new worker—Ashley Baxter. The young woman was on a search of her own, it seemed. When Charlie would come to visit, he noticed that Ashley cared deeply for the residents. Especially for his mother. Ashley had restocked his mother's peppermint tea, and she'd done something else.

She had found a box of old photos of Hank and Irvel, and she hung them on the walls of his mother's room.

That was the same year Audra Anne moved back to Bloomington for her junior year at Indiana University. She stopped in often to see her Grandma Irvel, and she reported back to her father the same thing Charlie had seen.

Even still her grandmother spent every afternoon waiting for Hank. Believing he was out fishing with the boys and that he would be home any moment. Irvel grew very fond of Ashley Baxter. Charlie had a feeling the connection was mutual.

In 2005, Ashley was one of the few people outside the family who attended the funeral of Irvel Holland Myers. Charlie sat with Peggy and Audra, and watched as Ashley set up a large photo on the casket. The picture was of Charlie's parents. His mother in her nursing attire, and his father in his marine combat uniform. The two of them clinging to each other for dear life.

For dear love.

No one would've ever known the real story of Hank and Irvel Myers, except for Audra Anne. She inherited her grandparents' house, and she lived there while she finished her undergrad and master's degrees in writing. She stayed in the old house after that when she started work at the university. Audra even lived there after she married Tom Mitchell two years after Irvel's death.

In 2012, Charlie retired, and he and Peggy moved back to Bloomington so they could be near Audra and Tom.

But it wasn't until three years after that, in 2015, when Audra and Tom's twins turned two, that the couple decided to remodel the house. And that's when they found the videos. The five tapes that held a story Audra could hardly believe.

She shared the videos with her parents, and then she wrote the book. She found an agent through her connections at the university, and a year later she had a contract.

"I think people are going to love your book," her editor told her. "I haven't read one like it."

The woman was right. There had never been a story like Irvel and Hank's and there never would be again.

Theirs was a love that truly could only happen just once.

• • •

AGAIN, AUDRA SET the book down. She stared out the window and a thought occurred to her. Until now, she and her family and a few guests from the OSS ceremony were the only people who knew about her grandparents.

But after next week, all the world would know.

Audra could see her grandparents up in heaven, somewhere near a window. Aware that their story was about to be shared with the public.

She could almost hear her grandfather. "This is where it gets good." He would grin at his precious Irvel.

"Yes, my love." Her grandmother would lean her head

on his shoulder. "So very good. Our story will live on forever now."

"It will." Her grandfather would reach for her grandmother's hand, and together they would watch the story come to life again.

Audra smiled. That's exactly what was about to happen.

She could hardly wait.

Dear Reader Friend,

I wanted to journey back to World War II and tell Irvel Myers's story ever since I met her at the imaginary Sunset Hills Adult Care Home, years ago when I was writing about the Baxter Family. Older people intrigue me and move me. They remind me that the gift of days will at some point take me to their places, their tired recliners and days of remembering. It is our common destiny, if we are blessed to live long enough. One day we will have hearts full of yesterdays to keep us company as we wait for heaven.

There were roadblocks to telling Irvel's story. I've never written a novel set this far back in time, and I wanted my first to be utterly accurate. That meant doing a deep dive into very specific details regarding World War II. From history classes I'd taken long ago, I understood the war on a surface level. The names of famous battles were familiar, as were the rough dates that represented the start and end of the war. But I had much to learn if I was going to set a love story in that time. What would it have been like to be twenty years old when Pearl Harbor was hit, and how would a guy like Sam Myers make it from Bloomington to the battlefields of the European theater. What trains and ships might take him there, and what would be the next steps once he arrived?

Along the way I stumbled onto the Office of Strategic Services, the clandestine organization that was the first attempt at today's CIA. I read about General William

Donovan and his belief that spies might be one way to help the United States and Allied Forces win the war. The idea hit like the most beautiful reality. Irvel Myers had been a spy! Of course, she had! This, then, led to even more research. I watched documentaries on the members of the OSS and especially the 4,000 women involved. I learned about code breakers and their part in key battles in the Pacific, and finally after months of research I was ready to write the story of Hank and Irvel.

I hope you love it as much as I do.

One thing I took away from Irvel's fictitious story was an even more real appreciation of the freedoms we have living in the United States. At least in my family, we are still a people who believe in that freedom, and the truth that to live free is a God-given gift. This year—like all years—we will hang the American flag from our front porch on all the right holidays, but I will take a moment longer to appreciate the real-life men and women who made our freedoms possible. People like Hank and Irvel and Sam.

I hope you do the same.

I must say, I wept writing the end of this story. The idea of Irvel losing her brilliant mind and seeing memories of so many beautiful times fade to dark was overwhelming at times. But it was another reminder to hold tight to today. The gift of this one sunrise and sunset. God alone knows what the future holds for any of us, but He has called us to appreciate this life, and to thank Him daily for it. While we still can.

As you close the cover on this book, do me a favor. Please think about who you can share it with. A friend who never overcame something from her past. A sister who can't seem to forgive herself for something she did. Someone looking for hope in the midst of a world gone mad. Or just that person who loves to read. A book dies if it's left on the shelf. So please share it.

By now you may have caught my No. 1 streaming show on Pure Flix—*A Thousand Tomorrows*. You will probably see my first theatrical movie, *Someone Like You*, when it releases in spring 2024. It is the first feature film from my new Karen Kingsbury Productions. As of this publication, we are still waiting to know when and where *The Baxters* will air. Please join me in praying that we will have answers soon, as three seasons of the show are filmed and ready to show to a viewing audience!

Visit my website, KarenKingsbury.com to sign up for my free weekly newsletter and find out more about *Someone Like You*, *The Baxters*, and about my other books and movies. These emails come straight to you and offer stories, devotions, and news you will not find anywhere else. There are no ads, so sign up today! You can also stay encouraged by following me on social media.

Remember, stories like the one between Hank and Irvel connect us. The characters become like family as they draw our hearts together. Thanks for taking the journey with me. Until next time . . . I thank God for you.

Much love!

JUST ONCE

KAREN KINGSBURY

1. What did you learn about World War II while reading *Just Once?*

2. What did you learn about Alzheimer's disease?

3. If you had been in Irvel's shoes, facing the loss of your memory, would you try to capture your story the way she and Hank did? Write an outline of the highlights of your story up until now.

4. Hank and Irvel regretted decisions they made when they were young, decisions to date other people. Share about a regret you have from your late teens or early twenties. How has that situation turned out today?

5. Did you have a childhood love? If so, share about it. How did that situation turn out?

6. Irvel Myers was a spy with the Office of Strategic Services. Did you know this organization existed and that four thousand spies during World War II were women? What did you learn about the OSS?

7. Would you have wanted to be a spy for the US government during World War II? What about today, would you want to be a spy? Why or why not?

8. How has American life changed since World War II? Give examples.

9. What is the most important way a person can pray for the United States? What about the world? Talk about this.

10. If you had served during World War II, where would you have wanted to be—the European theater or the Pacific theater? Explain why?

11. Do you have family members who fought in World War II? If so, what stories did you hear from them and what did you learn?

12. Is it important for schools to keep teaching the facts about World War II? Why or why not?

13. Irvel took one weapon with her on the hundreds of missions she undertook as a spy in World War II. That weapon was the Word of God. By memorizing Scripture, Irvel always felt the presence of the Lord with her. She was never alone. Have you ever memorized Scripture? How did that experience go for you? Challenge yourself to memorize Psalm 23.

14. How do you use the Bible today? Do you read it, share it, study it? Talk about the Bible and its importance in your life.

15. Do you believe Scripture is God's living Word? Why or why not?

16. Talk about the role of memories in the love story of Hank and Irvel. How did you see that memories were important to them throughout their lifetime?

17. What memories are important to you and how do they still impact the relationships you share with the people you love?

18. Irvel and Hank were separated throughout World War II, yet the distance only made their love stronger. Why do you think that is? Have you ever experienced distance between you and someone you love? How did that turn out for you?

19. Why is it important to tell your personal and family stories to the next generation? Have you done that, and if so, how? Make a plan to capture your memories and share them with the family members coming after you.

20. Right up until she died, Irvel remembered her handsome marine, Hank Myers. Even though she had lost all other memories to Alzheimer's. What memories from your life do you think you will have till the day you die? Talk about those.

ACKNOWLEDGMENTS

Just Once took me back in time, far longer than most novels. I could feel the sway of the troopships crossing the Atlantic, sense the damp deck beneath my feet, and hear the explosions on Guadalcanal. From now on, when I thank a serviceman or servicewoman for their military sacrifice, my gratitude will always run deeper than before. I will forever better understand the evils of Hitler's Nazi regime and his maniacal hatred toward the Jewish people. I will see the families huddled near train stations, the wide eyes of the children and concern of the parents as they were whisked off to death camps they knew nothing about. Researching the Holocaust gave me the reason for creating Irvel's friend, Ruth Cohen. Lest we ever forget the darkness mankind is capable of wreaking. Yes, World War II will forever be personal to me because of Hank and Irvel and Sam.

Now I am honored to thank the many people who helped make *Just Once* possible. I simply cannot leave the battlefields of the Solomon Islands or the harsh winter conflict that raged across Europe without giving thanks where it is so deeply deserved.

First, thank you to my amazing Simon & Schuster editor, Kaitlin Olson, and my publishing team, including the keenly talented Suzanne Donahue, Ifeoma Anyoku, and Lisa Sciambra, along with so many others! It's an honor to work with you!

Also thank you to Rose Garden Creative, my design team—Kyle and Kelsey Kupecky—whose unmatched talent in the industry is recognized from Los Angeles to New York. Very simply you are the best in the business! My website, social media, video trailers and newsletters—along with so many other aspects of my virtual conferences, signature events and film pieces—are cutting-edge and breathtaking because of you two. Thank you for working your own dreams around mine. I love you and I thank God for you every single day.

A huge thanks to my sisters, Tricia and Susan, along with my mom, Anne. You give your whole hearts in helping me love my readers. Tricia, as my executive assistant for fifteen years, and this year as Line Producer for Karen Kingsbury Productions. And Susan, as the president of my Facebook Official Online Book Club and Team KK. Also, Mom, thank you for being Queen of the Readers. Anyone who has ever sent me an email and received a response from "Karen's mom" is blessed indeed. The three of you are making a tremendous impact in changing this world for the better. I love you and I thank God for you always!

Thanks also to my son, Austin, for coming onto my staff as my event director. I couldn't have finished this book down the stretch without all the work you took on.

I treasure hitting the road with you, Aus. May you know just how much you are loved by God and by me!

Thanks to EJ for praying for me every day while I was writing this book, and for helping out in the office! Also to Tyler for doing more than his share of the heavy lifting on our film projects while I camped out on the deck of the USS *Solace*.

Also, thank you to my office assistant, Aurora Galvin. You create space for me to write! My storytelling wouldn't be possible without you. May God bless you and your family for the work you do in helping me tell stories like this one.

I am grateful to my Team KK members, who step in at the final stage in writing a book. The galley pages come to me, and I send them to you, my most dedicated reader friends and family. This time around that team is Hope Burke, Savannah Dudzik, Shannon Fairley, Sheila Holman, Renette Steele, and Zac Weikal. You are my volunteer test troop! It always amazes me, the typos you catch at the final hour. Thank you for loving my work, and thanks for your availability to read my novels first and fast.

My books only happen with the help of my family, especially my amazing husband, Donald. Honey, thank you for your spiritual wisdom and leadership in our home, and thanks for talking through books like this one from outline to editing. The countless ways you help me when I'm on deadline make all the difference. I love you!

And a special thanks to a man who has believed in my career for two decades, my amazing agent, Rick Christian.

From the beginning, Rick, you've told me to dream big, set my sights high. Movies, TV series, worldwide reach. All of it for God and through Him. You imagined this, believed it and prayed for it alongside me and my family. You saw it happening and you still do! While I write, you work behind the scenes on film projects and my future books, the Baxter family TV series and details regarding every word I've ever written. You are brilliant and driven, compassionate and dedicated. I used to dream of having you as my agent. Now Tyler and I are the only authors who do. God is amazing. Thank you, Rick, and thank you for praying for me and my family. That most of all.

Finally, my greatest thanks to God Almighty, who is First and Last and all things in between. I write for You, through You and because of You. Thank you with my whole being.

YOU WERE SEEN MOVEMENT

His name was Henry, and I will remember him as long as I live. Henry was our waiter at a fancy restaurant when I was on tour for one of my books. Toward the end of the meal something unusual happened. I started to cry. Slow tears, just trickling down my cheeks. My husband was with me and he looked concerned. "Karen, what's wrong?"

"Our waiter," I said. "He needs to know God loves him. But there's no time. We have to get to our event, and he has six other tables to serve."

Henry was an incredibly attentive server. He smiled and got our order right and he worked hard to do it. Everywhere he went on the restaurant floor, he practically sprinted to get his job done. But when he was just off the floor, when he thought no one was looking, Henry's smile faded. He looked discouraged and hopeless. Beaten up.

That very day I began dreaming about the "You Were Seen" movement. Many of you are aware of this organization, but I'll summarize how it works. Very simply, you get a pack of You Were Seen cards and you hand them out. Where acceptable, tip—generously. From my office in the past few months more than 250,000 You Were Seen cards have gone out. We partner with the Billy Graham Evangelistic Association's plan for salvation and other help links.

Today, it is really happening! People like you are truly seeing those in their path each day. You are finding purpose by living your life on mission and not overlooking the delivery person and cashier, the banker and business contact, the server and barista, the police officer and teacher, the doctor and nurse. You are letting strangers see God's love in action. Why?

Because Christians should love better than anyone. We should be more generous. Kinder. More affirming. More patient. The Bible tells us to love God and love others. And to tell others the good news of the gospel—that we have a Father who is for us, not against us. He loves us so much that He made a way for us to get to heaven.

Hand out a pack of You Were Seen cards in the coming weeks and watch how every card given makes you feel a little better. Go to www.YouWereSeen.com to get your cards and start showing gratitude and generosity to everyone you meet.

Always when you leave a You Were Seen card, you will let a stranger know that their hard work was seen in that moment. They were noticed! What better way to spread love? The You Were Seen card will then direct people to the website—www.YouWereSeen.com. At the website, people will be encouraged and reminded that God sees them every day. Always. He knows what they are going through. Every day should be marked by a miraculous encounter.

www.YouWereSeen.com

ONE CHANCE FOUNDATION

The Kingsbury family is passionate about seeing orphans all over the world brought home to their forever families. As a result, Karen created a charitable group called the One Chance Foundation.

This foundation was inspired by the memory of her father, Ted C. Kingsbury. Ted always said, "Life is not a dress rehearsal. We have one chance to love, one chance to truly live!"

Karen often tells her reader friends, "You have one chance to write the story of your life!"™ Now, with Karen's One Chance Foundation, readers can join her in the belief that all of us have one chance to make a difference in the lives of orphans.

In the Bible, James 1:27 says people with pure and faultless religion look after orphans. The One Chance Foundation was created with that truth in mind.

A donation to the One Chance Foundation was given for each of the dedications below. If you are interested in giving to Karen's One Chance Foundation and having your dedication printed in one of Karen's upcoming novels, visit www.KarenKingsbury.com. Below are dedications from some of Karen's reader friends who have contributed to the One Chance Foundation:

- Dedicated and in loving memory to our father, L. D. Suttle who served in WW11 from 1942-1945. He landed on Normandy Beach, (D Day) and was in the Battle of the Bulge and Central Europe campaigns. –Love, Mr. and Mrs. Louis and Jeannie Suttle and Mr. and Mrs. Melvin and Brenda "Suttle" Stewart
- CPT Preston Millison-Army - Sentinel at Tomb of Unknown Soldier - Badge #633 Nick-LEO - Katie Masters-911 Dispatcher –Love, Lisa Millison
- Devada, I love you –Kenzie
- To my precious twin Barb ~ Love you forever ~ Bev
- In honor of Jerry & Sharon Crisp who shared their special love through Marriage Encounter. CYH, Dave & Jan Miller-Kukkola
- In Jesus name! –Alexandra
- To my father, Rolland Strain, who proudly served his country as a Marine in WWII. –Maurine Dalluge
- In memory of my beloved husband, dad & grandpa, Stephen G. Yonker. Thank you for loving us so big!!
- To my husband Ivan York in Heaven. My heart misses you each day! Love, Judy
- Dedicated to our Grandpa Steve Yonker in Heaven.

We miss you! LOVE YOU ALWAYS! Lindsie Marie, Karlie Rose, & Lauren Elizabeth

- To Diane Sweet, amazing mother, best friend & encouraging loving soul! Thank you for my beautiful life! Love forever, Melissa Dubuque
- Happy Mother's Day to Denise Wensink and JoAnn Holland. Happy reading! We love you! Amber and Jason
- To Karen Kingsbury and the Baxter's biggest fan. Amie, you deserve the best birthday! We love you!
- To my beloved Kurt…we live JUST ONCE, so let's continue to make every precious moment count. I love you to beyond infinity and beyond!! Sheila
- Keep shining your light for Jesus, Natalie! I am so honored to be your Momma. You are 1 in a million!
- Elizabeth & Abigail Abraham, you are our sunshine, joy, and Philippians 4:8. We love you!
- To the best mom & wife, Kathy Treible. You are loved!
- To Jerome Boge, for teaching me to love Jesus. Love, Your Butterfly
- Adopted and grateful! –Linda Deuth
- To my blessed family. AMR
- Darice Jamison, we are so proud of you and the Godly and beautiful lady that you are, inside and out! We love you, Mom and Dad (Doris & Rhonnie Smith)
- Happy B'Day Sarah Davison! Love, Tim

- Mom, thank you for always being there in my life and always looking out for me. You always made me feel special and encouraged me all along the way. I may not have always appreciated this when I was young but as I raise Levi and Wyatt it is clear to me how important this was. I hope that I can be half the parent that you were to me. Love Chris, Levi, and Wyatt
- Glenda & Larry. My precious In-laws. Love You! Andrea
- Dean, always on my mind...forever in my heart. Love, Kathy
- I love you, Bill Fischer!! Love, Valarie
- To Bonnie, the absolute best sister-in-law! Thank you for always being there for me! Love, Melanie
- In memory of my loving Husband Jon Schilling from his dedicated family and wife Velna.
- In thanksgiving for answered prayer. Diane Weimer
- I have been abundantly blessed by God. He sent Jon & Nicole Saure, Rozlyn Olson and Andrew, Jordan & Quinn Saure to show me joy and unconditional love in my life. Deb Crisalli Saure
- In loving memory of my brother Charlie T. Gazaway! Love, Linda
- For the love of my life, Tim. Passed 9/11/22. Love, Susan
- Hank & Sandy White - mom & dad. Your gift of loving Jesus, family and each other for 60+ years has blessed generations. Love, Lisa

- To my Dad, Donald Getz, who served our country in WWII & loved his family. Love Patti
- From Clara Perkins to my husband Jim and my children, Shane, Stefanie, and Jared. You have blessed me and I am so grateful!
- Love and miss you - Janet Proch (9/26/22) and Marc Proch (12/15/22)
- My sister Elaine loved good reading. 'Til we meet in heaven, love you! –Joyce
- Matthew Conte, it was our honor to be your parents. You were taken too soon. We will never forget our gift from God.
- To Lt's Paul & Olivia, So proud of your service for God & country! Love, Mom
- For mom/Sherry- big fan of Karen's books! Love, Kristi
- To Mom and Dad! With Love, Kim
- In memory of Jim, wonderful husband, dad, friend, policeman, submariner, coach. Love you always! -Marilyn
- Carmen 2023 Honoring family who served
- Josh, I'm proud to be yours. Thank you for your service. Know that I'm by your side, ever supporting you. I love you. –Rachel
- To Gerry Matsushima who enjoys love stories as much as I do. My BFF! Love, Mona

- Dalton, Aaron, & Madison. I love you so much. Mom (Cindy Womack)
- Barbara Matley. Your love of reading inspires me. Love, Pam
- To John and Ruby McCormack who loved our country.
- I would like to dedicate this book in memory of my Dad John Wesley Johnson.
- Thanks to our family who fought for us in WWll: our Dads; Harold Dickson & Hal Pierce, our Granddad, Conrad Frisch; our uncles Bill & Wes Pierce; Ernie, Freddie & Art Frisch; Albert Lang & Jim Harrison! Love always, Annette & Charlie
- Mama, Thanking God for the blessing you are in my life! I love you! Debra
- Cancer took Jim at 47 & Chelsea Diener at 14 from us but they will Forever be in our Hearts! Teresa, Brittani, Cody, Chelsea & Moose
- In memory of: James McFalls Jr, Ronald and Hazel Meekins, Ella & Joseph Miller, Ira McFalls, Riley Buchanan and Marsha Insley.
- Stephen and Judith Speidel were two faithful parents who loved their family well! Thank you, Jesus, for giving them to us girls!
- Missing my Bro, Calvin Eacott. Hug Mom and Judy for me. Love, Becky

- Elizabeth (God's Promise), Abigail (My Father's Joy), & Luke (Light-Giving). You are our gifts from the Lord. xoxo Mom & Dad
- To my once-in-a-lifetime love, Master Sergeant Rick Rounds. ILYM April
- To one of my dearest and best friends, Debbie Paget! Love, Linda
- Carol/Leroy, thanks for being such a support these 2 yrs. We love you! G&J
- Chesney K - May you never lose your love for reading. Love, Mom xo
- Lori Prince, you do so much for others! Love, Pam
- Vickie C, you are the greatest blessing to our family! We love you so much!
- To: Suzanne Lair, Lauren Roberson, Catherine Herndon. You embrace Christ in all! You are wonderful daughters! Love, Mom and Dad
- To My Baxter Girls- Abby, Bailee & Kamryn. Love God, Love People! Mom/Debby
- Special thanks to Mary Anne Hamilton, whose late-husband Laurens Morgan Hamilton served in WWI. His great-great grandfather was Founding Father Alexander Hamilton, who was also General Hamilton, the senior officer of the U.S. Army when General Washington died in December, 1799 until June, 1800. Love, Helena